BY SUSIE DUMOND

Queerly Beloved

Looking for a Sign

Bed and Breakup

BED AND BREAKUP

BED
AND
BREAKUP

a novel

SUSIE DUMOND

THE DIAL PRESS
NEW YORK

The Dial Press
An imprint of Random House
A division of Penguin Random House LLC
1745 Broadway, New York, NY 10019
randomhousebooks.com
penguinrandomhouse.com

A Dial Press Trade Paperback Original

LIBRARY OF CONGRESS CATALOGING-IN-PUBLICATION DATA
Names: Dumond, Susie, author.
Title: Bed and breakup / Susie Dumond.
Description: New York, NY: The Dial Press, 2025.
Identifiers: LCCN 2025000814 (print) | LCCN 2025000815 (ebook) |
ISBN 9780593596296 (trade paperback; acid-free paper) |
ISBN 9780593596302 (ebook)
Subjects: LCGFT: Lesbian fiction. | Romance fiction. | Novels.
Classification: LCC PS3604.U494 B43 2025 (print) |
LCC PS3604.U494 (ebook) | DDC 813/.6—dc23/eng/20250113
LC record available at https://lccn.loc.gov/2025000814
LC ebook record available at https://lccn.loc.gov/2025000815

Printed in the United States of America on acid-free paper

1st Printing

BOOK TEAM: Production editor: Cara DuBois • Managing editor: Rebecca
Berlant • Production manager: Meghan O'Leary • Copy editor: Hasan
Altaf • Proofreaders: Julie Ehlers, Catherine Mallette, Bridget Sweet,
Bonnie Thompson

Book design by Susan Turner

The authorized representative in the EU for product safety
and compliance is Penguin Random House Ireland,
Morrison Chambers, 32 Nassau Street, Dublin D02 YH68,
Ireland, https://eu-contact.penguin.ie.

In memory of Nila Dumond

I died, and was born in the spring;
I found you, and loved you, again.

—MARY OLIVER, "Hummingbirds"

BED AND BREAKUP

1
MOLLY

IF YOU'D TOLD ME AT ANY POINT IN THE PAST SEVEN YEARS THAT I'd wind up back in Eureka Springs, I'd have laughed in your face. There are far too many ghosts in that town—not just the "real" ones tourists pay to hear about, but personal ones too. Eureka's signature way of living in the past is less fun when it's full of memories you're desperate to forget.

Yet here I am, driving through the Ozarks on a winding highway that feels all too familiar.

It's not exactly the same, of course. Some of the old antique shops are now axe-throwing studios and medical-marijuana dispensaries. I spotted a few electric-car charging kiosks where there used to be gas stations. Most of the Confederate flags have been replaced with signs for far-right politicians. But the exposed rock formations along the road, the surprise waterfalls around random curves, and the verdant summer growth all remind me of the breathtaking beauty ahead. I have to travel through the worst part of Arkansas to get to the best.

"Rise and shine, Marmalade. We're almost there," I say to the fat gray cat in a carrier in the passenger seat. She's too deep asleep to notice. After spending the past seven years on the road, Marmalade is more comfortable in my car than out of it.

As soon as I turn in to Eureka Springs' historic downtown, I feel like I've traveled back in time. That's the town's appeal, what's drawn visitors for decades. People go nuts for the Victorian architecture, the Prohibition-era lore, the restaurants built in caves. And crowds flock to the natural springs, long rumored to hold mystical healing powers that have led to a whole industry of quirky woo-woo shops touting spiritual cleansing, tarot readings, and crystals.

Personally, I'm not time traveling back to the turn of the nineteenth century like the tourists admiring the Gothic Revival architecture. I'm flung back to 2012, when I thought I'd found the place where I was meant to be. And to 2018, when I was proved monumentally wrong. When my wife gave up on our marriage, our shared business, and our future in Eureka. When I learned I was meant to be alone.

Unprepared to face my destination, I spend half an hour tooling around the twisty streets, finishing the last chapter of my audiobook, a historical mystery involving a library and a lady detective. Cars move at a crawl near downtown thanks to Eureka's refusal to install traffic lights, and out-of-towners in shorts and tank tops fill the sidewalks. It's a relief to see the town isn't completely the same. Some of the old hotels have gotten a makeover. Restaurants have changed owner-ship. The old stage at Basin Park has a fresh coat of paint. Maybe it's not exactly the place I left behind. But it's also a reminder of how long it's been since I left. How much I've changed too.

Once my audiobook ends—I *knew* it was the sketchy antique-book collector—I debate starting another one just to put off the inevitable. But it's getting late. I need to stretch my aching back, feed Marmalade her dinner, and see if my old art studio is still in shape for the work I need to do.

I take a right onto Magnolia Lane, and from there, it's muscle memory. I pass the old brick bank and the trolley stop, loop around a rocky bend of mountain, and there it is. The pastel-colored Victorian home that changed my life, looking just as gorgeous as I remember it.

Heading up the driveway, I feel ripped in two. On the one hand, my skin is burning like a sinner in church. This place is *bad* for me. But on the other hand, I can't help but swoon. I fell in love with this building the first time I laid eyes on it. Its intricately carved gingerbread trim painted playful shades of pink and green and blue, its wraparound porch that invites you to pull up a rocking chair and stay for a while, and the enormous, gleaming stained-glass window in the front, a portrait of a hummingbird paused mid-flight. Even now, it seems to be looking right at me and chirping, "Welcome home."

Still, I hesitate to open the car door and set foot on the inn's grounds. I left this place heartbroken. Even years later, those feelings haven't completely healed. Why am I doing this? How did my best friend talk me into coming back here?

Marmalade meows from beside me, blinking away sleep now that the car has stopped.

"Sorry, Marmee," I say, unlatching the front of her carrier. "Take a look around. Lord knows you could use the exercise."

I open the driver's-side door. Marmalade walks across the console, pauses to stretch on my lap, then hops to the ground with a thud. She takes a few curious sniffs of grass, then spots a butterfly and makes a lazy pounce for it, missing by at least a foot. Never a very good hunter, my Marmalade.

"Do you remember this yard?" I ask the cat. "This is where we met. You were a lot smaller then. I was probably a little smaller too."

Marmalade looks up sharply at the house, then goes galloping toward it.

"I guess you do." I haven't seen her move so fast in a while. Just last week in my New Orleans studio, she hardly even looked up when a mouse ran right past her nose.

I grab a couple of bags from the back seat but freeze in place when I see a figure on the front porch. The inn should be empty. Is it a nosy neighbor? A squatter? One of Eureka Springs' famous ghosts? It's probably a trick of the light. But then I spot Marmee rubbing herself against its ankles. Oh god, it *is* a real person.

"Marmalade? Is that you?" says a voice that sends a chill down my spine.

I can't believe it. This *must* be a nightmare.

The figure bends down to stroke Marmalade's back. I pinch myself, refusing to admit I'm wide awake, and accidentally drop my bags in the process, drawing her attention.

We make eye contact, and I know immediately that my worst possible nightmare scenario has somehow come true.

It's the scariest ghost I could imagine: my ex-wife. Robin. Here, at the Hummingbird Inn.

There are a million things I want to say to her, but the only word I manage right now is "fuck."

2

Robin

"FUCK," I SAY, JUMPING LIKE I JUST SAW A GHOST. "MOLLY?"

"What are you doing here?" we say at the same time. Dammit. Seven years apart and we're still jinxing each other.

As if moving into the Hummingbird Inn after all these years isn't enough of an ego check, now my ex-wife turns up? Okay, universe. I get it. I screwed everything up. Can't I have a moment to catch my breath?

"I have a right to be here," I say defensively as Molly edges toward the porch. "I'm still a co-owner, you know."

"Oh, believe me," Molly says, her tone scathing. "I know. I would have sold it years ago if it didn't require talking to *you*."

"So you'd rather let it sit here and rot than make a phone

call?" I ask. Actually, selling the inn has crossed my mind too, considering the dire financial straits I've been in lately. But I wasn't going to be the first to reach out after years of radio silence. I'd moved on. I assumed Molly had as well. But based on how it seems like smoke might start billowing out of her ears any second now, maybe she hasn't.

"Nothing with you is ever simple," Molly says. "Besides, I figured you were busy with your *restaurant group* and your *reality TV series* and your *brand partnerships*." She makes my accomplishments sound like a list of biblical plagues. "How'd you find the time to visit?"

I try not to visibly cringe. I'm not here by choice. But I'll be damned if I give her the satisfaction of knowing that. "I'm returning to my roots," I say vaguely. "For inspiration for my next project. Could use a little peace and quiet for my creative flow."

Molly looks me up and down, clearly skeptical. I can't avoid noticing how different she looks than the last time I saw her. For one thing, she looks stronger. Tougher. Grounded in her body in a way she wasn't before, shoulders back, feet firmly planted in her Doc Martens. And more tattooed, with new art stretching around her forearms and thighs. The fine lines on her face suit her, especially against her youthful freckles. Her naturally brown hair has teal streaks now, the same shade she had back when the Hummingbird hit it big, when we filmed that episode of *Inn for a Treat*.

"Well, you're going to have to find somewhere else for your 'creative flow,'" she says, lifting her bags onto her shoulders. "Because I'm working here for the next six weeks."

Seriously? This was supposed to be *my* secret lair for the

next six weeks. Could be six months, if I can't get my shit together and figure out where to go next. "Well, I was here first. So . . . dibs."

Molly scoffs. "This isn't a 'dibs' situation."

Marmalade meows, upset that I'm not giving her the welcome home she deserves. I scoop her into my arms, and she immediately purrs and rubs her head against my chin. She's a lot heavier than the last time I held her. I worry that cuddling the cat will lose me some ground in this standoff with Molly, but then I see she's irked at how pleased Marmee is to see me. I snuggle the cat closer, reveling in how it makes Molly's eyes narrow.

"Easy solution. There are a lot of nice hotels I'm sure you could stay at while you're doing your handywoman projects or whatever," I venture, remembering how Molly taught DIY skills to half the business owners in town when we lived here.

I can tell right away that I accidentally struck a nerve. "I've been commissioned to make custom stained-glass windows for several businesses in town," Molly says, standing straighter. "So I need the studio space in the shed. You, though, can work in any number of kitchens."

Is that what she does now? Stained glass? I remember when she taught herself to repair the broken panes in the inn's colorful windows and figured out how to make a few new ones of her own. If she's managed to make a career out of it . . . I have to admit I'm impressed. But it also explains why she'd need a free place to crash. She's probably a starving-artist type.

"I already stocked this kitchen for what I need," I fib as I place Marmee back on the porch. I've only been at the Hum-

mingbird for two days now, most of which I've spent loung-
ing around in pajamas feeling sorry for myself. Molly didn't
believe I could become an internationally recognized chef
back then, so I'm certainly not giving her the chance for an
I-told-you-so. "But hey, it's a big house, right? Nine bedrooms. Four floors. We probably won't even see each other.
At least for a couple days while you figure out somewhere
else to stay."

"While *you* figure out somewhere else to stay."

I widen my stance on the wooden planks, trying to convey a sense of ownership over the building I left seven years
ago without looking back. "That kitchen is mine. I'm not
going anywhere."

Molly purses her lips. "We can argue later," she says.
"Can I please just put down these bags? They're harder to
hold than a greased hog."

I bite down a laugh at the phrase, one of many she got
from the old-fashioned Southern grandmother who raised
her, then step aside, gesturing grandly to the inn's front door.
"Be my guest."

3

MOLLY

THE NERVE OF THIS WOMAN, INVITING ME INTO A BUILDING I own. Keyana only barely convinced me these six weeks in Eureka Springs were a good idea, and I'm already regretting it on day one. But I made promises, and I can't go back on them now.

I shift my bags on my shoulders and push past Robin toward the entrance to the inn. "Come on, Marmalade," I say to the cat, who betrays me by plopping down next to Robin's feet, belly up.

Fine. If she wants to forget which one of us took care of her and which abandoned her, that's her choice. She'll come running back to me when Robin leaves again.

As soon as I make it into the inn's entryway, I freeze, nearly dropping everything I'm holding. What the hell happened to the Hummingbird? The paint job on the exterior looked a little faded, but mostly the same. The inside looks completely different. The beautifully refinished wooden floors we labored over, sanding and staining and polishing for weeks after buying the inn, have been covered with cheap laminate. Keyana's gorgeous floral murals have been painted over with a neutral pale gray. All the painstakingly restored antique furniture is gone, the sturdy oak check-in desk and hand-carved breakfast buffet replaced with ready-to-assemble pieces made of plastic or cheap particleboard. In place of the old crystal chandelier is some atrocity with bulbs on metal bars pointing in all directions. Even the wooden banister on the staircase is now a nondescript white. Walking into the Hummingbird used to take my breath away. Now the inn's vintage charm is gone; the whole place looks soulless.

"What in the ham sandwich?" I blurt out.

From behind me, Robin says, "I figured this wasn't your style."

"How could the management company do all this without my permission?" I say, fuming. Sure, I approved some minor design updates the company suggested might help boost bookings after the lull of the pandemic, but this cheapskate nightmare flip is *not* something I would have agreed to. I feel an overwhelming rush of guilt that I let myself get so far removed from the inn, let strangers strip it of what made it great, let the beloved staff members who stuck it out be subjected to all that. I *know* Caro and Jesse must have fought against this.

"Who did you hire to manage the place when you left? They must have been some real tasteless morons," Robin says. I don't turn around, because if I see even a hint of smugness on her face, I might spontaneously combust.

"Whatever. I'll take the Zinnia Room," I say, starting up the stairs to the second floor and hoping that it still has the Jacuzzi tub and the great view of the back gardens.

"I'm using the Zinnia Room," Robin calls from the base of the stairs.

I pause at the second-floor landing, fuming and calculating which room is the farthest from that one. Technically it's the penthouse suite that used to be our apartment together, but it'll be a snowy day in hell when I face that room again. "Fine. The Snapdragon Room, then," I grumble. It's a floor higher, but it has a lovely bay-window reading nook. I added a thematically floral stained-glass pane across the top once I figured out how to make my own designs. Surely the management company didn't go so far as to remove those.

It takes two trips up the stairs to unload my things, and another trip around the back to drop off equipment in the shed-turned-studio. Robin watches from the porch with a beer in hand, not offering to help, while Marmalade the Traitor lounges at her feet. Each time I return to the car, the sight of her drives me up a neutral gray wall. What is she really doing here? Isn't she too rich and famous for Arkansas now that she's a hot celesbian chef? Didn't she say loud and clear that Eureka wasn't enough for her?

I'm doubly thrown by how different she looks in person compared to what I've seen on TV. I admit I followed her career for a while. Who could pass up the chance to stalk their C-list-celebrity ex online? But I eventually stopped looking because it hurt too much. Key even taught me how to block her name with a Google extension. But for those first couple years after she left, seeing how different she looked onscreen from the Robin I knew actually helped me face reality and get some distance. I fell in love with a messy-haired, makeup-free, baby-faced lesbian I met while working at the West Little Rock Home Depot. When I saw her guest-judging what seemed like every single show Foodie TV could come up with, I decided the Robin I married had clearly been abducted by aliens and swapped for some hot clone with an artfully styled pompadour, contoured cheekbones, and a crisp white chef's coat.

But the figure on the porch in front of me looks closer to the Robin I used to love, with a baseball cap pulled over unwashed hair, baggy jeans, and not a smidge of makeup. Infuriatingly, she doesn't have any new wrinkles or signs of aging on her face, but her body shows the years a little more. She's not as lanky as she used to be. A little weight has settled around her hips, and she's got thicker arms and legs, like she's spent a decade building muscle by kneading dough. Robin looks better like this than when she's all done up for the cameras.

Once I've unloaded my car and filled Marmee's food and water bowls, I debate saying something else to Robin. Telling her I'm headed upstairs for the evening. Asking what she's working on while she's here. Breaking the seven years' worth of ice between us with some nod at politeness. But no one ever said I was nice. I stomp up to the third floor without another word.

4

Robin

MOLLY'S ARRIVAL DOESN'T JUST RUIN MY LONG-TERM PLANS for my stay at the inn. My short-term ones are trashed too. I'd expected to spend tonight eating junk food and watching old episodes of *SpongeBob* on the big-screen TV in what used to be the dining room. But there's no way I'm letting Molly catch me moping. I have a single crumb of pride left that I'd like to protect. And from what I can tell, she has no clue I'm a bankrupt, humiliated failure.

Determined to at least make myself *look* busy, I wander toward the kitchen and pull out the random ingredients I grabbed at the store on the way into town. It's a little slim, but I've got the basics: flour, sugar, eggs, milk, butter. I scrounge up some dried herbs and spices from the dusty pantry. They're old, though. Probably purchased when Jesse was still in charge of the kitchen, before the management company fired the cooks and started serving store-bought pastries. At least that's what I gather happened, based on a binder of reheating instructions I find in a drawer. I can't help but laugh when I spot my brand of frozen quiche cups among the pages. I guess, in a sense, my dishes were still getting served.

Luckily, my old tools are stashed in boxes in the hall closet. And although the garden has grown wild and unruly, some of my fresh herbs are still going strong. I opt for a quiche. A little basic, sure, but given I've hardly made anything beyond a PB&J since my last restaurant closed, something simple is just what I need.

Making the rough puff pastry at first feels like I'm watching someone else's hands do the work. But as I roll it out into a crust, noticing the flecks of butter that will steam up to create flaky layers, I begin to get my groove back. I may have failed at a lot of things lately, but this I can handle.

While the crust chills in the fridge, I chop an onion, then caramelize it slowly on the stove until it reaches a deep, rich amber. It's meditative in a way, finding just the right pan temperature without any bits burning. I throw the crust in the preheated oven to parbake, then use an old blender to create a slurry of fresh herbs and olive oil. It tastes delicious: bright and tangy and complex.

When the crust is a light golden brown, I pull it out to cool while I whisk together the egg mixture and fold in the onions. I pour that into the crust and swirl the herbs into a marbled pattern on top. Once it's in the oven, all I can do is wait.

Waiting is the hardest part of baking. Wondering if all

your work will turn out. Hoping things rise like they're supposed to. And you can't even open the oven to check without messing up the temperature. This is the step where my brain starts spinning out of control, worrying about everything that could go wrong, and not just with the food. Can I keep up appearances until Molly finds somewhere else to stay? Will she laugh in my face if she finds out all my work to become a renowned chef landed me in the gutter? Surely she won't be able to stand living in a home with me for long, even if it sleeps up to eighteen people. I feel bad for her, really. She's probably on a tight budget and planned to crash here for free during a rare paying gig. Unfortunately, I'm even more strapped for cash.

I try to quiet my mind by cleaning up the mess I made. Scrubbing my knives, cutting board, rolling pin, and food processor as I think through options for making a quick buck. Wiping down the counters as I remember all the emails from my manager, Edgar, that I've blown off over the past month. When that's done, I start to check social media before realizing that's the absolute worst thing I could do for my mental health. My accounts have been quiet lately, which is better than trolls mocking my collapsing businesses. But I'm still likely to see plenty of my chef friends celebrating new restaurants and TV appearances and awards. I'm avoiding those until I can find it in me to be happier for them than I am sad for me. Pity parties are tacky as hell. That's why I came to Eureka to mope in private.

Instead, I focus on deep cleaning the refrigerator. It's a great distraction, scouring every corner until I can forget my personal failings. So good that the quiche gets a smidge overbaked before I notice. I kick myself internally as I pull it out of the oven. It'll still taste fine, and it's not like I'm serving it to any paying customers. But come on! Can't I have one win?

I finish cleaning the fridge as I wait for the quiche to cool. While picking at a spot on the back wall, I hear a creak of floorboards that makes me jump and hit my head against a shelf. I step back, holding the top of my skull, just in time to see Molly's back disappear around the corner.

"Trying to scare me off?" I say, still wincing.

Molly lurks back to the doorway. "No," she says, not even pretending to apologize. "I was going to look for something to eat, but I see the kitchen is occupied."

I can't eat this whole thing alone, and even though she's my bitter ex, I hate thinking about Molly going to bed hungry. I decide to be the bigger person. "I'm about to cut into this quiche. Want a slice?" I offer.

"I'm good," she says. "I'll go out and find something."

I look at my watch. "It's almost midnight," I say. "What are you going to do, drive half an hour to the McDonald's in Berryville? Just take it. It's caramelized onion with an herb swirl."

I can see Molly practically drooling. "It's fine. I'm not even hungry, really."

A loud rumbling sounds from Molly's stomach. I raise an eyebrow.

She sighs. "Fine. I'll take a slice."

Of course she will. Who could resist the smell in here? Buttery pastry, earthy onions, pungent rosemary and basil. I pull out plates, forks, and a knife. After plating two slices, I garnish them with a drizzle of the olive oil and herb mixture and a sprig of parsley, styling it like I would for TV out of habit. The camera would pick up on the overly browned crust, but it would also miss out on this ridiculously tempting scent. Some things can never be experienced through a screen.

I pass a plate to Molly. Before I can say a word, she takes a bite. Her eyes close as soon as the quiche reaches her lips. Then her face flips through a bunch of conflicting expressions, her eyelashes fluttering and lips pursing with delight and relief and frustration and maybe a dash of longing. Watching her taste my cooking awakens some ancient sleeping beast inside of me. I want to know—*need* to know—what she thinks. Maybe eating together can heal some of what happened between us. Not that there can ever be an "us" again, but maybe we can be something that vaguely resembles friends, if you squint. Turning to grab my own plate, I say, "I know the new tables in the dining room are cheap and flimsy compared to the the old walnut ones, but maybe we can sit and—"

My words hang in the air when I turn back, realizing she's already left the room. I hear footsteps running up the stairs a second later. So much for sharing a meal.

Was the quiche bad? I grab a fork and take a bite. It's fucking fantastic. Guess Molly hates me so much she can't even stand to eat in the same room as me.

"You're welcome," I say bitterly to the empty kitchen.

5

MOLLY

ON THE MORNING OF MY FIRST FULL DAY IN EUREKA, I BURST
through the door to Key to Happiness Art Studio with such
force that the two elderly customers and shop employee inside jump in alarm.

"Sorry," I say, sheepish.

But my rage is back in full force by the time I reach Key's
office in the back.

"Did you know she was here?" I demand as soon as I see
my potentially traitorous best friend.

Keyana pauses mid-brushstroke, turning away from the
praying mantis on her canvas. "Know who was where?" she
asks, taking stock of my clearly dangerous mood.

"*Robin,*" I spit out. "At the Hummingbird."

"Holy shit." Key turns from her easel and deposits her brush on a side table. "Why on earth would Robin come back here?"

I search Key's face for signs of some kind of *Parent Trap* scheme. Outside of myself and the inn's employees, Key was the most devastated by our breakup. Robin and I met her in that sparkly honeymoon phase of our relationship when it seemed like we'd be together forever, just after we moved to Eureka, and she used to be equally close to both of us. I'm lucky she chose my side in the breakup, because without her, I might have come completely untethered and floated off into space.

Seeing no signs of deception in Key now, I deflate. "No clue," I admit. "Something about 'getting back to her roots' and 'creative flow.'"

"Typical," Key says. "Using the inn for her own career advancement without taking any responsibility for it."

"Wait a second. I forgot the important part." I walk over to Key and wrap her in a tight hug. "Hi. I missed you," I say into her shoulder.

Key squeezes back. "Welcome back to Eureka," she says. "It feels more like home with you here, even if you're grumpy."

"When did you arrive?" I ask.

"Couple weeks ago," Key says, stepping back and brushing at the bits of dried paint from her apron that stuck to my shirt. "Just long enough to get the studio set up and hire a few new employees. Don't even think about coming to the duplex I'm renting. Everything's still in boxes. Yesterday I found my French press, but couldn't find my mugs, so I drank the coffee out of a vase."

"Invite me over when you've got a free evening," I say. "You know I love organizing storage closets."

Key raises her eyebrows. "Sounds like you've got your own complicated living situation to deal with first."

"This is *beyond* worst-case scenario," I say, pacing the length of the room. "I can't just make stained glass anywhere. I need the studio's natural light and my workbench to cut and lay out the glass, and the utility sink and ventilation for the soldering and patina. Meanwhile, Robin insists she *has* to be there too, even though there are a million kitchens that are bigger and nicer."

"Oh, I feel you," Keyana says, nodding toward her own highly specific studio arrangement. "You've seen how long it takes me to set up a new painting space. But can't you stay somewhere nearby and just use the shed during the day?"

"It's June in Eureka. I called around, but every hotel in the county is at capacity." I drop into an empty chair, burying my face in my hands. "How am I supposed to share a house with her? For at least a month! I don't know how to survive this."

"She really won't leave?" Key asks.

"She says she's legally just as entitled to the inn as I am. And she's not wrong."

Key fiddles with the brushes next to her easel for a moment, then looks up as if she's had an idea. "So make it impossible for her to stay."

I arch an eyebrow.

"You were together for, what, six years? Surely you know how to press her buttons. Scare her off."

Huh. Key might be on to something. If I made Robin

miserable during our marriage simply by being myself, what
could I do if I was actually trying?

"How's the inn, besides Robin?" Key asks. "Do my murals need a touch-up?"

I groan, remembering the horror that greeted me upon
entering the building yesterday. "It's awful, Key. That management company ruined everything. Painted over all your
work. Got rid of the furniture and decorations and turned
the whole place into some soulless chain hotel. Seriously, it
looks like an IKEA catalog. Not in a cute way."

"Even the one of all the different flowers in the entryway?" Key says, looking appropriately horrified. "That's
tragic!"

"Tell me about it."

"Are you going to fix it?"

"Why bother?" I sigh. "It's not like I'm going to open it to
guests. It's just a place for me to crash while I work."

Key gives me a knowing smirk. "Yeah, we'll see how long
it takes for you to take on a project or four."

I look at the praying mantis painting Key's been working
on. She's penciled in a burst of marigolds in the background
that's going to look stunning. Her style has evolved since I
first met her. I hardly knew anything about fine art when I
met Keyana, but now even I can recognize her skill. "How
are you doing, being back?" I ask.

After being separated for too long working on projects in
different cities, last year Key and I schemed to get commissions at the same time in New Orleans. We were sharing an
apartment and studio space there when she got the news
that her father's Parkinson's had taken a turn for the worse.
Key lived in Conway for the last few months, helping care

for him until he passed. I wrapped up our affairs in Louisiana, then made it to Key's hometown in time for the funeral. Afterward, Key told me her plan to move back to Eureka Springs, a town she first visited with her dad as a kid and where she'd started her art career around the same time Robin and I bought the Hummingbird. She wanted to buy the storefront she used to rent for her gallery, and she wanted me to come with her, at least at first, to design a custom window for her business. I couldn't say no. I asked Roxie, the agent Key and I share, to clear my calendar of commissions, then headed back to Arkansas. Key's been there for me through every up and down. I want to do the same for her. Even if it means returning to the town that broke my heart.

Key tilts her head from side to side, considering my question. "It's all right so far. A lot of emotions to work through. But that's good for my creativity, in a way."

Knowing all that Key's been through lately, I'm sure she's got more to get off her chest, and I'm guessing she could use a walk. I remember the new bakery down the street owned by an acquaintance of Key's. I promised I'd also make a window for that shop while I'm here, and I've been meaning to check it out in person. "Want to tell me about it over donuts?" I suggest.

Key's eyes light up. "At Thembi's place? Oh hell yeah. I'm in."

A few minutes later, we're swimming through crowds of tourists on Main Street, dappled sunlight cutting through the trees around us. "How's your mom doing?" I ask, remembering how drained and unlike herself she had seemed at the funeral.

"About as good as she can be," Key says with a sigh. "It's a big change. She's never lived alone."

"Wow. She met your dad when she was a teenager, right?" I ask, matching Key's leisurely pace.

"High school sweethearts. Forty-two years together and it still didn't feel like enough."

I can see it hurts Key to think about her mom's loneliness. Heck, it hurts me to think about, especially considering my own catastrophic marriage situation, which doesn't hold a candle to losing someone who had been your spouse and best friend for decades. Deciding I'll give Key some space to process that later, I change the subject. "How's the business bureau going?" I ask.

Key visibly perks up. "Really well. Thembi and Louis joined their first board meeting last week, and they're thrilled to get to work. We're planning some advertising and recruitment in Little Rock, Conway, Jacksonville, and Pine Bluff."

Part of Key's goal in moving back to Eureka Springs was to start a Black Business Bureau with some friends and create a safer space for people of color in the mostly white town. Eureka is an oasis for old hippies, making it a pretty liberal place. The city council endorsed gay marriage in 2012, the same year Robin and I bought the Hummingbird Inn, and the town voted to make weed the lowest possible priority for local law enforcement back in 2006, way before either issue got nationwide support. But getting to and from Eureka requires driving through former sundown towns and a neighborhood that still proudly calls itself "the birthplace of the KKK."

It was Key who drew my attention to the real history of

Eureka, the stuff they gloss over in the walking tours. The healing natural springs had long been a sacred site for the Osage people when the federal government pushed them off the land. Then Eureka became a kind of safe haven for previously enslaved people, with numerous Black-owned businesses and hotels and schools. But that all changed in the mid-nineteenth century, when white politicians decided to position the spot as a wealthy retirement town, pushing Black people out of the community they'd help build. Now Key's leading the charge to bring that Black history and heritage back.

Key talks me through updates on her business development efforts as we turn down a stairway carved into the mountainside, leading to the street below. "You know my friends-and-family discount for anyone on the bureau has no expiration date," I say once she's finished. "Assuming Robin skedaddles again soon, I'll come back anytime."

"I bet folks will take you up on it," Key says. "Especially once they see whatever windows you come up with for Thembi and Louis and me." She pauses before adding, "Too bad the Hummingbird isn't open so you could offer a discounted place to stay too."

I roll my eyes. Keyana gives me constant grief for letting a gorgeous historic building we both adore sit empty because I'm not willing to pick up the phone and work through the details with my ex. To her credit, Key's totally right. To *my* credit, Robin is an unrepentant asshat who walked away from our life together and never looked back. Who can blame me for not wanting to open that can of worms? Besides, when I hit the road with my stained glass, I was surprised by how much I could charge for my work. I may be leaving money on the table with the inn vacant, but I don't actually *need* income from the Hummingbird.

Key and I take a right, squeeze past a group of people watching a street performer with a banjo, and there it is: Drizzled Donuts. I immediately pull out my phone to get pictures of the long window running above the storefront, the one where I can already picture my stained glass on display. I think I recognize this building as what was once our favorite local pizza place, where our old friend Clint was a server. That is, when he wasn't working at the hardware store, or the florist's, or the gay bar, or Keyana's studio. A real jack-of-all-trades, Clint. I make a mental note to ask Key if she's seen him since she's been back.

I'm pulling a tape measure from my bag when a tall, smiling woman with long box braids appears at the door. Key greets her with a hug, then introduces her to me as Thembi, the owner of Drizzled Donuts and treasurer of the Eureka Springs Black Business Bureau.

"So nice to meet you," I say, following Thembi inside and pushing down a wave of nostalgia at the familiar layout and hexagonal-tiled floor. The old booths have been refinished with pink velvet fabric and the walls painted a minty green. Nevertheless, my head is swimming with memories of cuddling up to Robin at the table in the back corner where we always used to sit, play-fighting over the last garlic knot. I forcefully push the images from my brain. I came to this town for my art, not for my messy feelings.

"Key's told me so much about you," Thembi says, waving us toward a table. "And she showed me some of your windows. I can't wait to see what you create for the shop. Getting affordable custom art is like winning the lottery for a small business owner."

"I can't wait to get started," I say. "I've had a long run of commissions for banks and hotels and old rich dudes' mansions lately, so I'm itching for a passion project. I'll grab measurements today, plus some pictures of your display case for inspiration."

"Oh, I've got just the muse for you. Fresh out of the oven."

Thembi returns a minute later with a box of vibrantly colored donuts, scents of chocolate and vanilla and hot sugar glaze wafting from them. As soon as a bite of a raspberry-cheesecake-stuffed donut hits my tongue, I'm in heaven. They almost taste good enough to make me forget what I'll have to face when I return to the inn.

6

Robin

I SLEPT LIKE ABSOLUTE SHIT LAST NIGHT, TOSSING AND TURN-
ing, thinking every creak was something haunting me, one of
the Hummingbird's many infamous ghosts or, more likely,
Molly. After finally falling asleep around sunrise, I wake up
at the crack of noon to find the house empty. I don't want to
be caught lurking around in sweatpants when Molly returns,
so I shower and get dressed to wander into town.

Beyond one short grocery trip, I haven't set foot outside
of the inn since I arrived days ago. Frankly, running into old
acquaintances while at rock bottom sounds only slightly
more pleasant than Molly's death glares. I throw on a baseball cap and sunglasses in the hope I won't be recognized,
then walk toward the outskirts of downtown, trying to avoid
the thickest crowds of summer tourists.

It's aggressively sunny outside, everything green and flowering. Rude of the weather to be so lovely when I feel like a hair ball Marmalade coughed up. I'm scowling at a particularly lovely rosebush outside an old bank when I hear a walking-tour guide approaching. Based on the voice hoarsened by years of cigarettes, I can tell it's good ol' Dorothy Baxter, part of the town's hippie generation who moved here in the 1970s and never left.

"Now, you might've heard about Eureka's Prohibition-era history," I hear Dot say to the tourists following her like ducklings. "During the heyday of speakeasies and illegal gambling rings, we had a special advantage: underground tunnels. Eureka's two main streets were originally built lower down in a gulch, but they flooded so often the locals started to call Main Street 'Mud Street.' So in 1890, the city raised the streets. What was once the entry level in all these buildings became the basement level, and these limestone passageways between the old and new roads could help you get around without being seen. Popular place to hang out for gangsters and bootleggers, like Al Capone, who was rumored to spend some time in those tunnels. Used to be I could take tour groups through there to catch a glimpse of the ghosts in person. Now it's supposedly 'unsafe,' but ask me again after a beer or three."

I'd usually love catching up with Dot. She's hilarious, and her stories of Eureka's lesbian drama in the 1970s always kill. But right now, I'd rather face the ghosts. So before she spots me, I run up the nearest staircase built into the mountainside.

These stone stairways are all over town, cutting steep walking paths between roads. There are even storefronts tucked away in the hills halfway up the staircases. Eureka is a nightmare for anyone with mobility issues. Ask me about the month when I had a sprained ankle and couldn't go to half the places in town—including my own fourth-floor apartment.

Just when I thought I'd escaped, I hear Dot and her tour group turning onto the bottom of the stairs. *Dammit.* Looking around for places to hide, I spot a restaurant sign at the top that looks unfamiliar. Figuring it's less likely to be full of people I know than the old-favorite Eureka spots, I take the stairs two at a time and throw myself in before Dot can point me out as a former local, now washed-up celebrity.

"Welcome to Counterculture," a server in a burlap apron says, appearing out of nowhere and almost giving me a heart attack. "Table for one?"

"Um, yeah. Sure," I say, realizing it's my only option. As the rich smell of freshly baked bread and roasted garlic hits me, my stomach gurgles.

The server grabs a menu and leads me to the only open table, right in the front window. Not a great spot when you're trying to avoid, oh, everyone. "Actually, could I just sit at the bar?" I ask.

The server, unbothered, nods and hands me the menu. I creep over to the darkest corner of the room, which is decorated tastefully with potted plants and copper statement pieces. Climbing onto a stool, I pull down my hat brim and broadly avoid eye contact, just in case.

It's not until I start scanning the menu that I remember I'm broke. I have no business being in a restaurant that charges eighteen dollars for portobello grits. I'm searching for the cheapest dish—a side of Broccolini for ten dollars? Yikes!—when the bartender comes for my order.

"I'll have a cup of coffee and a side of home fries, please," I say. "Plus a slice of lemon and side of garlic aioli, if you have it?"

"Holy shit," a voice says from behind me as the bartender walks away. "Robin Lasko? Are you fucking serious right now?"

As much as I want to avoid interacting with any living soul, I can't possibly be upset to hear that voice. "Jesse!" I say, hopping off my barstool for a big hug.

"I have missed the shit out of you," he says, squeezing me so hard I think my eyes bug out a little.

I take a moment to appreciate his familiar wavy brown hair, his kind eyes, his big, warm smile. Then I clock his white chef's jacket. "Wait, you work here? That's great, dude!"

He beams with pride. "Actually," Jesse says, "I own it."

"You . . . own . . ." The revelation hits me and I'm ripped in two, half thrilled for this guy I adore, half brokenhearted about my own failed restaurant ventures. I give myself an internal shake and lean into the happy-for-Jesse feels. "Freaking incredible!" I say, gripping him by the elbows. "I would say I can't believe it, but I absolutely can. You deserve all the success in the world."

The bartender returns with my coffee. "Gia! Do you know who this is?" Jesse says to her, wrapping an arm around my shoulders. "Robin Lasko. *Let's Do Brunch* winner. Foodie TV. She taught me everything I know."

"That's an exaggeration," I say, shrinking as heads across the room turn in my direction.

"Oh yeah!" Gia says as she looks at me again. "I thought I recognized you."

"Seriously though, dude," Jesse says to me, his face brimming with sincerity. "You gave me my first shot. Took me in when no other kitchen would. I owe all of this to you."

I gulp, moved but also embarrassed by how the tables have turned. Jesse was my first sous-chef at the Hummingbird, hired with essentially zero experience or professional training. But the Arkansas culinary world was too distracted by the fact that he was a trans man to notice he was bursting with talent, even at eighteen. "Anyone paying a lick of attention would have seen your potential. I'm lucky Caro introduced us," I say with quiet gratitude.

"Caro," Jesse says, his eyes widening. "Oh shit, I have to call Caro. They're going to freak out. Our house is just up the street."

"You two are still going strong?" I say, my voice wobbling from the influx of bittersweet memories. Caro was our earliest employee at the inn and pretty much the only reason we held it together when we accidentally became a hit LGBTQ+ travel destination and the waitlist went bananas. Maybe my marriage was a bust, but if that makes Jesse and Caro the queer power couple in Eureka these days, it's a silver lining.

"Fourteen years next month." Jesse whips out his phone and starts typing. "Hey, I've gotta get back to the kitchen, but, Gia? Give Robin anything she wants on the house. Actually, I'll send out a chef's tasting menu. No fennel, right?"

"You don't have to do all that," I say, although both my stomach and my wallet are relieved.

Jesse waves my words away. "How often do I get to show off for a world-class chef?" He disappears into the kitchen as a voice in the back of my head says, *World-class loser.*

7

MOLLY

IT'S AFTER NOON BY THE TIME I LEAVE DRIZZLED DONUTS, AND I'm considering asking Thembi to pay me for the stained-glass window in baked goods. She's got a real gift, especially with bold, colorful frosting patterns, which gets my own creativity flowing. I couldn't ask for better inspiration.

Key has to get back to her studio, but before she does, she walks me around the curving Main Street to Wild Card, the other business I've agreed to work with for a friends-and-family discounted window design. She introduces me to the owner, Louis, before heading out. Louis is just as quickly swept off by a couple of customers with questions about the shop's monthly Dungeons & Dragons campaign, so I browse the store's impressive supply of tabletop games, dice sets, and gifts to craft my vision. I've already got an idea brewing, inspired by classic board games. Stained glass is a perfect medium for this quirky Victorian town: a vintage aesthetic with plenty of room for modern design and color choices. It blends the old and the new, proves that some things are worth the trouble of preserving.

"Sorry about that," Louis says when he returns, straightening his fashionably retro glasses. "Find anything you like?"

I look down at the game in my hand, a colorful card game about patternmaking. I hadn't intended to buy anything, but when I saw that this one could be played solo, I was intrigued.

"Excellent choice," Louis says. "It's got beautiful illustrations, and it's super relaxing. Designed by an artist in Missouri. If you like it, I'll hook you up with the expansion pack."

"Can't wait to try it," I say as Louis walks me to the register. "So, tell me about the shop."

His face lights up instantly. "Wild Card, well, it's my whole heart in one building," he says as he scans my game. "I worked at a gaming chain store in Chicago for years and always dreamed of how I'd do it differently. How I'd make it more than just a place to buy stuff. A place to build community and experience the magic of play with your neighbors. I only opened the store six months ago, and yeah, running a small business feels damn near impossible most of the time. I'm working sixteen-hour days, and hardly find the time to eat, and still worry about breaking even. But I look around at the family of gamers I've already brought together, and it amazes me. I'm getting ready to hire a new staff member who can lead a second Dungeons & Dragons campaign, because our waitlist is a mile long. And when I sell someone a game I know will bring them joy and let them spend quality time with their friends? Nothing compares to that feeling. Oh, speaking of, your total is $28.56."

"I can tell how special this place is, even just being here for a few minutes," I say, tapping my card to pay. "I want to create a window for you that brings the same enthusiasm and . . . unique energy that you do."

Louis laughs shyly. "You can say it. I'm a big old nerd."

"A nerd is the best thing a person can be," I say. "It means you're passionate about something. As someone who's spent a lot of time in dusty garages learning my old-school craft, I'd say I'm a pretty big nerd too."

"Go nerds!" Louis gives me a high five.

"So Chicago, huh? How'd you end up here?"

"My husband and I are rock climbers," Louis shares. "We heard Eureka was a good climbing spot, and super queer. We actually wanted to stay at this famous queer bed-and-breakfast we saw on TV, but turns out it closed a few years back. Didn't stop us from visiting town anyway, and then we were hooked. Now we're lifers."

I'm on the verge of confessing that the bed-and-breakfast he saw on TV was *mine*, but I can't quite manage the words.

"So you like it here? Even being all, you know . . . Arkansas?" I ask. I've always had an uncomfortable relationship to my home state. I don't have any family here anymore, not since my gram died. Yet I still feel tied to it in a way that sometimes feels comforting and sometimes hurts, especially when conservative politicians spew nonsense about queer people being the devil. I hear there are kinder places to live, even if I'm too scared of airplanes to see them for myself. My work has taken me all over this area of the country. My biggest commission yet involved installing steel-and-glass pieces across three states on Route 66. Even after years on the road, I can't imagine really leaving Arkansas for good. But I also can't imagine *choosing* to live here after growing up somewhere different.

Louis shifts his head and shrugs in a way I take to mean "it's complicated." "Is it perfect? Definitely not," he says. "I've encountered racists and homophobes. But they have those in Chicago too. And they don't have the same mountains, cool history, and queer hidden gems as Eureka. I love this weird little town. It may not be perfect, but I can build something here that makes it a little bit better. A community that plays together, that fosters creativity and connection and joy. That's what gaming's all about."

Hearing Louis echo all the things I love about this town makes me feel guilty for walking away from it seven years ago. As much as I've learned from my years on the road, as much as I've grown as an artist, I've still harbored some discomfort about leaving the inn, our employees, and our faithful guests. We built something special, a community kind of like what Louis is talking about, one I thought was meant to last. Did it make Eureka better? And if it did, was my impact erased when I packed my bags and ran?

I thank Louis for his time, grab the game I purchased, and walk back to the Hummingbird. Slowly, the sights, smells, and sounds of the Ozarks pull me out of my head. There's something extra magical about Eureka in June. Everything is blooming and green. The air smells like honeysuckle. Every restaurant and storefront has a Pride flag in the window, and queer tourists come from all over to hold hands and wander the town in their short shorts and crop tops. Back when the Hummingbird was at its peak, June was our busiest month. Some of our most loyal guests would book their stays for Pride years ahead of time.

When Robin and I first bought the Hummingbird Inn, I never dreamed it would become an LGBTQ+ travel destination. Robin and I never really felt like the Pride-celebrating, rainbow-flag-waving, "Born This Way" kind of gays. My grandmother never made me feel like an abomination for being a lesbian, and she also didn't turn into some outspoken queer advocate. To her, my sexuality was just a neutral fact about me, like my freckles or my shoe size, which is its own kind of progress, I guess. Robin's parents are similar, which is more surprising considering they're lifelong Republicans. But it was hard for both of us not to absorb some generalized shame about our queerness growing up in Little Rock. It felt like something to keep private, something that, if brought up around strangers, would likely bring more harm than good. But then I found Eureka Springs. I was suddenly surrounded by queer people, had access to spaces where Robin and I could hold hands in public, and was given the chance to attend drag performances like the one taking place in Basin Park as I walk by on my way home. When people started calling the Hummingbird a queer destination, I realized I actually felt proud of that label.

But the whole lore of the inn was founded on Robin and me, as a unit, as two people in love. *That B&B owned by the lesbian couple.* What was I supposed to do when she ran off to Portland with another woman? Convince tourists that *the B&B owned by one recently abandoned and heartbroken half of a lesbian couple* was just as romantic? Spend the rest of my

days in the penthouse apartment we'd shared, haunted by
memories of all the tiny celebrations we held and the cute
little love pranks we pulled on each other, watching alongside the rest of the Internet as Robin moved on to the hot
new chef of the week?

Louis's words about building a community that makes
the town he loves a little better are still echoing in my head
as I round the corner onto Bridge Street and spot the inn. I
want to hate this place. Maybe my life would improve if I
sold it to the first person to make a cash offer and washed my
hands of it forever. But when I see that hummingbird window gleaming in the sunlight, my heart beats faster. There's
something about this old building that sticks. I knew from
the moment I laid eyes on that stained-glass window thirteen
years ago that I was meant to find it, meant to give it the love
and care it deserves.

My grandmother loved hummingbirds, always had feeders for them on the front porch, would spend hours watching
them. She was a rather serious person, raised on a struggling
rice farm during the Great Depression. Gram didn't talk or
even smile much, but those tiny, flittering birds enchanted
her. Even though she passed before I found this place, I believe her spirit is in these walls. I took all the love still cours-
ing through my veins after her death and channeled it into
the inn. As I admire the exterior of the building in the afternoon sun, I remember how each repaired patch of drywall,
each new shingle on the roof, each coat of paint was my love
letter to her.

Or was it my love letter to Robin? Even now, I can't tell
where my feelings for the Hummingbird end and my history

with Robin begins. I fell for Robin and the inn in one life-altering tumble on a weekend getaway to Eureka just two weeks after we met. Looking back at that time, it's hard not to see myself as a grieving, vulnerable twenty-two-year-old, searching desperately for somewhere and someone to make me feel like I belonged. I'd just lost the only person who had ever truly loved me, ever tried to understand me. All it took was one of Robin's earnest, wide-eyed "I'm listening to you" faces and I would have followed her off a cliff. The Hummingbird Inn just happened to be the nearest one. Its owner, Miss Addy, who had been recently widowed and reminded me just a little too much of my own grandmother, was looking for someone to buy the inn so she could retire. It felt like fate. I fixed up Gram's house and sold it, Robin convinced her dad to let her access her trust fund, and suddenly we were two young idiots in charge of a decrepit historic property in need of a *lot* of work.

But what does it matter? I tried to make this place better, but whatever misplaced love I funneled into the inn is gone, replaced by cheap furniture and mass-produced "art." The pastel-painted exterior of the house may look mostly the same as how I left it, but inside, all the vintage charm I worked so hard to preserve has been erased in favor of decorations like any other vanilla hotel's. And now, in an effort to support my best friend and the town that built me, I have to face the two greatest failures of my life: my marriage and my B&B. Even if there *were* a world where I could fix up the Hummingbird and restore it to its original glory, I certainly can't do that with Robin lurking about. She's useless with a tool kit and was more of a hindrance than a help when we renovated the inn. Back then I found her DIY incompetence cute. Now I think it would toss my sanity down a garbage disposal.

I step onto the porch, readying myself for the frustrations waiting behind the front door, when I suddenly have an idea. What was it Key said about pushing Robin's buttons?

8

Robin

BY THE TIME I FINISH MY LUNCH AT COUNTERCULTURE, EVERY customer and employee in the place has figured out who I am, even if they've never seen me on TV. There's no way I can keep a low profile after this. I wave and smile politely at the queer twentysomething trying to discreetly take pictures of me with their phone, and step out onto the sidewalk. *Fuck.* My plans to hide out in Eureka are ruined already.

At least I've got a full stomach. Jesse's gotten *really* good since I last shared a kitchen with him. He kept the dishes coming for over two hours, and I didn't even notice until the fourth course that everything was vegan. Complicated puff pastries, even, with no butter. He's a goddamn magician.

I would be lying if I said I wasn't a little jealous. Honestly, I never thought a restaurant with Michelin-star potential could survive in the Armpit of the Ozarks. But one table of out-of-towners told me while I was autographing their napkins that they'd come to Eureka *just* for Jesse's restaurant.

Honestly? I'm hella proud of him. I knew from the beginning that he had the taste and determination to make it as a chef. All he needed was one mentor to give him a shot. I'm just the lucky bastard who said yes after all those transphobes turned him down.

But as I take the long way back toward the inn, visions of my own failed ventures throw off my balance, making the asparagus tartlets and piquillo-pepper canapés lurch in my stomach. Jesse created a smash-hit experimental vegan restaurant in a tiny town in a red state. I couldn't keep a trendy brunch restaurant open in the most hipster city on the continent.

But eating Jesse's food also reawakened something in me, a yearning to bust out of my comfort zone, to get my hands dirty, to create something that feels new. Jesse's black currant mousse gave me this idea for a trifle I'm dying to make. God, when was the last time I felt this much genuine excitement about cooking something? It feels like years.

I make a detour to the nearest grocery, and by the time I make it back to the inn, I'm practically buzzing. I think I have enough fresh mint in the garden out back to make a—

"What the hell is going on in here?" I blurt, batting my way through layers of plastic drop cloths taped over the kitchen doorway. Once I've untangled myself, I find Molly on a stepladder carving an enormous hole in the wall with a jigsaw for some godforsaken reason.

Molly turns off the saw and pushes her protective eye gear to the top of her head. "There's a leaky pipe in this wall," she explains. "I need to repair it."

I look disappointedly at the grocery bags in my hands. "It had to be fixed *now*?"

"Would you rather it burst and flood the whole kitchen?"

"No," I grumble. "But Jesus, you couldn't warn me first? I just bought all these ingredients to workshop a recipe."

"I noticed the water damage on the cabinets today," Molly says. That's when I realize there's a chunk of cabinets missing from the wall next to the sink. I spot them spread out along the opposite side of the kitchen. "The pipe was a ticking time bomb."

I pull off my baseball hat, ruffle my bangs, and put it back on. "How long do you think it will take to fix?" I ask, trying to hide how peeved I am by this leak ruining my plans.

Molly turns back to the massive hole, almost large enough to ride a bike through, and starts pulling off even more chunks of drywall. "A couple weeks? Maybe more, if there's damage under the tile." She shrugs. "Honestly, you're lucky it's stuff I can handle alone. If we had to call in a plumber and contractors to fix it, it could take months."

I blow out a frustrated sigh. "Well, what am I supposed to do in the meantime? Bake scones over a bonfire in the backyard?" I ask, wondering if I've really fallen so far that I'll have to return to the cooking techniques I learned as a kid at Girl Scout camp.

Molly pulls the trigger on the jigsaw, which makes a short buzz. "Like I said yesterday, there are plenty of kitchens in Eureka Springs. Surely you can find somewhere else. Maybe a suite at the Crescent Hotel, unless that's not classy enough for you these days." Molly pulls her goggles back down and fires up the saw. There's no time for a witty retort before dust starts flying and I'm forced to pull the neck of my shirt over my nose and mouth. I throw the whole bag of groceries in the fridge, even the things that are shelf-stable, then stomp out the back door onto the porch for some fresh air.

Not classy enough for me these days. As if I haven't spent the past few months eating ramen while watching the last dollars in my bank account circle the drain. I make my way over to the gazebo in the middle of the backyard, muttering the whole way about the groceries I blew twenty bucks on and now can't even use. She couldn't have sent me a text? Classic Molly. Always focused on the next project, never thinking about who gets screwed over when she turns off the water or switches the breakers or takes a door off its hinges.

I listen to the birds sing for a moment, thinking about my options, then get out my phone to do the scary but unavoidable thing. I call my manager.

Edgar answers with a weary "Hey, Robin. How's your retreat?"

That's how I've been selling my disappearance. I didn't run away to hide from my failure! I'm on a creative retreat!

"It's, uh, something," I say, unable to come up with a quick lie about how I'm thriving. "How's L.A.?"

"Oh, you know L.A. in June. All the locals go out of town to avoid the tourists coming *here* for vacation."

Edgar pauses for a moment, probably hoping I'll tell him I'm ready to get thrown back into the mouth of the Hollywood monster. He found me a couple guest-judge spots on some cooking competitions after Kindling closed, but I couldn't bear to show my face in public, so I turned them down. I mean, how would they even introduce me? *Please welcome our guest, owner of several short-lived restaurants, former star of various canceled and un-green-lit TV shows, chef Robin Lasko!*

When I don't say anything, Edgar asks, "So, any decisions on what you'd like to do next? We probably won't get more TV offers until the market picks up again in the fall, but now could be a good time to start talking to potential investors for a new restaurant."

"'Good time' seems like a stretch," I say, skeptical.

"Hey, even if Kindling never made it into the black, it got great media coverage and reviews. We could leverage that," Edgar says, almost exactly the same wording he's used every time we've talked since April. "It would help if you had an idea to pitch, though."

"Still working on it," I mumble. "But is there something low stakes I could do in the meantime to get some quick cash? Sell some recipes to some food magazines? Maybe a cookbook deal?"

"Honey, book deals are probably the slowest way to make money," Edgar says with his signature sass, which lets me know, even if he's annoyed with me, we're still in this together. After all, he only gets paid if I get paid. "Would you be willing to do a gig short-term as a guest chef? Dinner for a charity gala or something like that?"

I'm not sure why I hesitate, but I manage to say, "Maybe in a few more months."

Edgar takes a breath, then offers, "I could probably round up a few more social media partnerships."

I groan, thinking about how my platforms have been nothing but sponcon for weeks. But I know he's right. If I'm not willing to leave my hiding spot in Arkansas or commit to a bigger project, it's my only option. "Yeah, that would be great. The sooner, the better."

Edgar promises to keep me updated, then hangs up. He's a smart manager. Serving a fancy dinner at some fundraiser is an objectively good idea. Low commitment, high visibility. Some TV appearances or conversations with potential investors would also be good career moves. So why can't I bring myself to do any of it, even with the threat of going broke hanging over my head? I look back at the inn, admiring the pastel-painted trim and how the different stained-glass windows in the guest rooms shine in the afternoon sun. From here, you can almost forget everything the management company did to ruin the interior. But even with their bad choices, I'm grateful for a place to hide out and lick my wounds. I feel weirdly safe in the Hummingbird, even though my ex is currently inside tearing through the walls because the pipes are threatening to explode.

It's only then that I realize: I didn't see any water stains on those cabinets.

9

MOLLY

I'M STILL RIDING THE HIGH OF RUINING ROBIN'S DAY WHEN I hear her yelling again, somehow even louder than the buzzing of the jigsaw. I take my finger off the trigger and turn to find Robin hopelessly tangled in plastic drop cloths by the back door. Just as she manages to escape one, the other pulls off the wall and the loose tape sticks to the plastic on Robin's back, making it even harder to escape.

Could I help her? Yes. Will I instead enjoy watching her struggle? Obviously.

I'm barely holding back a laugh by the time she rips her way out, cursing, her face bright red. "Is all this really necessary when you're working on the other side of the goddamn room?"

I shrug. "If you want drywall dust and moldy insulation all over your cooking utensils, be my guest."

Robin takes a step forward, and static makes a plastic sheet cling to her leg. She tries to kick it away, but it only further attaches to her jeans. I watch wordlessly, trying not to notice the inches of skin between the hem of her shirt and the waistband of her pants, as she grabs the sheet and throws it with all her might. It floats for a moment before landing only a couple inches from her feet.

"Did you need something?" I ask with calculated non-chalance.

Robin points at the hole in the wall. "Where's the leak?"

It takes great effort not to roll my eyes. "Where do you think? It's where I cut the hole."

Robin comes closer, her whole body tensed as she stares into the void. "So why is it dry?" she says. "You said there was enough water damage for you to spot it, but I don't see any moisture."

"Because I already turned off the water and removed the damaged drywall," I say as if explaining it to a third grader.

Robin turns to the row of cabinets I removed earlier, now organized on the floor against the opposite wall, and says, "You said the water was soaking into the cabinets." She leans over to examine them, running a finger down a white-painted board. "But they're bone-dry."

"I wouldn't expect *you* to see the damage when you didn't even notice half the lightbulbs were burned out in here," I say primly. "Once I replaced them, the leak was obvious. Now, if you don't mind, I've got work to do. And you shouldn't be in here when I cut the pipe unless you've got safety goggles and work gloves."

"You don't even *do* plumbing," Robin says in a gotcha tone. "We always had to hire professionals for that."

I descend the stepladder, put down the jigsaw, and pull off my eye protection. "I didn't realize you kept track of the new skills I've learned in the seven years since you *left me*," I say, my iciness melting into a steamy rage. "Is it so hard to believe that after renovating this place nearly single-handedly, teaching myself to patch drywall and refinish floors and shingle roofs and weld and whittle wood trim and repair antique decorative windows, I was capable of learning to fix a leaky pipe?"

"I didn't say you were *incapable,*" Robin says, looking a little frightened but also unwilling to back down. "It just feels convenient that right now, when I need the kitchen for my work, there's suddenly some giant invisible leak that takes the whole room out of action."

I stare at Robin with such intensity that I wonder if I've manifested the power to shoot lasers from my eyes. "You're accusing me of lying? You think I tore open this wall for *fun*?"

"I wouldn't put it past you, no."

Furious, I turn my back on Robin and stomp right up to the hole, then turn around and gesture for her to follow. She does, although she maintains enough distance to make it harder for me to strangle her. I splay a hand across the drywall to the left of the opening. Robin stares at me like I've lost my marbles. "Put your hand on the goddamn wall, Rob," I say, the once familiar nickname surprising me as it leaves my mouth. Robin visibly stiffens. It started as a term of endearment, but became something I called her only in moments of irritation by the end.

Robin concedes, placing her palm against the wall several feet away from me.

"Not there." When I grab her hand to pull it closer, it's like the whole world flips upside down for a second before righting itself again, leaving me dizzy and disoriented. It's our first skin-to-skin contact in years, and it feels like my body has been spun through one of those starship rides at the state fair. Does she feel the same?

I pull back as if I've been stung. Robin leaves her hand where I moved it, just to the side of the jagged square. I clear my throat. "Waterlogged drywall feels cooler to the touch. See how it's cooler closer to the pipe there?"

Robin slides her hand back and forth along the flat surface, looking uncertain. "Maybe?" she says.

I sigh and unclip a flashlight from my belt. "See how it's dark and discolored? There's clearly some water absorbed into these wooden support beams," I explain. "It's lucky I caught it when I did. I can run a dehumidifier in here, dry it out while I patch the pipe, and we won't have to replace any of the structure. This could have been a five-figure repair cost if the pipe had fully blown."

Something in Robin's posture seems to shift, shrinking by inches. "Fine. Do what you need to do," she concedes.

"That's all? No apology for calling me a liar?"

Her eyes flit up to mine for a moment before falling back to the floor. "I'm sorry I questioned your expertise," she murmurs.

I know my smile is smug, but I can't stop it from unfurling across my face. "Now, if it's all right with you, I'm going to try to get this kitchen back in working order ASAP."

As soon as she's out of the room, I release a huge sigh of relief.

A burst pipe is never a good thing. A completely fine pipe that I can pretend is burst? That's a different story. Sometimes you have to be the leaky pipe you wish to see in the world. Besides, Robin's right. I have no idea how to fix plumbing.

I do, however, know how to act like I know what I'm talking about when it comes to home repair. I also know how to draw out a DIY project until Robin's sick to death of the inconvenience. When I told her I'd have the kitchen back in order ASAP, I meant "as slowly as possible." Only one of us can live at the Hummingbird this summer, and I'll move heaven and earth to make sure it's me.

10

Robin

I DRAG MY FEET UP THE STAIRS, LOCK MYSELF IN THE ZINNIA Room, and collapse onto the bed. I'm such an asshole. How could I think Molly came up with some fake plumbing scheme just to mess with me? Here she is making sure our shared property doesn't fall to pieces and all I can do is complain about what an inconvenience it is to me personally. Talk about self-centered.

Maybe Molly's right. Maybe I should just find somewhere else to lie low for a while. But where else can I stay for free while I figure out what to do with my life next? I've cashed in every available favor in L.A. and the whole Pacific Northwest at this point. While pouring every dollar I earned back into my restaurants, I wore out my welcome with every industry acquaintance with a guest room. I've let most of my friendships from my pre-TV days wither to dust. But there must be someone who would be happy to see my face on their doorstep, right?

My parents are the obvious answer. A year ago, I'd have sooner slept in my car than move into my parents' basement. But here I am, facing down the decision, and . . . well, my car doesn't have wifi, or a refrigerator full of gourmet olives.

I heave myself up and find my dad's number on my phone, ready for my second miserable call of the afternoon. I give myself a pep talk with my thumb hovering over the call button. *It's your dad. He loves you. Sure, he shows it in some pretty annoying ways, but if he knows you need help, won't he be more than willing to give it?*

I press the button. It only rings twice before I hear my dad's voice.

"Birdie!" he says. One word and I'm already cringing. I hate that nickname. It makes me sound like an eccentric old lady who sexually harasses servers at bingo night. But Dad continues, unaware of the face I'm making on the other end of the line. "Been a long time since I heard from my only daughter. Thought you might have gotten too famous for your old man. Sharon, get over here! Robin's on."

"You know I could never get too famous for you, Dad," I say, my jaw tense around the fake smile intended to make my voice sound friendlier.

"Robin, honey?" I hear my mom's voice grow louder as she gets closer to the phone. "Is everything all right?"

"Of course everything's all right," I lie, wanting to ease into asking the favor. "Just wanted to see how things are going in Little Rock."

"You know us, always busy," my mom says. "Gabriel is

mad at us for letting Annalise and Bradford watch your old VHS of *The Nightmare Before Christmas* while they were here last weekend. Apparently Annalise still won't let them turn the lights off at bedtime."

I snort, picturing my introverted younger brother lecturing my parents about which movies are appropriate for his kids. "Four and one do seem a little young for Tim Burton," I admit. I'm still scarred from when we watched *The Sixth Sense* when I was nine and Gabe was seven. My parents assumed it was a kids' movie because it starred one.

"Eh, they'll be fine," Dad says, unbothered. "Hey, have I told you my new practice in Bryant is opening next month? It's close to the golf club, so I'll always make it to tee time."

Can my parents hear me roll my eyes? "Sounds great, Dad," I say.

"Speaking of the club, did you hear Penelope Ratcliffe got a divorce?" my mom says.

"I haven't talked to Penelope since college, Mom. How would I know that?" I've gone from polite to surly in under a minute, a new record.

"I heard about the whole gay marriage getting legalized thing, but when did they pass gay divorce?" my dad says in his amateur-stand-up-comic voice.

"Ha ha."

"Maybe you should give Penelope a call," my mom says. "Catch up. You're not with that hippie anymore, right? What was her name . . . Georgia?"

"Georgina," I say tightly. "We broke up. And she's not a hippie, she just lives in Portland." I can feel a headache brewing. "Anyway, I thought y'all should know I'm in Eureka Springs for a bit."

"Eureka! I've found her!" my dad says, and my mom laughs in the way only a wife can. "You filming something new up there? When can you come down to see us?"

"Not filming," I say, massaging my forehead with one hand. "I'm using the Hummingbird Inn's kitchen for some recipe testing."

"Recipe testing?" my dad asks. "For that camping restaurant?"

"You know that place closed," I say, failing to curb the annoyance in my voice.

"What was it called again? Scorcher? Burned Out?"

Hearing my dad joke about my passion project, the restaurant I poured my heart and soul into, stings. I've known my dad long enough to get that humor (especially bad humor) is his love language, but *really*? Can't he joke about, I don't know, literally anything else? "It was called Kindling."

"Up in Flames would have been a better name for it," he says in a muffled voice, like he's talking more to my mom than to me. "Since it, you know, went up in—"

"Oh, look at that, my manager's on the other line," I blurt out. "Sorry, I've got to run. Love y'all, I'll try to make it down soon!"

I slam the end call button and throw my phone across the room.

Well, that was a terrible idea. If I can't spend five minutes on the phone with my parents, there's no way in hell I can *live* with them. Molly may be a hostile roommate, but I guess I choose her over my parents' laughing at every mistake I've ever made. Or calling me too sensitive when I don't find being the butt of the joke funny.

I look around the Zinnia Room, which no longer has any

evidence of why we gave it that name in the first place. Molly and I bought the inn from an antiquer named Miss Addy. When we first visited, the rooms had the most horrifyingly tacky themes. Roosters. Gone fishing. One room was decorated head to toe for Christmas all year long. And worst of all: the porcelain doll room. I had literal nightmares about it for years. Even though it was my job to sell all the old decorations on eBay, I had to beg Molly to deal with the creepy dolls because I couldn't even look at them without hyperventilating.

When Molly and I bought the inn from Miss Addy, we wanted room themes that felt simple but impactful, timeless but also relevant. Ultimately, the hummingbird window inspired us. For the guest rooms, we chose eight different flowers that hummingbirds love, and we decorated accordingly. We chose zinnias, petunias, lilacs, and honeysuckles for the second floor, sunflowers, lilies, azaleas, and snapdragons for the third. Molly's grandma had left her a bunch of handmade quilts with floral patterns that fit pretty close. We paid Keyana to paint murals of the flower of choice in each room, and Molly made stained-glass windows to match. When I took charge of the gardens, I planted the same flowers so we could arrange them in vases and use them for decoration when they were in bloom. The garden had the side benefit of drawing more real hummingbirds to the inn. Guests ate it up.

But now the Zinnia Room looks just like all the others. Instead of Keyana's colorful mural, there's a light gray wall and a mass-produced painting of some footprints on a beach. No fresh flowers on the dresser. No lovingly handmade floral quilt. Just Molly's stained-glass window of a bouquet of pink, orange, and yellow blossoms without context. It may be a lifeless imitation of what this inn once was. But for now? For *free*? I guess it'll do.

I hear the doorbell, then the sound of Molly talking to someone else echoing up the stairwell. Too nosy to ignore it, I stick my head out of the Zinnia Room door. I'm surprised to recognize the voice of an old friend.

"Jesse and Caro told me Robin was in town, but I didn't know you were here too!" I hear the voice say to Molly.

"Clint!" I say, nearly tripping down the steps in my excitement. "You're still in Eureka!"

"Of course I am," Clint says, pulling me in for a hug when I reach the porch. "I'm a lifer."

"Holy shit, dude," I say, pulling back to examine his outfit. His three-piece suit is a major change from the denim cutoffs and tank tops he used to wear for his dozens of part-time jobs around town. Seems like he's moved up in the world, but he's still got the same scrappy charm and contagious smile. "You look great. Is that Hermès?"

"Oh, stop," Clint says, smoothing back his already perfectly styled dark hair. "I just came from a meeting with some investors. Had to get dolled up."

"Investors?" I say, blinking.

"I own One More Round now," Clint says like it's old news. And maybe it is, but not to me. One More Round was a little run-down back in the day, but still the best gay bar in Eureka. And Clint was everyone's favorite bartender, always good for a heavy pour and a little gossip.

Molly freezes, the dirty rag she was using to wipe her hands going still. "You *what*?" she says, equally shocked.

"May I come in?" Clint asks, and we both usher him

through the door. Clint hugs me, then turns to Molly, but seeing how covered in dust and drywall she is, opts for a pat on the back instead. "Yeah, I bought out the bar a few years back. It was really struggling and the owners were desperate to get rid of it. I used all the renovation and design stuff you taught me at the inn—thanks again, Molly—and now it's less hole-in-the-wall and more sleek, trendy club people travel from out of state to visit."

Molly looks as astonished as I feel when she says, "That's incredible, Clint. I'm so happy for you. I'll have to visit while I'm in town."

"You must! Drinks on the house." Clint pauses for a moment, taking in the dull gray hellscape around him. "Speaking of house . . . what the hell happened here?"

Molly and I muddle through an embarrassed explanation of the management company's poor choices. It's strange to be on the same side of an issue after how much we've been butting heads, but there's no denying their redesign was a major downgrade.

Based on Clint's overly theatrical response, I'm guessing he'd heard rumor of the makeunder from Jesse and Caro, but seeing it in person is a whole other kind of shock. After all, he was here for the Hummingbird's glow-up. Miss Addy had used Clint as a handyman, and Molly kept him around to help with some of her projects when she realized how embarrassingly unhandy I was with power tools. "That company should be run out of town for ruining this place," Clint declares. "It looks like if Eeyore decided to take up interior design. *After* going off his antidepressants. You're planning to fix it, right?"

My glance meets Molly's for a moment before we both

look away like eye contact is lava. "We're here for . . . other reasons," I say.

Clint points toward the plastic tarps hanging from the kitchen doorway. "But . . ."

"Just fixing a leak," Molly says.

"That's a shame," Clint says with a sigh. "I've been thinking about expanding my portfolio in town. Buying a restaurant, or a spa, or, I don't know, maybe an artfully quirky vintage bed-and-breakfast with national name recognition among queer travelers."

If I were a cartoon character, my pupils would be dollar signs right now. "You'd think about buying the Hummingbird?" I ask.

Clint waves a hand toward the horrible exposed-bulb light fixture on the dining-room ceiling. "Not like this. Sorry, but I saw how hard y'all worked to get it in shape last time, and I'm still burned out from renovating the bar. I'm not looking for this much of a fixer-upper. But if you two were to flip it again together . . . y'all *are* back together, right?"

"No," Molly and I say in unison.

"We're, uh, here to work some things out. Separately," I add.

Clint looks back and forth between us. "Okay, then," he says skeptically. "If you decide bringing the inn back to its former glory and selling it will help you 'work some things out' . . . " He pulls a business card from the inside pocket of his suit jacket and hands it to me. "Call me. Anyway, got to run. Some luxury liquor salesmen invited me to a tasting in a cave. Seriously, come to the bar soon. Good to see y'all back in town!"

After Clint leaves, I look down at the thick, matte, gold-embossed card in my hand—*Clint Boswell, innovative entre-preneur, style icon.* I turn to Molly, thrilled at the possibility of Clint's offer, only to be met with a stony look.

"Absolutely not," she says, then spins around and disappears through the kitchen door.

"Can't we talk about it?" I ask, but I can't even finish my sentence before I'm cut off by the roar of some power tool.

I guess that easy money won't be as easy as I hoped.

11
MOLLY

"NO," I TELL ROBIN FOR WHAT FEELS LIKE THE MILLIONTH time as I linger outside the door to the basement, a basket full of dirty laundry in my arms. Everywhere I've been this week—working on stained glass in the shed, repairing the supposedly burst pipe in the kitchen, searching high and low for a moment of peace—Robin keeps managing to corner me to try to convince me to accept Clint's offer.

"But why?" Robin asks. "Aren't all the gray walls and tacky light fixtures and canvas prints of beaches killing you?"

"Of course they are," I say, readjusting the basket on my hip. "But I didn't come here to renovate the inn again. I have work to do."

Robin paces across the floor of the dining room, bumping into one of the cheap folding café tables. "Sure. But with the money we could make from selling the inn, you wouldn't *need* to work for a while. When's the last time you took a vacation?"

"I'm not the vacationing type."

"Fine," Robin says. "Then I'll do it myself."

I don't intend for my laugh to sound harsh, but I've never heard such a harebrained idea. "You don't even know how to use a power drill," I say.

Robin looks offended. "Sure I do."

I put down the laundry and produce the yellow-and-black bag from where I stored it under the check-in desk. "Okay, then," I say, pushing the bag into Robin's hands. "Show me."

Robin straightens up and rolls her shoulders back in a move I can tell is meant to convince herself of her competence just as much as me. She pulls out the drill, holds it with two arms fully extended like a sheriff in a Western, and presses the trigger. It makes a whirring sound, and Robin smirks at me like she deserves a round of applause.

I cross my arms. "Won't you need a bit?"

"Uh . . ." Robin turns the drill around and sees the blank space at the chuck. She digs in the bag to find a bit, inserts it, then pulls the trigger again. The bit, predictably, falls to the floor.

My point proved, I pick up my basket and walk downstairs to the basement.

"This conversation isn't over!" I hear Robin's voice echo behind me. "You'll see reason at some point!"

We've been having this fight for almost a week, and I don't intend to come around to Robin's view. The job of fixing up the inn sat largely on my shoulders last time, and I'm not falling into that trap again, especially if Robin intends to take half of the money in the end. Sure, she helped with some painting and cleaning, but she spent most of her time selling Miss Addy's antiques, getting all the business licenses squared away, building our website, and testing recipes for breakfast service. None of which would be necessary this time around. Besides, haven't we been fighting enough without a massive, high-stress project on our hands? My only path back to sanity is getting Robin out of here, not committing to several more months together. Especially because this disagreement is reminding me of a different kind of tension we used to have. One that's decidedly more . . . heated.

I try to shake the encounter from my head and focus on my dirty clothes. I haven't been down in the basement since I returned to the inn. First, because it's creepy. It's dark and shadowy and smells like mildew and for some reason there's a random horse saddle? If anywhere in this house is haunted, it's the basement.

Second, though, is because it's where Robin and I used to sneak away to make out early on when the inn was full of guests. We even had sex down here once. Okay, more than once. And yes, the horse saddle was sometimes involved. But we stopped when we realized it wasn't worth getting cobwebs in our underpants.

I get a little flushed remembering all that sweat and heavy breathing and intensity. But I shove a load of laundry into the machine and slam the door shut on those memories. It's been a long time since I got laid. It's hard when you're on the road, working on commissions, sore from welding and soldering. Maybe some people manage to find hookups while traveling for work, but it's not my style. I like to get to know someone first.

And unfortunately, I know Robin *quite* well. I know exactly what happens when I kiss that spot where her neck meets her collarbone. I know how her callused yet soft hands feel against my skin. I know the precise gasp she makes when I use my tongue to drive her right to the edge, and how to keep her there until she's ready to burst.

I wipe away a bead of sweat and fiddle with the buttons on the machine until I find the right setting. As I press start, it occurs to me that maybe I *don't* know Robin like that anymore. We've now been apart slightly longer than we were together. My body has changed since the last time we saw each other naked. Hers probably has too. I wonder if that birthmark on her rib cage still looks like the Little Dipper. If her breasts still fit perfectly in my palms like they were made to go together. If she'd still make that irresistible low moan if I ran my fingernails up the inside of her thigh.

Whew, I think the AC is broken down here. I tie my hair into a messy knot on top of my head and fan the back of my neck with a file folder of old documents I grab from a nearby cabinet.

This level of horniness is not sustainable. I can't think about Robin like this when she's walking around right over my head, so close but untouchable. I've got to figure out a way to defuse this sexual tension, and fast.

At least I can distract myself for now with this mess in the basement. I elbow through the piles of boxes and old furniture around the machines. It looks like the management company didn't get rid of everything, thankfully. If I hadn't been faced with the more pressing problem of co-habitating with my ex-wife, finding out what happened to all this stuff would have been my top priority.

Poking through the storage, it only takes a minute to find a box with all the old quilts that used to be on the guest beds, each one handmade by my gram. I took my favorite one with me when I left, but losing the collection would have felt like losing her all over again. For a moment, I get lost in running my fingers over her careful stitches, admiring her choices of colors and shapes to create sprawling floral patterns.

I peek into more boxes, sorting some of the contents and clearing more floor space in the basement. It looks like most of the antique decorations are here, lamps and framed art and knick-knacks. The dining room furniture is stacked under the stairs, along with some of the chairs and bedside tables from the guest rooms. I find a folder with a key to a nearby storage unit and a list of larger furniture supposedly held there. As staunchly opposed as I am to restoring the inn with Robin, it's hard to look at all this stuff and not feel nostalgic.

Even more unsettling are the boxes of our personal things that got left behind. The tacky bunny mug Robin gave me for our first Christmas. The two-seat kayak we bought once we hired enough staff to take days off to spend at the lake. The oversize guest book from our wedding.

Just when I've had enough of wandering down memory lane, the washing machine buzzes. I switch my clothes over to dry and head back upstairs with plans to start cutting glass for the board-game store's window. But then I smell burning plastic coming from the kitchen. I push my way through the drop cloths to find Robin at the same moment the smoke detector starts beeping.

"What the hell?" I pull down two pieces of plastic to reach the window above the sink and immediately push it open. Then I work on untangling Robin from the staticky drop cloths to find the source of the burning smell. She'd somehow managed to carve out a bubble in my construction zone around the stove. "Get out of there!" I demand.

Robin emerges from the gap in the plastic sheets, coughing and holding a smoking pan. "Whew. That did not go as expected," she says lightly, as if she didn't just nearly give me a heart attack.

I pull more of the sheets from around the hot stove to redirect another cloud of smoke. "Do you have any idea how fucking dangerous this is?" I shout over the alarm, fanning until it stops shrieking.

"I know, I know," Robin says. "I could have messed up your drywall or whatever. But hey, I made grilled cheese! Want one?"

"You could have *died*," I say, shocked that she can be so cavalier while my adrenaline is pumping. I may hate her, but I was fully prepared to drag her from the building and perform mouth-to-mouth resuscitation. "You turned on a gas stove with zero ventilation. You could have suffocated. You could have caught yourself on fire!"

Robin grimaces. "Well, that's why I turned on the hood vent. But then it created a weird vacuum and the plastic got stuck on the burner and . . ." She trails off and starts waving away the smoke with a couple of oven mitts.

I massage my temples. "You don't have the common sense God gave a goose."

Dropping the mitts on the counter, Robin says, "I should probably be offended by that, but it's the goofiest way of insulting someone I've ever heard." She steps closer to where I'm bundling up damaged plastic drop cloths, analyzing my expression. "Were you worried about me? Is that it? Look at me. I'm fine. So is the kitchen. I made a little mistake, but we're good."

Instead of admitting that she's right, I *was* scared she'd get hurt, I focus on the building. "You could have burned down the whole inn. Miss Addy is probably rolling over in her grave."

Robin's face goes pale. "Her . . . grave?"

"She passed in 2022," I say, quieter when I see how devastated she is by this news. "Heart attack. I forwarded the obituary and funeral details to your assistant."

"I never saw them," Robin admits, voice hoarse. As I watch her make the decision to put her feelings away and move on for now by busying herself with the pan on the stove, I remember how she's never been good at sitting with grief. When her favorite aunt died, she wouldn't talk about it, just put on a smile and spent a week obsessively polishing the silverware. Now she clears her throat and holds out the pan, where two only slightly overcooked grilled cheeses are still steaming. "Well, then, should we have lunch?"

I blink at her, knowing pain was behind the emotional U-turn I just witnessed but unable to fully make it with her. "The sandwiches you risked life and limb to make? I'll pass."

"Well, what am I supposed to do?" Robin says, her falsely calm exterior finally slipping. "I have to eat, and you already closed up the drywall, but you just want me to starve to death waiting for you to say the kitchen's finished?"

"The spackle is drying, and I still have to add another layer tomorrow, sand it, paint it, reattach the cabinets," I say, counting off the tasks on my fingers. "Dust will go everywhere. It's not something I can rush."

"But," Robin says, an obnoxiously hopeful look swinging back onto her face, "with all that, you'll have basically renovated one room. We'll just need to do eight more, and then we can sell the inn to Clint. Right?"

"Wrong!" I say, my temporary feelings of sympathy evaporating in favor of the old, familiar resentment. "Eight guest rooms, eight guest bathrooms, the hallway and check-in area, the dining room, and the penthouse? That's more like twenty rooms. And fixing the pipe in the kitchen has already put me behind on my glass projects. Renovations take a ton of time. Time *I* don't have, even if you've got all the time in the world to test recipes and make my life miserable."

Her lips are pressed together in two thin lines. "It never took you this long back in the day."

"Are you kidding me?" I say with an unamused laugh. "It took *months*."

"But no hole in a wall took more than a couple days, three max!" Robin says, outright yelling at this point.

"If you know so much about leaky plumbing and drywall, fix it yourself!"

"Maybe I will!"

I don't know when it happened, but suddenly we're less than a foot apart, my face turned up toward Robin's, her looking down her nose at me, engaged in the glaring match of the century. Robin's gaze is intense, her golden-brown eyes blazing like hot copper foil. My rage is simmering dangerously close to the surface. It may only be one small spat, but with this crackling energy between us, it feels like I've traveled through a time machine and been dumped out right in the middle of our fights back in 2018. She'd try to convince me to move to Portland with her to open a restaurant and I'd try to convince her to stay here and appreciate what we'd already built. Both of us so certain we knew what was best for each other, what could keep our love alive when we'd grown so far apart.

But it's not 2018. Our marriage is already wrecked. I don't have to stay here and keep reliving the year that proved I was doomed to spend my life alone. I break eye contact, turn on my heel, and stomp out of the kitchen.

12
Robin

I WATCH THROUGH THE KITCHEN WINDOW AS MOLLY BLAZES across the yard and locks herself in the shed. I really thought that kitchen encounter was going to end differently for a second. It's been a long (*long*) time since I've kissed Molly, so maybe I forgot how close that about-to-make-out vibe is to fighting. The extended eye contact. The physical intensity. The way her lips get all pouty and I can hardly keep myself from running my thumb along them to see if they feel as soft as they look.

Nope, that was definitely a fight. And our relationship is messy enough already. Kissing is, objectively, a Very Bad Idea.

Especially because I'm angry at Molly, I remind myself as I shake the frustration out of my body like a wet dog and carry my lunch to a table in the dining room. She's not the only one here allowed to be upset. I have just as much right to hold a grudge as she does. We had a chance at a shared future, an opportunity to build something bigger than this inn, this town, this soul-crushingly red state, and she didn't believe in me, or in *us*, enough to try. Maybe my restaurants would have succeeded if we'd built them together. If I hadn't been fighting to get them off the ground alone.

And just because she's afraid of planes and decided the Hummingbird Inn was her safety blanket doesn't make her the sole arbiter of its fate. Sure, she managed it without me while I was filming and for a few months after I moved to Portland. Yes, she did the lion's share of the renovations and upkeep. But I painted some of these walls. I cleaned up the yard and planted the gardens. I interpreted all the legalese in the mortgage and contributed half of the down payment. I helped keep Miss Addy's legacy alive, even if I didn't know until now that she died and dammit, I'm heartbroken because she was special to me. But this is *our* inn, not Molly's. And if she's going to rip a hole in the kitchen wall, I think as I take an aggressive bite from my grilled cheese, I should at least get some say.

Besides, I still have my doubts. I did some googling, and I'm not convinced I saw a leaky pipe in that wall. I wouldn't put it past her to try and inconvenience me enough to scare me off. But if she'd seen my bank account, she'd know I have a compelling reason to stick it out.

I'll admit it: I suck at living on a budget. I grew up in the old money part of Little Rock, going to the best private schools, never went to bed hungry. If my parents and I fought over buying new clothes, it wasn't over the price, but because I wanted the dykiest ripped-up jeans and flannel shirts I could find, while my mom thought I should always be dressed for surprise stops at the country club. It was honestly shocking how well they handled me coming out. But even now, I think they wish I were a different sort of lesbian. More like Penelope Ratcliffe, who fits in networking with doctors and lawyers better than playing pool with dishwashers and line cooks.

The worst part, I admit to myself while chewing on a bit of burned crust, is that they might have been right. Working some desk job probably would have been smarter. I couldn't swing it as a chef, and now I'm barely eking out a living on my last few paid social media partnerships. Looks like I'm barreling toward a career change, whether I want it or not.

Unless we manage to whip the inn back into shape and sell it to Clint. Then I'd have enough money to fuck out of Molly's life forever. Isn't that what she wants? To never see or speak to me again? Isn't that why the inn has sat here unused for so many years, because she'd rather let it rot than face me? But no, apparently, I'm hopelessly incompetent because I don't know how to attach a stupid drill bit.

So maybe what I need to do, I think as I look around at the poorly redecorated dining room, is prove I'm not a useless idiot. Take some initiative. Even if Molly's refusing to renovate with me, I can stake some claim and show her I have just as much right to be here as her.

After I've polished off both grilled cheeses and made Marmalade do some cardio by chasing a string on a stick, I hear Molly come in through the back door. She walks down the hallway right by me, not even glancing my way, goes upstairs for a few minutes, then leaves through the front door.

I peek through the hummingbird window to watch her walk toward downtown. Once she's out of sight, I go back to the kitchen, which still smells like burned plastic, and gather a portable cooktop, a slow cooker, a pressure cooker, a giant toaster oven, and an armful of cooking utensils. If I can't have the kitchen, I'll create my own makeshift workspace.

The dining room has lots of natural light for photographing dishes for social media. And the check-in counter is the perfect standing height for food prep, so I find an extension cord and start plugging in all the small appliances I gathered. The fact that Molly will have to walk right through my new kitchen setup every time she comes downstairs is a bonus. I'm so proud of myself for this plan that I almost forget that I don't have a real reason to test any recipes.

13

MOLLY

THE MOMENT I WALK IN THE FRONT DOOR OF THE INN AFTER my meeting at Wild Card, I know exactly what Robin's doing. She's rearranged the whole dining room and reception area specifically to get a rise out of me. It clearly can't work as a cooking space. There's no sink. Or refrigerator. Or stove. Yet somehow she's got a pan with garlic and rosemary sizzling away, sending billowing steam through my whole front hallway.

This room isn't properly ventilated; the heat and smells could cause permanent damage. I want to demand that she clear this stuff away immediately. I want to shut this whole thing down. But another fight is exactly what she wants. So instead, I purse my lips, turn around, and walk up the stairs to the third floor. I close the door to the Snapdragon Room behind me. And then I scream into my pillow.

I thought I'd moved on completely, accepted that I'd spend my life without attachments, grown into a more independent, coolheaded, unflappable person. Yet two weeks with Robin has me all kinds of flapped.

I can't help being reminded of how I felt when I first met Robin, back when we were both only twenty-two. I thought I had adulting totally figured out. In some ways, I did. I'd always been ahead of my peers in the maturity department, uninterested in childish drama, less likely to throw fits over minor inconveniences, more aware of how much toys and candy and extracurricular activities cost and why that meant I couldn't always get what I wanted. That's what happens sometimes when you're born to teen parents: You end up raising yourself. But at twenty-two, I still had a lot to learn about who I was and what I wanted out of life. I had to realize that the only person I could ever really trust was myself.

With a sigh, I decide to stop pouting and get out my sketchpad to work on my design for Wild Card. But even with a pencil in my hand, my mind wanders to my parents, who split up before I reached kindergarten. Who could blame them? They were still kids too. My dad became a long-haul trucker, always on the road, occasionally sending my mom a check for my upkeep. Mom and I lived with my gram, and Dad would drop by once or twice a year. It would always take me a minute to remember who he was. He faded out of my life so gradually that I never thought to ask when he'd return.

Mom and I were closer, even if she felt more like an

older sister than a parent most days. But when I was in middle school, she got sucked in by some evangelical church. She saw being "born again" as a chance for a new life, an opportunity to erase all her past mistakes—mistakes like me. By the time I started high school, she'd found a pastor husband and moved all the way to South Dakota near his new church, starting over with a fresh set of kids while I stayed in Arkansas with my grandmother. I scribble away at my sketchpad as I think of the three half-siblings I've never met, could only maybe recognize by the Christmas cards I used to receive once a year before I sold Gram's house and neglected to send my mother my new address. It was less painful to lose touch than know she had the means to reconnect and chose not to. The last time I heard her voice was shortly after high school graduation, when Gram convinced me to come out to Mom as a lesbian, suggesting that revealing my truth might bring us closer together. Instead, Mom suggested I "pray the demons away." I was crushed and gave up on having a relationship with her entirely. But I didn't realize until years later, when I was going through Gram's desktop computer after she died, that she'd sent Mom a fiery letter about her response, defending me tooth and nail. The phrase "she's not full of demons, *you* are full of shit" was a real standout, especially considering Gram rarely cursed.

Looking down, I realize that instead of a board-game-inspired window, I've accidentally sketched my favorite of Gram's quilt designs, the sunflower one I brought with me on the road when I left the inn. She's the only person I ever really needed. Gram was always there for me: to change my diaper when my parents were grossed out, to teach me to ride a bicycle, to celebrate when I got my first job at Home

Depot. She showed up at every occasion where parents were expected to support their kid, to make sure I never felt alone. And I took care of her too. I taught myself to fix things around our house, covered some of our bills with my meager pay-checks, drove Gram to her doctors' appointments when her heart started acting up. When my high school friends went off to college, I threw away all my fancy pamphlets with pic-tures of green quads and big brick libraries, picked up more hours at Home Depot, and focused on trying to convince Gram to follow a heart-healthy diet and give up her stressful job at the post office.

And then, quick as lightning, she was gone. While the rest of my friends were getting drunk at frat parties, I was ordering death certificates for various insurances and debt collectors and taking Gram's will to probate. Alone. Mom, who was eight months pregnant at the time, didn't even send a condolence card, much less travel down for the funeral. It made more sense after I discovered the letter Gram sent to her after I came out, but it still stung.

I was still reeling from my loss that day at Home Depot when Robin wandered in, looking devastatingly hot in her ripped jeans and vintage Toad Suck Daze festival T-shirt, her messy dark-blond hair sticking out from under a red beanie. Perhaps any cute lesbian who asked me for a barn-door-mounting kit with a mischievous gleam in their eye could have changed my life that Thursday afternoon. I was desper-ate for someone to cling to, to keep me afloat. It just so hap-pened to be Robin who walked in and became my life raft.

By the time I met Robin, I was an expert at getting left behind, so I should have been ready for her to abandon me at the inn six years later. If I could survive my dad leaving, then my mom, then losing my gram, always somehow coming out stronger on the other side, I knew objectively that I could make it through Robin running away in pursuit of fortune, fame, and a hotter, more ambitious woman. I had already suspected there was something going on with her and Georgina, her competitor on *Let's Do Brunch,* the series she spent six weeks filming about a year before our split. The best reality TV producers in Hollywood couldn't have made that romantic arc up. When I confronted her, Robin said she'd been pushed to talk about her natural connection with Georgina and the production team cut all the confessional footage of her talking about me. Her wife. Whether or not that was true, the effect was the same. I was humiliated, heartbroken, and furious at myself for not seeing it coming.

Robin's betrayal hurt worse than any of the ones before it, I realize as I flip over on the bed and turn a page in my notebook. At some point in our six years together, I'd let my guard down. I'd started to believe that we really could be together forever. That I really wouldn't have to go through life by myself. Shocking that I could still be so naïve after all I'd been through. It's a mistake I won't make again. You come into this world alone, you leave it alone, and you might as well spend the time in between alone too.

If only I could be alone in the Hummingbird like I planned. Robin's presence is messing with my head, making it impossible to keep my emotions carefully locked away. While I start a fresh sketch of the streets of downtown Eureka as a board-game map, I think about how I should focus on my work, support Keyana, and get back on the road as quickly as possible. Even though Robin's driving me bananas, as I trace the familiar streets, I can't deny that Eureka feels like where I'm supposed to be right now. I've given up on putting down roots, but being here brings back a tiny bit of the youthful optimism that drew me to the inn in the first place. Maybe there is something I need to do here.

Pausing my work, I look up at the sad gray walls and mass-produced furniture in the Snapdragon Room. To be honest, my fingers have been itching to tear out the ugly fake flooring and cheap light fixtures since I first laid eyes on them. Clint's idea isn't bad. I *do* want to return the inn to its former glory and leave it in trustworthy hands. I just don't want to do it with *her*. Too many distracting memories of those sweaty, exhausting, blissful months after we first bought the inn, of falling deeply in love as we worked our way through the long list of necessary repairs and figured out what to do with all of Miss Addy's antiques, of hiding little surprise gifts and silly notes for Robin in unexpected corners, and of how full my heart felt when I uncovered her goofy, sweet pranks in return.

I sit up from where I've spread across my bed, pencil still in hand as the memory gives me an idea. I grab my empty laundry bag and run down the stairs to the basement, not sparing a glance in Robin's direction as I pass her new kitchen setup. Then I dig past all the items I organized earlier until I find the one I'm looking for: a dusty old box pushed to the back corner under the stairs. Peeling back the layers of tape, I pull open the box to find a dozen sets of glass eyes, staring at me like they've been waiting a decade for this.

It's time for the revenge of the dolls.

14
Robin

MY ALARM GOES OFF BRIGHT AND EARLY ON TUESDAY MORNING.
Now that I've got a workable cooking space set up, I actually
have something to wake up for. The savory stuffed crêpes I
made yesterday turned out pretty great, once I got the hang
of the heat settings on the portable cooktop. So what if I'm
not menu planning for a new restaurant? Maybe I'll get a
guest spot on a TV series soon. Or perhaps I can sell a recipe
to *The New York Times*. The sky's the limit.

And if me bustling around in my makeshift kitchen at
dawn annoys Molly? Even better. She didn't say a word about
it yesterday evening. That's how I know I *really* got to her.
There's something delicious about pissing her off again after
all these years.

I roll out of bed, my head foggy. When I lived in the inn before, I was always up and at 'em before the sun. Serving gourmet breakfasts was my whole purpose in life. Or at least it was once we had staff to deal with guest check-ins and room cleaning and whatnot. My schedule didn't change much when I opened Robin's Egg in Portland afterward; I had to be in the kitchen by four A.M. to get dough rising and pastries baking. Being a morning person worked out with my TV appearances too, since call time was often absurdly early. But when I opened Kindling, it was the first time in years I had the chance to sleep in. I embraced nightlife. If I was up at four A.M., it was because I was still out unwinding after the dinner shift.

Maybe eventually I'll get back in the habit of waking up early. But right now, I feel like a slug. I practically crawl to the en suite bathroom and pee without turning on the lights. After ripping off my undies and the old, oversize Toad Suck Daze tee I use as a sleep shirt, I pull back the shower curtain to turn on the water and gasp.

I whip it right back into place. Surely I didn't just see what I thought I saw. There's no way. It's my half-asleep brain playing tricks on me.

I turn on the light, my heart racing, and blink a few times to focus my eyes. *Chill, Robin,* I tell myself silently. *Nothing is there.*

Gathering my courage, I push the curtain back again, then let out a terrified yelp, jumping several inches off the ground. Covering my eyes with one hand and my boobs with the other (since everything is scarier when you're naked), I try to logic my way out of this. *It's a toy,* I think. *It's not haunted*

by the ghost of a Victorian child. It's just some porcelain and
fabric and creepy glass eyeballs and fake hair. God, I hope it's
fake hair.

I peek through my fingers, hoping the doll has somehow
disappeared during my inner pep talk. But no, it's still there,
perched eerily on the ledge of the tub against the wall. It's
got a faded, lacy green dress, a mass of blond ringlets topped
with a white bonnet, and big, unblinking blue eyes that, although of course I know better, appear to be staring right
into my very soul and thinking about sucking it out of me. Its
head is at a jaunty angle and, oh god, is that a crack across its
cheek that's been glued back together?

Unable to survive its cold stare for another moment, I
draw the shower curtain and back out of the bathroom slowly.

My rational brain knows that this has to be Molly's doing.
She's the only person who knows about my phobia, and I always had a lurking suspicion that she didn't actually take the
decorations from Miss Addy's doll room to the antique store
like I asked, considering she was in the middle of retiling all
the bathrooms. She also happens to have a motive for trying
to scare me off.

My irrational brain, meanwhile, is saying, *That doll is*
going to cast a dark magic spell to make you trade bodies and
then throw the porcelain version of you out the window so your
very real brain is smashed on the sidewalk. Run. Run as fast as
you can.

I tell my irrational brain to get the fuck out of here and
refocus my adrenaline rush on Molly. How dare she take advantage of my most secret fear? I need to disrupt her REM
cycle immediately.

I pull my shirt and a fresh pair of underwear on and

stomp to the hallway. I rip open the door, ready to give Molly a piece of my mind, and hoooooly shit there's another one right there, sitting on the hardwood floor of the hallway outside of my room like it was waiting for me. It's wearing a striped nautical outfit, and its shiny brown hair starts disturbingly far back, making it somehow look like a balding middle-aged man trapped in a young girl's body. Before I can think about what I'm doing, I kick it out of the way like it's a ticking time bomb, then run in the other direction, taking the stairs to the third floor two at a time, my fury and fear reaching an all-time high. I'm preparing to yell Molly's name when an unearthly screech leaves my mouth.

They're . . . *everywhere*. The whole landing is covered with dolls. A clown-faced one. Another in a rain jacket with an umbrella. A matching cowgirl-and-cowboy set. There are at least a dozen, all turned to face the top of the stairs like a highly attentive audience of demons who feed off my fear.

I'm blurting out a string of curse words, some of which I might have just invented, when Molly cracks open the door to the Snapdragon Room with a mischievous glint in her eye.

"Wurdaflockarjoosinty," I spit out, not even sure what I was trying to say but shaking so hard the floor under me is creaking, my eyes jumping from doll to doll, my pulse pounding in my ears.

Realizing I'm on the verge of a full-blown panic attack, Molly's expression turns from glee to concern. "Jesus, Rob," she says as Marmalade appears behind her, stretching and then walking toward me through the crowd of dolls. "Breathe. They're just toys."

I've backed myself all the way against the wall, not on purpose. Pressing my palms against my eyes, I say, "Make them stop looking at me like that with their soul-sucking eyes and their gremlin smiles."

"I will, one sec." I hear Molly's footsteps, but I can't look. That sight is already going to haunt my nightmares for the rest of my life.

"Okay, you're good," she says after a moment, but how can I trust her? Closer now, Molly's voice says, "It's just me." I feel her fingers brush against my wrists, then gently pull my hands from my face. "They're covered, see?"

I cautiously look to see that Molly has pulled a sheet from her bed and thrown it over the dolls. That's a little better, although irrational brain is screeching that the monsters are still there, even if I can't see them. My body doesn't know what to do with all this adrenaline, so as I accept the fact that the dolls aren't a threat, my fear does a quick pivot into rage.

"What the *fuck*, Molly?" I say, pulling away from her grasp. Even though I can tell she's trying to help me now, I wouldn't need comforting if it weren't for her prank. "I know you don't want me to be here, but are you trying to *kill* me?"

Molly steps back. "It was supposed to be a joke."

"A joke?" I say. "You *know* how much dolls freak me out. This is straight-up cruel."

"I said I'm sorry, okay?" Molly says, her tone switching from soothing to defensive. "I get it. I went too far. Kind of like *you* took it too far by taking over the whole first floor without asking me."

"Which I wouldn't have had to do if you'd stayed out of my kitchen," I fire back. "And that's not even close to deliberately triggering my worst fears."

"They're just dolls, Rob!" she yells. "Not rattlesnakes!"

"Get rid of them. Right now," I demand.

Molly puts her hands on her hips. "Only if you get rid of all the cooking stuff in the dining room."

Both of us narrow our eyes, daring the other to fold first. And then, at the same moment, our gazes shift to look below each other's faces and we realize we're half naked. I'm in my sleep shirt and neon green briefs. She's wearing a short robe with navy pinstripes that falls barely below her hips, hanging open to reveal a black sports bra and bikini-cut underwear. Even as I try to avoid looking at her, I get caught on a colorful set of flowers painted across her chest beneath her clavicle, a tattoo I don't recognize. She must have gotten it after I left for Portland. I spot some bees and honeycomb partially showing over the top of her panties. Her upper thighs are ringed with a stained-glass pattern. I have the bizarre urge to peel off her robe and find out what other art is hiding under there. I glance up toward her face to see she's just as distracted by my body, her eyes taking in the screen-printed logo across my breasts, trailing down to my bare thighs.

Suddenly self-conscious, I tug down the hem of my shirt. The motion seems to snap Molly out of it too, because she pulls her robe together in the front and crosses her arms.

"I want the dolls out of the house," I demand again, trying to forget about all of Molly's skin, right there in front of me, almost within reach.

"Then move your kitchen setup to the penthouse."

"The . . . penthouse?" I say, surprised by the idea.

"It has a sink," she says. "And a small fridge and oven. It makes way more sense than the middle of the main floor."

I'd completely forgotten about the kitchenette in our old apartment. Or maybe I hadn't so much forgotten it as intentionally pushed it out of mind. From the moment I returned to the Hummingbird, I put mental CAUTION, DO NOT ENTER tape around that whole floor, assuming the air up there was still toxic from all the fighting Molly and I did before I left. Or, even worse, that seeing it could trigger a flood of memories about the good days. And seeing Molly like this, half-dressed with pillow creases on her cheek and teal-streaked hair in a frizzy bird's nest atop her head, already has me hella confused.

"I'll think about it," I concede. "But only if the dolls disappear, like, *right* now."

"Fine." Molly shifts from one bare foot to the other. It seems like she's waiting for me to go downstairs first, but I haven't forgotten about that creepy sailor doll outside my door. No way am I going near that thing again. Recognizing my refusal to budge, Molly rolls her eyes and bends down to gather up the dolls in the bundle of sheets. Her robe shifts up, and before I can avert my eyes from possibly seeing the demon toys as she knots the sheet into a bundle, my gaze snags on the stained-glass tattoos at the top of her thighs. God, I'm even more drawn to her body at thirty-five than when we met at twenty-two.

But I won't let my distraction keep me from getting back at Molly for the doll thing—which is easier to say once I'm on the second floor and she's out of sight. This was an act of war.

15

MOLLY

AFTER THROWING THE DOLLS IN A BOX ON THE CORNER with a FREE TO A GOOD HOME sign—I know they'll go quickly with all the antiquers in this town—I lock myself in my studio. So maybe I went overboard. I thought the prank would be funny, if a little mean-spirited. But I wasn't laughing when Robin cowered in the hallway like the dolls could actually murder her. In fact, I felt an unexpected need to protect her.

Maybe it was because she was in her underwear, her hair sticking up in every direction, looking as naïve and confused as the day we met. She was even wearing the same shirt as that day at Home Depot, I recall as I start clearing and wiping down my workspace, hands clumsy with Robin still in my head. With her bleached-blond TV hair growing out and her natural light brown showing at the roots, how am I supposed to remember how much she's changed?

I've got to focus. I came here two weeks ago with a job to do, and between tormenting Robin and daydreaming of renovating the inn, I've let myself get off track. I need to snap out of this and get to work.

Luckily, it's time for my favorite step in making stained glass: cutting pieces to size and piecing them together. I finished my design for Wild Card yesterday while scheming about the dolls and texted it to Louis, who gave it a big thumbs-up.

I'm dressed in my usual glass-cutting attire: a long-sleeved tie-dyed shirt, loose cargo pants, and oversize square-framed glasses to protect me from flying shards. There's just enough space to spread out my hand-sketched outline on the floor. After spending some time chatting with Louis and browsing his impressive stock of board games, I was especially inspired by a corner display featuring several barrels of dice. Not just standard dice with six faces—eight- and ten- and twenty-sided dice in a wide array of colors and sizes. I made them the centerpiece of my design, with a trail of colorful squares winding around them like a Candy Land board, subtly placed like the streets of downtown Eureka. The effect is geometric and vibrant and perfect for such a fun, playful shop.

Now for the good part. I put in my headphones, press play on my audiobook, some nonfiction about the science of bees that Keyana recommended, and start tracing and cutting shapes out of glass. Each piece must be trimmed down to fit its place in the puzzle of my design. It's meditative. The back of my brain keeps up with the audiobook while my hands stay busy, scoring and breaking each bit of glass, wrapping the edges in shimmering copper foil, and, once all the pieces are ready, soldering them into place in the larger picture.

It feels so much like the weekend afternoons I used to spend quilting with Gram. I didn't notice the similarities when I first started working with stained glass; I was too focused on repairing old windows without cutting or burning myself. But when I started making my first original pieces—the floral windows for the bathrooms in the guest suites—it felt eerily similar to cutting and piecing together various fabrics. Gram would always turn on a book on tape, usually a mystery novel, and we'd get to work. As a little kid, I was in charge of sorting the fabric scraps into rainbow order, just like I've organized the recycled glass I'm using today. Gram had a gift for color selection, putting together unexpected shades that sang when combined. I like to think I inherited it from her, that I'm using the same instincts to place this tangerine shade next to that rich eggplant. As I grew up, I graduated to measuring and cutting fabric, then to running the sewing machine. She eventually let me help create some of her patterns, sitting shoulder to shoulder with her as we envisioned the individual pieces coming together into one picture.

But then I turned sixteen and got my driver's license and my first crush, and suddenly, spending my weekends quilting with my grandma seemed less fun than buying too many lattes at the coffee shop where Raquel was a barista. And then I had to get the job at Home Depot to pay for all those lattes. And then, in what felt like the blink of an eye, Gram was gone. I wish I could remember the last time I helped her with a quilt. But like so many things—my last bicycle ride with training wheels, my last drink at my favorite lesbian bar before it shut down, my last casual good morning kiss from Robin before we split—I didn't realize it was something I would never have the chance to do again.

Still, every time I piece together a stained-glass project like this, soldering together disparate pieces of glass that likely would have ended up in the trash but are instead finding a new future, I feel like Gram is here with me. She's watching over my shoulder as I place the final triangle on the twenty-sided die at the center of the window, smiling at how the blues and yellows and reds play against one another, how each small piece plays a role in creating something so much grander. Gram is the voice in my head telling me *try that indigo next to the emerald,* she's the sense of calm I feel when a crucial piece of glass cracks and I know just how to fix it, she's the sunlight that gleams through the finished product, turning it into a spectacle of dancing color.

Glass demands your focus. Besides the audiobook, which weirdly helps me concentrate on the work at hand, there can be no distractions, or else accidents are sure to happen. Pieces broken, flux spilled, cuts, burns. I've got the scars to prove it.

As much as I insist my head is in the right place for this project, the glass says otherwise. By the time I finish today's work, my fingers are covered in Band-Aids, blood droplets stain my paper outline, and my mind is still stuck on Robin in nothing but her underwear and that damn Toad Suck Daze T-shirt. Even alone in this shed, sweating over the art I love, I can't escape thoughts of her, regret over the prank I pulled swirling with a desire to get a rise out of her again. I can't figure out if it's that I want her to leave or that I, simply, want her.

Want what we had, the future I pictured for us all those years ago, the one that's maybe still possible in some alternate universe where things had gone very differently.

What happened to the new Molly? I spent years trying to move on, and these two weeks have made it abundantly clear that I failed. I need to end this chapter of my life so I can truly dedicate myself to the next one. Robin, the Hummingbird Inn, Eureka . . . I need to move on from all of them.

It's time to do my least favorite thing and admit that Robin is right: We need to sell the inn.

16
Robin

IT TOOK PRETTY MUCH ALL DAY YESTERDAY FOR MY BLOOD PRES-
sure to recover from the doll incident. Between that and
filming some video promoting a food delivery app that I've
never used but was contractually obligated to say was the
best in the game, I didn't get a chance to test out Molly's idea
of using the penthouse kitchen. So this morning, I hop in the
(doll-free) shower, get dressed, duck under the plastic sheets
in the kitchen to gather supplies, and head up to the fourth
floor to get the lay of the land.

As much as I hate to admit it, Molly could be right about
the penthouse apartment. I really could use a sink. And an
oven, even a tiny one. It would mean dragging all my kitchen
tools up three flights of stairs from my current setup, but it's
worth considering.

I climb to the attic and open the door with a shove. It always sticks in the summer humidity. When it swings open, I gasp.

While every other room in the inn has been touched by the management company's IKEAfication, the penthouse looks exactly how I remember it. The same morning light shining on the vintage floral wallpaper. Same scuffed wooden floors and faded blue-green rug. Even the same furniture Molly and I moved from Little Rock back in 2012. It's like a time capsule, perfectly preserved. Well, not perfectly. It's dusty as hell.

Memories come rushing back. Molly and me collapsed on the floor, sweaty and exhausted after dragging all our stuff upstairs. Molly and me playing gin rummy in the armchairs by the window. Molly and me getting dressed for our wedding, anxious and excited and a little overwhelmed by my family members filling the inn's guest rooms.

I try to push away the pictures from my past, refocus on what I came here to do. The kitchenette is small but functional. I turn on the faucet and the water runs clear. The fridge and stove are unplugged, but when I reattach their cords, the lights blink on. All seems to be in working order.

But I can't spend hours up here cooking. All the history is too distracting to ignore. Our literal wedding outfits are hanging in garment bags in the closet. With my brain still stuck on Molly in that untied robe, battling the urge to take a closer look at all those tattoos, there's no way I can get any actual work done here. I need a fresh slate.

The trouble is, fresh slates cost money.

Luckily, Edgar's got a few more social media gigs up his sleeve. Posting sponsored content feels so fake right now, but I need those checks, even if they're small. I need to take pictures in some bulky pocket-covered aprons I'm supposed to model, and then I need to showcase my food on dishes from some trendy serving-ware company. I hoped to use the crêpes I tested a couple nights ago after getting inspired by Jesse. They were delicious, but not photogenic enough. So it's back to the drawing board, and my creative well is running dry. Particularly since three-quarters of my brain is currently focused on being frustrated with Molly for refusing to even *discuss* fixing up the inn to sell, and that last quarter is traitorously thinking about all the times we had sex in that bed, *right there.*

I suffer through it anyway, taking some photos with the apron where I'm not visibly grimacing and whipping up a boring eggs Benedict to show off the plates. After the first shot of the dish, I realize it would look better with some fresh greens, so I run down to the back-porch planters to grab some chives, sage, and thyme.

On my way, I hear Molly doing something in the kitchen. She calls my name, and I'm fully prepared to ignore her after Dollgate, but I decide to be the bigger person. I step into the doorway, giving my best "what the fuck could you possibly want from me" face, and am surprised to find Molly has pulled down some of the tarps I saw earlier this morning and is on a step stool, holding up a giant cabinet.

"Can you help me with this?" she asks.

I jog over to help balance the cabinet against the wall. It's kind of heavy and definitely awkward. I'm surprised she got it this far on her own. "What do you need me to do?" I ask.

"Just hold it there while I drive the mounting screws in,"

Molly says. "And keep the doors all the way open so I can get to the back. Please."

This is the chance I've been waiting for to prove I can be more than moral support during a DIY project. I hold the cabinet as carefully as a soufflé fresh out of the oven, when any bumps or shakes could make the whole thing collapse.

Once Molly puts in the first two screws, she clears her throat and says, "So I've been thinking."

I wait for her to continue, but she doesn't. "About life on other planets, or . . ."

Molly takes a breath, then says in a rush, "About reno-vating and selling the inn." She pauses to drill in another screw.

I nearly jump in excitement, then remember I have a job, so I keep the cabinet steady. "It could be good, right?" I say carefully. "I mean, we're both already here, and with a few months of work, we'd never have to talk to each other about it again."

Molly powers up the drill. "You can let go now, I think it's secure enough," she says.

I pull away slowly and the cabinet stays in place. "So in all that thinking, you've decided . . ." I prompt her.

Molly pulls more screws from her pocket, then looks down at me, blinks, and says, "I'll do it."

"Yes!" I spin in a circle, then punch the air above me. I almost grab Molly in a hug but think twice for several rea-sons, including the fact that she's holding a power tool I don't want stabbed in my eye. I have a feeling this decision is par-tially an apology for the doll thing, but no need to push it. "This is great. Oh, Molly. Thank you. You won't regret it," I

say, already calculating how long it'll be until I see more dig-
its in my savings account.

"But I'm not doing it alone," she says quickly. "And I also
don't think we should work too closely together. So we don't,
you know—"

"Kill each other," I finish for her. "Agreed."

"We'll have to figure out how to divide and conquer,"
Molly says. "I can start by finishing up the kitchen. Repaint-
ing. A deep clean of the floors and appliances. Maybe putting in a new backsplash. And you can start with the grounds,
since you already know how to handle them."

I nod immediately. I may not know my way around a drill
bit, but gardening I can do. When Molly first suggested I
take responsibility for the yard back in 2012, I thought it was
a terrible idea. My parents hired landscapers when I was a
kid, so I'd never even powered up a lawnmower. But as soon
as I gave it a shot, started weeding the flower beds closest to
the inn and putting in fresh mulch and seedlings, I was
hooked. Being out in the sun and helping a patch of dirt
grow into something cultivated and beautiful was even more
therapeutic than scrubbing the kitchen. Better yet, I could
grow my own ingredients. Big, juicy Arkansas tomatoes next
to leafy clusters of basil, tart blackberries and raspberries on
sprawling bushes, hardy root vegetables like shallots and
leeks. Fresh produce and herbs became a huge inspiration
for me as a chef. I kept some aspect of the interactive nature
of gardening alive in all my restaurants, like customers picking their own parsley and rosemary and thyme garnishes
from planters in the dining rooms. Maybe a figurative and
literal return to my roots is just what I need. *And* it's a way to
show Molly I'm not afraid of a little dirty work.

"On it, Coach," I say to Molly. "I can start tomorrow."

"Once we're done with those, we can make a list of everything else we need to do and split it up," Molly suggests. "But you'll probably need to learn some new skills, because it has to be a fair division of labor. And of cost. We'll need to buy all the supplies. Paint. Spackle. Varnishes. Tools."

I wince. There goes all the money I'll make from my social media ads before it even hits my wallet. But I'll do anything to keep Molly aboard the Sell the Inn Express, even if it means finding a part-time gig somewhere in town. "Of course," I say. "We'll split it."

"And I can't dedicate a hundred percent of my time to this," she continues. "I've still got to finish the windows I promised to Key and her friends."

"Sure. I'll have stuff to do too," I say vaguely. "But we'll figure it out. Together."

Molly's lips tighten, and she looks away from me back to the cabinet. "Right. I'm going to finish this and get a coat of paint on the walls. Can you call Clint to let him know we're interested in selling?"

"Absolutely. I'll do it right now. And hey—" I put a hand on Molly's shoulder, preparing to thank her. She doesn't see me coming and, surprised by my touch, jolts so hard she loses her balance, nearly falling off the step stool. I catch her by the waist just in time, lowering her to the ground next to me. It takes a minute for me to realize I'm still holding her, staring into her big green eyes, both of our hearts racing, cheeks pink from the scare, or maybe from something else. Holding Molly close, it's like entering the twilight zone of what could have been if she'd fallen, or if we'd worked things out back in the day, or if we forgot about all the fighting and time apart and kissed right now, all these crisscrossing possibilities. And then I let go. We both straighten our clothes, mumble apologies, and practically run in opposite directions to try to forget what just happened.

CLINT ENTHUSIASTICALLY GAVE US THE go-ahead, promising to meet up to work out the details soon. So the next morning, I put on ripped denim overalls over a sports bra, slather on some sunscreen, and head out to the yard. It's a sizable property, a little under an acre in total, with lots of green space to wrangle. The inn has a full wraparound porch with flower beds stretched across every side. The back left section by the kitchen is filled with herbs for cooking. Most of the flowers we used to grow in the rest of the beds—the same pollinator-friendly blooms we chose for room themes—have been choked out by weeds. There's overgrown grass I'll need to trim between the front porch and the sidewalk, stretching around both sides of the building. The backyard is bigger, with a round wooden gazebo in the center and stone walking paths leading to the raised vegetable and fruit beds lining the edge of the property. Behind that is a row of towering cedars and junipers separating us from a steep fall into limestone bluffs.

Having already raided my herb garden, I know it's survived the years of neglect pretty well. Not everything made it, but the chives, sage, thyme, rosemary, lavender, and mint are going strong. I start my weeding and pruning there before moving on to the rest of the flower beds, and then on to the fruits and veggies.

The produce has gone wild. Some plants, like the now enormous berry bushes, have overgrown their intended areas. My prized tomatoes have disappeared completely, but the asparagus and rhubarb have happily expanded into their space. Once I start digging around, I find garlic and shallots and leeks galore. This garden hasn't had a lick of attention in years, yet the fertile Arkansas soil has given these plants everything they need to thrive. I pull up weeds, trim back overgrown bits, and collect ripe fruits and veggies, talking softly to the flora as I go. Marmalade escapes through the cat door on the back porch to laze in shady patches of grass by my side.

It hardly feels like a whole day has passed by the time the sun ducks behind the mountaintops. The last thing I do before calling it quits is hose off the dusty hummingbird feeders dotted around the yard and refill them with sugar water. Guests used to spend hours in the gazebo watching the tiny birds they drew to the inn. I figure it will take a while for them to reappear after the feeders have sat empty for so long, but the moment I finish rehanging one, a hummingbird proves me wrong by flitting over and dipping in its long, thin beak.

"Clever bird, huh?" I say melodically. "Have you been watching me all day, waiting for me to remember to feed you?"

I hear a shifting in the tall grass behind me that I first assume is Marmee, but when I turn, I see Molly trekking from the shed back to the house. It hadn't even occurred to me that Molly was across the lawn all day working in her shed. She looks in my direction with an expression that I almost confuse for tenderness. But as soon as we make eye contact, her face shifts into a scowl. There's something that feels intentional about it, and I wonder if it might be for show. Maybe she, like me, can't remember if we're supposed to be mad at each other these days. Before I can say a word, she disappears through the back door.

Dammit. I'd finally sweat my way through enough manual labor to forget about that weird moment in the kitchen yesterday, and here I am again thinking about how it felt to have my arms around her.

I turn to the pile of fresh produce I collected, organized into a few wooden crates I grabbed from the basement. What am I going to do with this bounty? Even if I had a fully functioning kitchen, it's way more than two people can eat. But it's so fresh and colorful and delicious—I know, having snacked on some of it for lunch. It deserves to be handled by a talented chef and served up to people who will appreciate it.

I know just the place.

17

MOLLY

KEYANA MUST HAVE SOME KIND OF FRIEND TELEPATHY. JUST when I thought I was going to come apart at the seams watching Robin in those ridiculous overalls talking to a hummingbird, looking so much like her old self that I nearly forgot what year it was and walked right up to her and did something I'd regret, Key texted to invite me on a hike. The next morning, as I strap on a beat-up pair of boots, I begrudgingly admit that it's probably a good idea to get out of the inn and breathe some fresh mountain air. Even if it means getting eaten alive by mosquitoes.

Key picks me up at the inn in her vintage Jeep Wrangler with a fresh cold brew from Drizzled Donuts waiting for me in the cup holder. She knows me well enough to not start a conversation until the caffeine hits. Ever since I came out in high school and all my old pals stopped talking to me, I've been wary of friendships. But Key has always made it feel like the most natural thing in the world. Our silences are never awkward. No matter how long we go without seeing each other, it feels like no time has passed when we meet up again. And most importantly, she knows when to give me space, which is most of the time. I'm not really sure *why* Key wants to be my friend, considering I've had very few successful long-term relationships and can be pricklier than a cactus, but I'm glad she does.

She tools a couple miles north up winding roads as I sip my coffee. By the time she parks, I'm ready for human interaction.

"How's the studio?" I ask, opening the passenger-side door and stretching my legs.

Keyana sprays herself with sunscreen as she answers. "It's all right," she says. "I'm still doing most of my business online. Not too many customers have figured out I'm back yet. But being in my old space has been great for my craft. I've been looking back on some of the pieces I painted the last time I lived here for inspo, and it turns out I'm actually pretty good."

"Pretty good?" I say with a surprised laugh. "You're phenomenal. I knew that from the first time we met, when you were working on that painting of a beehive. Remember that one?"

"Of course," Key says as she pulls her curls through the back of a baseball cap. "I sold it to that tourist who was into all the kinky whipped-cream stuff."

"Oh my god, whipped-cream girl. I forgot."

"The money from that sale lasted a whole lot longer than

our fling. Which is fine by me. Whipped-cream residue is *very* sticky." Key locks the car and gestures to the start of the hiking trail. "Shall we?"

As we begin walking, Key explains our mission. She wants to paint a series of the unique rock formations in our pocket of the Ozarks, particularly ones with flowers sprouting out of their crevices. Apparently I'm here to make sure she doesn't fall down a cliff while taking photos. But the scenic views and friendly chat are lifting my mood too.

We find a few spots perfect for Key's purposes: bright red flowers that look like stars, a particularly colorful patch of lichen, and lovely light purple blooms Key identifies as Ozark wild crocus. She takes pictures of each before leading us farther down the path. After about an hour, we find a shaded rock looking out on a lake and decide to take a rest.

Key pulls out a couple of protein bars and hands me one. "How's it been cohabitating with Big Bird?" she asks, using the nickname we came up with when the breakup was so raw that even hearing Robin's name felt like being stabbed in the gut.

I flinch as I rip into the snack's package. "Awful. It's a big house. You'd think I could avoid her. But every time I turn a corner, there she is, being all infuriating and difficult and acting like nothing is ever her fault. I should already be done with the window for Wild Card and starting to design the one for Drizzled Donuts. I'm behind because I can't get a moment of peace from Robin, and it's only going to get worse now because . . ." I sigh heavily before breaking the news. "Because we're renovating and selling the inn."

"Wait, what?" Key says, twisting toward me, her eyes wide with delighted surprise.

I tell her about the day Clint stopped by the Humming-bird, the arguments I had with Robin about it, and how I finally caved.

When I finish, Key stares at me like I'm some modern art piece she's trying to interpret. "So why are you so upset about this plan? It seems like a tidy solution to your problem. The inn gets a cool new owner to reopen it, you get a check, and you never have to talk to Robin again."

I consider her words. As much as I want her to mirror my own irritation at the whole thing, a friend who lies to me to make me feel better isn't really a friend I want to have. "Sure, but it also means a *lot* of speaking to Robin now. And I'm already barely holding it together with her."

Key takes a chug from her water bottle while thinking this over. "It's less work than the first time, right? It's not a major fixer-upper, just bad design choices. Painting, changing out décor, that kind of thing?"

I shrug noncommittally, although I know she's right.

"If you're so upset about this, why did you agree to it?"

I kick at the dirt and pebbles at my feet. "I don't even know," I admit. "Being around Robin has me all tangled up. I thought I'd moved on, but all these stupid feelings are rushing back and I don't know if I want to slap her or ki—" I catch myself before making a truly humiliating confession. "I need to get the hell over her, over the Hummingbird. I've built a whole new life, but now my old one is getting in the way of it and I don't know who I am anymore. I need it to end."

"Sounds like your Pisces nostalgia is getting in the way," Key says, pulling a leaf from my hair. "Maybe this is a chance for the closure you and Robin never got. Quitting an ex cold

turkey is straight culture. You need to handle this the lesbian
way. Remember when I broke up with Alia and we went on a
breakup road trip to Amarillo to say goodbye? *That's* the lesbian way. Spending a weird amount of time together, taking
on a project, and perhaps, if you're brave enough, talking
through what happened."

"But you're pansexual."

"We borrowed the method from the lesbian toolbox," Key
says, waving away my comment. "Don't you and Robin have
some unfinished business, though? Wouldn't it be nice to
clear the air and get the inn out of your shared custody?"

I groan. "I know, I know. You're right. She's just so distracting. Always making messes, nearly setting the house on
fire cooking where she shouldn't, strutting around with no
pants on—"

"Ah," Key teases. "So that's what's distracting you."

"What? No! Anyone would be distracted by some pants-
less lesbian in their house, all loud and confident and . . ." I
drop my head into my hands, embarrassed to look at Key.
"Fine, she's fucking irresistible, okay? I feel like I'm a big
blob of walking hormones around Robin. What's wrong with
me?"

"There's nothing wrong with you," Key says, gently patting my shoulder. "Y'all have a lot of history. It makes sense
that your emotions and your body are all tangled up."

"I don't want to sleep with her. Right?" I say, recognizing
in the moment how pitiful I must sound. "I keep telling my
brain to get my body under control. But no matter how hard
I try, one look at her in some ugly old overalls and I'm un-
done."

"Oh, so overalls are your kink," Key jokes, but backtracks

when she sees my frown. "Look, maybe you just need to get laid. Get it out of your system so you can face Robin with a clear head. What are you doing Saturday night? We can go to One More Round like the old days. Except this time, we'll *both* be single and looking."

I chew my bottom lip, considering the idea. "Am I even capable of picking up some girl at a bar? I've never been good at that kind of thing."

"I know you can flirt," Key says. "I saw you at Mardi Gras. Plus, I'll be your wingwoman. I owe you after all the years you did it for me."

She's right. I've played the field a little since Robin left. Just because I've never gone cruising for dates in Eureka before doesn't mean I'm incapable of it. "What do I even do if I find someone, though?" I ask. "Bring them back to the empty B&B where I'm currently living with my ex? Isn't that weird?"

Key shrugs. "Maybe it will be good for Robin to see you with someone else. Show her you've moved on."

Honestly, I'll try anything to get the idea of kissing Robin out of my head. "Fine. Saturday night," I agree. "Now, this is supposed to be my break from Big Bird. Can we please get back to nature?"

"Absolutely," Keyana says with a grin. "Let's go stare at some more rocks."

18

Robin

I WAKE UP BRIGHT AND EARLY ON FRIDAY MORNING AND TOTE my crates of produce to Counterculture, figuring Jesse will be there even though they don't open until eleven. Everywhere else is, of course, closed. Eureka's a bit of a sleepy town, where shop hours change based on when the owner leaves to walk their dog or go visit with the bartender next door. But when you own a restaurant, you pretty much spend every waking minute there. Some of your sleeping minutes too.

I find the kitchen door in an alley halfway down one of the flights of stairs built into the mountainside next to Counterculture. Jesse answers, aproned and covered in flour. I offer him the lot for free, but am relieved and grateful when he insists on paying me like any of his local vendors. After I admit to having no plans until the garden store opens, he invites me into the kitchen to help him clean and prep the fruit and veggies for lunch service. It feels surprisingly good to be back in a professional kitchen, slicing rhubarb and chiffonading basil as Jesse tells me about this week's chef's special, chanterelle étouffée.

"How much longer are you in town?" he asks while caramelizing onions on the stove. "A celebrity chef like you must have a packed schedule."

"Not exactly," I say, shooting for confidently casual. "I came for a bit of a career reset."

Jesse looks up from his pan for a moment, giving me a knowing smile. "So you have something exciting brewing, huh? Knowing you, you're probably going to make a big announcement soon that blows the culinary world's mind."

It stings a little for Jesse to have so much faith in me when I don't deserve it, but I appreciate his vote of confidence. "I'll actually be around town for a while," I say, not confirming or denying. "I just agreed to renovate the Hummingbird and sell it to Clint." Leaving Molly out wasn't an intentional choice, but our weird housing situation feels like too much to explain at the moment.

"Dude!" Jesse yells, turning toward me. "That's the best news I've heard in years! If it can't be you and Molly running it, Clint's definitely the best person in town."

"Totally," I agree. "He was there in the beginning."

"Have you seen One More Round since he took over?" Jesse asks. "It's like a whole new bar. Swanky."

"Not yet."

Jesse's eyes light up. "We should go! And bring Caro! Oh, Caro's gonna do a happy dance when they find out you're fixing everything the management company ruined." Jesse shakes his head grimly as he starts inspecting mushrooms from a bin by the sink, then says in a quieter voice, "We fought like hell to stop them, but there was only so much we could do. Especially once they replaced me and the other cooks with dry-ass premade pastries."

My cheeks heat with guilt for putting Jesse and Caro in that shitty situation. I mean, Molly chose the management company, but that doesn't let me off the hook. I sent Jesse a lengthy email after I moved, apologizing for leaving him to run the kitchen alone without warning, but I didn't realize how bad things got. "Yeah, I'm sorry about that, bro," I say, rubbing the back of my head. "You deserved better. And you found it! Look at this place."

Jesse looks around the kitchen, his frown shifting into a proud smile as he turns back to stir the onions. "Yeah. It's pretty great, huh?"

An idea strikes me like lightning. I need cash. *And* I owe Jesse for leaving him high and dry. Maybe I can make things right with Jesse by helping him out during this busy summer season and also get paid. If Molly's got another gig going, it's fair game for me to have one too. "Since I'm here for a while, what would you think about hiring me part-time?" I ask. "To keep my skills sharp?"

"Are you kidding, dude?" Jesse says, knocking his hip into the handle of his pan as he turns around, nearly sending it careening off the stove. "Having you here would be incredible for business. A Robin's Egg residency! Or Kindling, but it involved open flames, didn't it?" Jesse starts pacing the kitchen, popping his knuckles. "We're probably not coded for that kind of thing, but I'm sure we could get creative with the concept. Maybe butane torches? God, the regulars will be ecstatic."

"Whoa, slow down." I move over to Jesse's pan of onions and stir them before they burn. "That's very generous of you, but a pop-up wasn't really what I had in mind," I say honestly. I can't afford to buy my own ingredients or pay any staff, and at this point, just getting a job at Counterculture feels like a big enough favor to ask, even if Jesse doesn't know it. I suggest, "Maybe something more like sous-chef. You're the vegan expert here. I could learn a lot from you. It wouldn't have to be full-time. A few days a week would be great." Normally, it would take a massive dose of humility to go from owner/head chef to line cook. But if there's anyone I want to see thrive, would do anything to help succeed, it's Jesse. I can proudly be his sous-chef. And I need the job, especially if Molly expects me to help pay for the renovations.

Jesse pauses near the dishwasher and gives me a questioning stare. "We do need a sous. But you could be a guest chef at any restaurant in the world. Why would you want to be second-in-command at some small-town place no one has ever heard of?"

"You're selling yourself short," I say. "I've seen the online reviews—people are planning whole trips to Eureka for a dinner reservation here. I respect the hell out of what you've built. And second, I'd love to be back in the kitchen with you. Like the good old days, only you're in charge this time." I mean every word, but can't help feeling guilty about hiding the rest of the truth from Jesse. Deep down, I know Jesse wouldn't judge me if he knew the truth of my money woes.

But I also can't stand the thought of him hiring me out of pity.

"It's not a glamorous job," Jesse says, seeming to hear my arguments, but his forehead is still wrinkled with concern. "A lot of laminating pastry and julienning carrots and cleaning artichokes. You're sure you don't want to do a pop-up instead?"

"Maybe someday," I say. "But for now, cleaning artichokes sounds amazing."

"All right, then." Jesse comes closer and gives me a heavy pat on the shoulder. "When can you start?"

I look down at the pan of onions sizzling in front of me, giving off a sweet, earthy scent. "It seems like I already did," I say.

Jesse laughs, and I feel lighter than I have in weeks. "Amazing. We open in three hours, and we've got a reservation for a group of twenty, so let's get chopping."

19

MOLLY

I'M SKEPTICAL OF KEY'S WINGWOMAN IDEA, AND IT'S BEEN A minute since I truly tried to look presentable, but as I give myself a last look in the mirror before leaving the inn, I admit I cleaned up pretty nice. I've got on a loose fuchsia crop top that contrasts perfectly with the teal streaks in my hair and might show a glimpse of the sunflowers tattooed across my ribs if I move just right. I paired it with high-waisted denim shorts that are a little frayed at the edges and black Doc Martens. My hair is in loose waves around my shoulders, and I've got pink topaz earrings to match my top. After touching up my thick black eyeliner, I look good enough to eat.

Walking to One More Round, I realize I haven't felt so confident in months. I strut down Spring Street to the tunes of a street performer, feeling like I'm in a movie. Why is Keyana always right about making me leave the house?

When I walk in the door of One More Round, I'm stunned by how my old favorite dive now looks sleek and expensive. Rich dark colors, leather booths, gold fixtures. Clint really gussied it up. Inside are more than just the queer regulars; there are as many tourists as locals, and a spread of ages and genders that means Clint has truly made this the hottest bar in town. Key spots me and makes a loud wolf whistle of approval over the bumping music. Every head in the place turns in my direction, and I feel both right at home and like an interloper. I weave through the crowd to Key's tall table, trying to stifle the part of me that feels like I don't belong here.

After a second, it's clear that I'm the only one making myself feel out of place. Good old Dorothy and Eleanor, two of my favorite townies, totter over right away.

"Molly Garner, what a sight for sore eyes!" Dot says, her raspy voice sounding like a familiar song to my ears. She wraps me in a hug that smells like cigarette smoke and cherry cough drops. "And is that you, Keyana? Why, the lost generation has returned!"

Dot comes around the table to Key while I greet Eleanor. "It's so good to see y'all," I say with genuine enthusiasm. "I should have come by to visit as soon as I got into town."

"You sure should have," Eleanor says with a fond grin. "I made your favorite coconut cake last week."

"The one with the caramel drizzle on top? Do you have any left? Let's go, I would trade a cocktail for a slice of that in a heartbeat."

Eleanor pats my cheek. "You know my cakes hardly make

it out of the oven before they're gone. I'll make you another one. You staying at the Hummingbird?"

"Yes, ma'am."

Eleanor squints at me sympathetically. "Not the same as you left it, huh?" She worked the check-in desk for us part-time back in the day, but retired before Robin and I left. She must have heard about the terrible redesign through the grapevine.

"Say, is Robin back in town too?" Dot asks. "Could've sworn I saw her last week on my way to the crystal shop. You two back together?" She wiggles her eyebrows suggestively.

"Yes. Er, no." I cringe, annoyed that my Robin-free night is already tainted. "She *is* back in town, but we're not to-gether."

Dot looks confused. "Where's she staying, then?"

My lips grow thinner as I bite back a grimace. "Also at the inn. Different rooms."

Dorothy and Eleanor glance at each other. "We'll see how long that lasts, eh?" Dot says under her breath.

I scoff. "I heard that!"

"I like that cane, Dot," Key jumps in, gracefully changing the subject before I start a fight with a senior citizen. "The leopard print suits you. You still guiding walking tours?"

"Sure am!" Dot says proudly. "Little slower moving these days, but I'll keep doing 'em long as I can stand."

"Even if I keep begging her to retire so we can take that Olivia cruise we've been talking about for years," Eleanor says, giving Dot one of those looks that only couples who have been together over half of their lives can share.

We chat for a little longer before Eleanor and Dot leave, saying it's past their bedtime. Key immediately gets us back on task, pointing out potentially single hotties. I've got my eye on a stranger near the jukebox with a buzz cut and an eyebrow ring.

"I need a drink first," I interrupt her. I head to the bar and, of course, immediately find another familiar face.

"Molly!" Clint ducks under the end of the bar to give me a hug. "You came!"

"Of course," I say, embracing Clint. "The place looks spectacular."

"Not as good as *you*, lady-killer." Clint holds me by the elbows and examines my outfit. "Jesus Christ, you're ripped. I'd almost go straight for you."

"Thanks, Clint. You look amazing too. I love the lip ring."

"Thanks, babe. And great news about the inn! Can't wait to work out the details next week. It's exactly what I need to build my empire," Clint says with a cheeky wink. Someone calls for him from across the room, but before he goes, he tells a bartender, "Get this woman an espresso martini, on the house."

The bartender starts mixing the drink, then does a double take before saying, "Molly? Is that you?"

I nearly fall over when I realize it's Kayla, the daughter of the couple that owns the garden store. She was learning to drive last time I saw her. "Kayla? I can't believe it. Are you old enough to work here?"

"I turned twenty-one last month," Kayla says, beaming. "Oh my god, are you and Robin back together?"

"What? No," I say, trying to keep my annoyance from spilling over. "Why would you think that?"

"Oh, sorry," she says. "I guess I just figured if y'all ever came back, it would be together."

"Nope," I say, chin held high. "I'm here for work. It has nothing to do with—"

"Robin!" a handful of people cheer closer to the entrance, jolting my attention to you-know-who striding through the front door.

Why does the universe hate me?

I examine Robin from across the room. She has the audacity to look just as good as me tonight. Maybe better. Her hair is slicked straight back, showing off her golden-brown eyes and life-ruining smile. She's got on a plain white dress shirt, sleeves rolled up to the elbows, unbuttoned low enough to be distracting. Her tight black pants leave nothing to the imagination. It's a simple outfit, but one that looks effortlessly cool and makes me worry that I tried too hard with my eyeliner and crop top.

She's quickly overtaken by queer tourists with pens and napkins in hand for autographs. I guess that's why she hasn't left the inn much. Robin manages to look both honored and embarrassed by all the attention. I, however, probably look like someone just stole my handbag. Alarmed, angry, and highly suspicious.

"So Robin *is* back in town," Kayla says as she pushes my drink to me atop the bar.

I drop a cash tip next to the glass. "I guess so. Thanks."

It takes me a while to navigate the crowd around Robin to get back to my table.

"Holy shit, Robin looks good," Key says as I sit down. "I totally get all the thirstiness you've been going through."

"What is she even doing here?" I grumble, ignoring Key.

"You know I'm Team Molly, but it *is* a public space," Ke-

yana says. "And anyway, why should Robin get in the way of
our mission? There are enough cuties to go around."

The person with the buzz cut I'd put at the top of my list
is currently staring at Robin with big heart eyes, so I'm not so
sure. But Key shoves me in the direction of someone nursing
a Bud Light at the far corner of the bar, seemingly uninterested in the celebrity sighting.

Gathering my courage, I chug my drink and sidle up to
the stranger. "Hey there," I say in a voice that I intended to
be sultry but comes out corny. "You a local?"

The person looks up through fashionable glasses, clearly
noticing me for the first time all night. They have a lopsided
haircut that screams gay. "Nope, visiting from Fort Smith for
the weekend," they say, seeming wary but curious.

"Cool," I say, feeling a bead of sweat drip down the back
of my neck. "Can I buy you another beer?"

The stranger's expression goes sympathetic. "Not unless
you want to buy one for my wife too," they say gently. "She's
in the bathroom."

I just now notice the half-empty Tecate to their left. "Eh,
why not." Grabbing Kayla's attention, I order a whiskey soda
and another round for the out-of-towners. I pass the drinks
over with an "Enjoy Eureka, y'all."

I'm halfway back to our table when I screech to a halt. Is
that *Jesse*? Without even thinking about it, I elbow my way
through Robin's audience to wrap my arms around him. I've
been at One More Round for an hour and have already
hugged more people than all last year. Something about this
town brings out the softie in me.

"Jesse! I'm so happy to see you!" I shout over the noise

around us. Jesse and his partner, Caro, were two of our first
employees at the inn, and two of my favorite people on the
planet. I kept up with them for a little while after leaving
town via text and the occasional FaceTime, but as much as I
adore them, seeing them thrive in the town where Robin and
I used to be so happy hurt too much. I let our communication fizzle out.

"Molly! Holy shit!" Jesse lifts me off the ground in his
excitement. He's gotten buff. "What are you doing here? Are
you and Robin back together?"

"No!" When I say it this time, I have an echo. I turn to
see Robin has taken an interest in our conversation.

"Oh. Sorry," Jesse says, looking contrite. "I just figured
since Robin's settling in here for a while, and you're here
too . . ."

"Settling in?" I look at Robin, my eyes narrowed.

"Didn't she tell you?" Jesse says. "She's my new sous-
chef!"

"Your sous-chef?" I say to Jesse. "Does that mean you're
a head chef now?"

He puffs up with pride. "Not just a head chef. I own a
restaurant. Counterculture."

I gasp and hug him again. "I can't believe it! But also, of
course I can. I can't wait to visit."

New information is crashing together in my brain. I'm
thrilled for Jesse and obviously want to support him. But
Robin has a job? Explains why she hasn't been around the
inn for the past couple days, even though she promised up
and down that she'd do her fair share of the reno. Also, she's
working for Jesse? I'm surprised her ego can handle working

for a chef she trained. Also also, is Robin checking me out right now? I reach up to smooth my hair, purposely displaying my bare midriff along one side, and watch Robin's eyes follow. She takes a heavy gulp, then walks away to the bar. The crop top strikes again.

Noticing the kerfuffle, Key comes over to join us. We chat with Jesse for a while as Robin's groupies follow after her. Then Caro shows up, and I feel another rush of unexpected joy. Caro was our first employee, a charmer at the front desk and a workhorse behind the scenes. They tell me that they're now the head concierge at a historic hotel much larger than our little inn, and while that job also includes lots of "other duties as assigned," they miss our little queer refuge. Caro's easygoing attitude and beaming smile always had a way of lowering my stress levels, and it seems to still work based on how easy it is to forget for a moment that Robin's in the same room. Until she wanders over to chat with Caro too.

After Key finishes telling the group about buying her old storefront, Caro turns to Robin. "So how were your first two days on the job?" they ask.

"Fantastic," Robin says. "Jesse's a great boss. He's teaching me so much about vegan pastries and sauces. It's only fair. Lord knows he spent years patiently listening to me blab on about sourdough techniques and the perfect egg-poaching temperature."

"One eighty," Jesse says right on cue. "I'll never forget it, even if I don't cook eggs anymore. And it's an honor to have you in the kitchen. I wouldn't be half the chef I am without you."

As much as I love Jesse, I barely stifle an eye roll. All this
fawning over Robin makes me want to hurl. Like the obser-
vant wingwoman she is, Key notices and grabs my wrist.
"Want to dance?" she asks.

I nod, grateful for the escape. We promise to catch up
more with Jesse and Caro later and wend through the in-
creasingly crowded bar to the bustling dance floor in the
back half of the room. With a couple cocktails down, moving
my body to the pop beats feels good.

As one song shifts into another, Key nudges me toward
attractive strangers bouncing to the rhythm around us. I try
to play along, shuffling closer to the cuties who seem to be
dancing alone, but I keep getting distracted by catching
glimpses of Robin across the room. She, Caro, and Jesse
grabbed a tall table by the front door, and she's still got a
cluster of fans at her side, batting their eyelashes every time
she smiles at them. God, is she signing someone's boob? She
makes avocado toast! She's not a superhero!

Then I notice Robin looking back at me, and I can't help
but use my midriff against her. I put my hands in the air and
wind my hips back and forth, feeling the warm air hit my ribs
and the weight of Robin's gaze on my skin. This is all very
unlike me, but I'm enjoying being someone else for the night,
someone more daring and unencumbered.

When I spin around and spot Robin again, her mouth is
hanging open like a cartoon character's. Our eyes meet long
enough for her to be certain I caught her watching. She looks
embarrassed at first, her lips quickly pressing back together,
but then I see her expression shift to smug when she realizes
that I wouldn't have noticed if I hadn't also been seeking her

out across the room. In a heady, intense moment, I read all of this on her face as clearly as she's probably reading mine.

I feel someone dancing against my back, and when I break the moment with Robin and shift to face them, I'm relieved to see they're cute. Or at least cute enough. I roll my body against theirs and lean in encouragingly as they run their hands over the bare skin at my waist. Robin's eyes are glued to my every move. I know because, whenever I'm not glancing at my dance partner, my eyes are glued to her too. My body is pressed against someone else, so why does it feel like I'm dancing with Robin?

"It's so fucking hot in here," the stranger says, their lips right up against my ear. Robin's watching, so I lean into them even more. "There's a bar at my hotel across the street. Want to come with me? I'll buy you a drink."

Their offer has the unspoken potential of a no-strings one-night stand, exactly what I came here for. I could get laid, get the sexual tension out of my system. But all I want to do is stay here on the dance floor and watch Robin's face turn different shades of red.

"No, thanks. I want to dance."

By the end of the song, the stranger disappears into the crush of people. Keyana's dancing with someone almost as gorgeous as she is. Feeling a little too warm, I leave her to it and wander outside for some fresh air.

The patio is classically Eureka Springs, a wooden deck with a low fence on two sides stretching to a wall of natural limestone looming partially overhead, beautiful and terrifying. Clint replaced the old fairy lights with sturdier round bulbs, and the outdoor couches and tables are new. But I hardly have a moment to take it all in, to let the memories of past nights here wash over me, before the door opens again.

"Molly," Robin says, walking purposefully toward me. "What are you doing?"

"Breathing." I turn to face her. "What are *you* doing? Don't you have a VIP meet and greet going on?"

"I mean, what were you doing in there? Grinding on some stranger? It's not like you. Have you had too much to drink?"

Getting Robin riled up was my goal, but I'm irked by her calling me out. "What gives you the right to tell me what is and isn't 'like me' anymore?" I shoot back.

Robin's jaw tightens. "Am I not allowed to care about your well-being?"

"You certainly didn't care about it when you walked out seven years ago."

"This again?" Robin starts to turn back to the door, then changes her mind and walks toward me with her fighting face on. "We both made choices. Why are you acting like it's all on me? You could stand to take some responsibility. Or at least be chill while we're both here and leave the past in the past."

I feel an angry wolf howl inside of me, and I let it out. "Don't you dare lecture *me* about responsibility. You left without even considering what a mess you were leaving behind. Do you have any idea how hard it was to run the Hummingbird alone, when you'd already had one foot out the door for months? When you were too famous to even be bothered to make a fucking checklist for someone else to do your job?"

"You left too!" Robin says, matching my anger beat for

beat. "Don't act like you're so brave for sticking around when you ran off, what, two months later?"

On another day I'd feel guilty about that, but there's no space for past regrets in this argument. "I left when everything was taken care of!" I spit back. "Caro and Jesse didn't want the responsibility of running the place, and after watching us tear each other to shreds over the inn, who can blame them? *I* hired the management company and brought them up to speed so our staff was in capable hands. They contacted *me* when they had to make decisions about the property. *You* were off gallivanting around Portland and rubbing elbows with celebrities. And if you were too cool for this quaint little town then, you don't belong here now. So do what you do best and leave."

Robin laughs mirthlessly. "By the looks of it, people are more excited to see me back here than you. So maybe *you're* the one who should leave."

I'm not sure if it's the alcohol or my all-consuming rage, but the sequence of events blurs together—screaming at each other, gesticulating wildly, poking my finger accusingly right in Robin's face—and the next thing I know we're inches apart. Robin's gaze slides from my eyes to my lips, and now my fingers are mussing up her slicked-back hair and her hands are under my shirt and my back is pressed against the brick exterior wall of the bar and she's biting my lower lip and instead of cooling off I'm a hundred and eighty degrees, the perfect temperature for poaching an egg, and everything makes sense and nothing makes sense.

It takes the sound of the patio door opening to bring me back to earth. A woman, the one whose chest Robin signed, is ogling us like she might take a picture and post it to a fan page. I shove Robin away from me and tug my shirt into place. How did I get here? What did we just do? And why do I feel like I'm about to catch on fire?

Sliding away along the brick wall, I say, "Nope. Absolutely not. This is *not* happening, now or ever." Then I hop the low wooden fence and run.

20

Robin

WHAT. THE *HELL*. WAS *THAT*?

Too flustered to talk to the woman who's been trying to slip me her number ever since I agreed to sign her body, which I regret, by the way, I hold my phone up to my ear and pretend to have a very important conversation with Edgar by the limestone wall.

All I wanted was a fun night out with Jesse and Caro to celebrate my new gig, and instead I'm dodging fans left and right, having a fight with Molly that's been brewing for weeks, then ending up with her tongue in my mouth. I don't even remember what either of us said in that argument; I couldn't hear us over the sound of my pulse racing in my ears after watching her dance with some handsy stranger. Jealous? Me? Hell no. I was *concerned*.

I yap about scheduling some fake flight until the woman goes inside, then tuck my phone back in my pocket and sit down on the ground, dropping my head into my hands. Yeah, okay, maybe I was jealous. But this is *our* bar. It's where we came to celebrate with our friends after I proposed. It's where we had the watch party for our first-ever TV feature, on *Inn for a Treat*. How can she hit on someone else here, right in front of me? What happened to the sweet, quiet, gentle Molly I met back in 2012? This can't be the same person.

Did she kiss me first? Surely. She's the one who's drunk and hyped up. I don't remember what happened exactly, but she must have thrown herself at me in a moment of confused passion.

But, if I'm being honest with myself, I also had a role in it. She's this fireball of fierce rage and tattoos and freckles and every time she looks at me, even in a scathing way, I feel the urge to grab her and . . . well, kiss her. So I guess there's the tiniest chance that I started it.

No. I'm too angry to admit that possibility. Somehow she gets off scot-free for hiring some terrible management company that did such a piss-poor job of running the inn that it's been vacant since the pandemic, *and* she calls dibs on the whole town where we both lived for years. I've got friends here too. Hell, I've got an actual *job* here, not just whatever she's been tinkering around with in the shed.

That kiss was quite the distraction, but I haven't forgotten the hell she's put me through these past two weeks. Tonight I get my revenge.

I let Molly have her head start. I stand up, brush myself

off, smooth my hair where Molly mussed it, and go back in the bar like everything is completely normal. After chatting with Jesse and Caro a little more, I sign a few autographs and tell Keyana that Molly left but I'll make sure she got home all right. Then I say my goodbyes and walk home, scheming the whole way.

Once inside the front door, I take off my shoes and tiptoe up to the third floor. Molly's gentle snores are audible through her door. She always sleeps like a rock after a couple drinks. That's perfect for me, because I can set up without tipping her off.

It takes a little over an hour to get everything together. Then I wait a while longer, because everyone knows the scariest time of night is between three and five A.M. I spend my time remembering when Dot first told us about the rumored ghosts of the Hummingbird, the ones she talks about on her walking tours. How, after she told us, Molly and I had to sleep on blankets in the dining room with the lights on for three nights because we were so freaked out. I'm hoping that fear is still lying dormant in Molly, ready to be reawakened.

When the moment is right, I connect my phone to a Bluetooth speaker hidden on the stairs between the second and first floors and play a track I found online of a girl quietly singing and laughing. God, kids' voices out of context are so creepy. This is off to a great start.

Except, after a few minutes, Molly's still asleep. I bump the volume up a notch; still nothing. Luckily, I know how to move around this house quietly, how to evade the creaky floorboards and squeakiest hinges. I tiptoe to the third floor and crack open Molly's door an inch to let in more of the sound.

I'm about to head back downstairs when Marmalade comes out of Molly's room, blinking her big eyes at me curiously. I give her a head scratch, and she chirps. The snores stop. I put a finger over my lips and, as if Marmee understands, she silently disappears up the stairs to the fourth floor. Good. It's best she stays out of this.

I sneak all the way down to the main floor on light feet. The soundtrack of the girl singing has looped back to the beginning, and even though I know it's fake, I still get goosebumps as I pass the disembodied voice.

Just as I reach the front hallway, I hear Molly's door open. *Let the games begin.*

"Robin?" I hear her say tentatively. "Is that you?"

I hit pause on the track, play a sound effect of a girl screaming, then hurl a sack of oranges to the top stair of the second-floor landing. It falls exactly as I hoped, noisily thunking down the steps back to me. I grab it and duck behind the check-in desk.

"Jesus Christ! Robin! Are you all right?"

I hear Molly run down to the second floor, then pause at the open door of the Zinnia Room to see it empty, my bed made as if I haven't yet come home from One More Round.

"Robin?" Molly says again, her voice more nervous this time. I hope she's thinking about that story of the little girl who won the Princess of the Ozarks pageant back in the 1950s, then fell down the stairs that very night and bashed her head in, still wearing her crown. Guests in Miss Addy's day claimed they saw the girl sometimes late at night.

Time for phase two. I connect my phone to the Bluetooth speaker I hid in the basement and play a track of glass
bottles clinking. Molly flicks on a light on the second floor
and slowly makes her way downstairs. I catch a glimpse as
she turns the corner onto the main floor. She's in her underwear and that short robe again, just like the morning of the
dolls. Her hair is in two messy buns, and her eyeliner is
smeared like a punk-rock raccoon.

When Molly realizes the sound is coming from the basement, I hear her mutter, "Oh, fuck this," then, more loudly,
"Robin? God, I hope it's you. But if it is you, I'll kill you." She
pauses to grab a lamp from a side table in the hallway and
holds it up as an improvised weapon, then flips the light
switch at the basement door and descends toward the sound
of clinking glass. I wait just long enough for her to get down
the stairs before slamming the door shut behind her and
using an app to kill the smart bulb I installed a couple hours
ago. Molly's scream is immediate and much worse than the
recorded one I played earlier. I imagine she's thinking about
the bootlegger rumored to have used the inn's basement for
his bathtub gin who poisoned himself with a bad batch.

I launch myself back behind the check-in desk and
power up the flat-screen above me with a message in an old-
school typewriter font: "THE END was written on my story too
soon. My business is not yet finished."

A moment later, Molly comes hurtling out of the dark
basement, breathing heavy, clutching the lamp to her chest
like a life vest. I assume she notices the screen because she
immediately screams again. Now she's probably thinking
about the story that gave us the most trouble, the one about

the typewriter salesman who built this house, accused of murdering his annoying mother-in-law by pushing a stack of typewriters onto her in the attic, now the penthouse apartment where we used to sleep. Anytime the old house used to creak, we'd both think it was the sound of a typewriter's keys, the sign of the mother-in-law's ghost saying she'd seek her revenge. I must be right, because Molly starts running back upstairs mumbling, "Oh no, not today, I do not mess with ghosts."

I'm hardly holding back laughter when I hear a loud crash, breaking glass, and Molly's pained grunt.

"Shit," I say, leaving my hiding place to find Molly splayed on the landing of the second floor, the lamp shattered next to her. "Molly! Are you okay?"

I'm almost to her when she holds out a hand to stop me. "Careful!" she says, looking at the scattered ceramic and glass shards between us. "I . . . I think I'm okay."

I step strategically around the mess to help Molly up and ask, "Are you sure?"

She pats her sides, shifts from foot to foot, and twists her arms around looking for damage. "I'm not hurt," Molly says. Then, realization dawning, she shoves me hard, but away from the stairs or the broken glass. "What the hell, Robin? You did all this?"

Stumbling to regain my balance, I say, "I . . . uh . . ."

"This is a new low." Molly's face is more furious than I've ever seen it, red, scowling, eyes narrowed to slits. "You're some kind of evil mastermind. I can't *believe* you."

I can tell that both of our hearts are still racing. "It's only fair," I say breathlessly, trying to organize my thoughts after worrying I actually hurt her. "The dolls. We're even."

She lets out some kind of indecipherable roar, then storms away up the stairs to her room and slams the door behind her.

Turns out revenge doesn't taste as sweet as everyone says. I don't feel better. Actually, I feel worse.

21
MOLLY

WHEN DID ROBIN BECOME THE PETTY ONE? ISN'T THAT *MY* thing?

There's no sleeping after all that. Hours later, I'm wide awake in bed in the Snapdragon Room, jumping at every noise, staring at a crack in the ceiling that I'll have to fix before we sell this place. I'd almost forgotten about the inn's ghost stories, but now they're running on a loop in my head, narrated by Dot's cigarette-tainted voice. It's drizzling outside, and somehow the rain sounds eerily like the click-clack of typewriter keys.

The worst part is that I can't even blame Robin. She's right. I had this coming after the doll stunt. I want to be furious with her, yet somehow the move makes me respect her more. I guess she has just as much right to terrify me to death as I do her. But after agreeing to the reno, shouldn't I get a free pass from retribution?

After endless tossing and turning, my heart racing at every tiny noise, sunlight begins to light up my room and I drag myself out of bed. My hangover is rearing its ugly head. Everything hurts. I pop a couple ibuprofen, chug some water, and try to sketch window design ideas for Drizzled Donuts. I've got a decent vision going, but my hands are too shaky to execute it. I need sustenance. I head downstairs to the now functional kitchen, trying to decide if I have the energy to scramble some eggs, when I hear Robin's footsteps behind me.

I turn around and spot a mug in her hand, and I can't ignore the rich, warm scent coming from it. "Oh my god, is that coffee?"

"I moved the coffee maker to my room while the kitchen was off-limits," Robin says, then takes a dramatic slurp and sighs contentedly. "Want a cup?"

"God, yes. I slept like shit because *someone* decided to turn our house into Ghost Disneyland."

Robin has the grace to look ashamed. "Hand me a mug?"

I reach into a cabinet and pull out the first cup I touch. As I pass it to Robin, we both freeze, spotting the corny cartoon rabbit on the mug at the same moment.

"You still . . ." Robin's voice fades before she finishes her sentence.

It's the bunny mug I found in the basement, the one Robin bought at a yard sale to give me for our first Christmas together. Annoyed as I was at Robin, I couldn't help but bring it upstairs to use. I clear my throat. "Yeah, I couldn't get rid of it."

After another awkward second, Robin grabs the mug and heads back upstairs. She returns a few minutes later with the promised coffee. The first sip makes me feel a little more human. "Thanks," I grunt. "I'm still not over the ghost thing, though."

"Fair. I'm still not over the doll thing either." Robin turns away from me and opens the fridge. "But I'm also fucking starving. Want some breakfast tacos?"

I wish I could hold on to my bitterness enough to say no. This chummy thing we have going on feels new, and I don't think I like it. But I start salivating at the very idea of Robin's cooking; I can't talk my empty stomach out of this. "Yeah," I say as casually as I can manage. "I do."

OUR BREAKFAST TOGETHER LIGHTENS THE mood. There's no big emotional heart-to-heart. We don't say much at all, actually. But sitting across the island from each other as we scarf down mushroom and shishito-pepper breakfast tacos makes me feel truly at home for the first time since I arrived. Between agreeing to work together on the inn and both getting a chance to terrorize each other, it appears we've reached some kind of truce. Or perhaps the surprise kiss at One More Round helped get some of the tension out, although we seem to be on the same page about acting like it never happened.

And now that my brain isn't preoccupied with hating Robin and/or thinking about kissing her, I can actually get some work done. I spend the day soldering together the remaining pieces of the window for Wild Card, then cleaning and polishing it and applying a copper patina to the seams.

All I need to do is buff it up with wax and it's ready for installation.

I'm so exhausted by the end of the day that I fall into a dead sleep as soon as my head hits the pillow. I must be in the middle of a REM cycle when I'm awakened around one A.M., because at first I think the tapping and creaking sounds are part of a dream. But once I crack open my eyes and situate myself, I realize the noise is coming from the attic.

The sound pauses for a moment, long enough for me to hope I imagined it, before resuming even louder. The tapping is too irregular to be dripping water, and the groaning floorboards suggest something's moving around up there. I'm trying to convince myself it's not a ghost or serial killer when I hear a loud crash.

I jump out of bed, my heart threatening to burst out of my chest, as I realize what's going on: Robin's pranking me again. Just when I thought we'd found peace.

I throw a robe over my underwear and race into the hallway, ready to run to the attic, murder Robin, and add a new ghost story to the Hummingbird's lore. But I don't make it that far, because Robin is already halfway up the stairs to my floor.

I go in on her. "Good grief, Robin, can you not give the ghost shenanigans a re—"

But Robin's shouting right back. "—thought we were even and now you pull *this* bullshit, scaring me half to . . ."

We freeze midway through our overlapping rants.

"Wait, that wasn't you?" I say, taking in Robin's wrinkled sleep shirt and the lined pillow imprints on her face.

Robin shakes her head, eyes wide. "I thought it was *you*."

"Then who . . ." My voice trails off as another creak emanates from the floor above us.

Robin and I look toward the ceiling, then back at each other. Too afraid of what might happen if we make another noise, we have a wordless, gesture-laden conversation about who's going to risk her life to confront the axe murderer in our attic.

Together? I mouth when we reach an impasse.

Robin nods, then looks around, I assume for a makeshift weapon. I tiptoe into my room, rummage through my toolbox, and return with a hammer and a crescent wrench. They won't do much damage to a ghost, but they might harm a more corporeal threat. Robin grabs the hammer, then moves toward the stairs, gesturing for me to follow. We both know how to creep up this flight to the attic without making a peep, skipping the fourth step, veering right on the eighth, left on the fifteenth. When we reach the top, the door is slightly ajar. Robin looks at me, her hand hovering over the doorknob, eyebrows raised in question. I gulp, lift my wrench above my shoulder, and nod. If we're about to get murdered, at least it will be together.

Robin flings open the door, and my life flashes before my eyes. We race in, weapons in hand, to see Marmalade streak across the wooden floor, chasing a tiny brown mouse into a hole in the baseboard.

"Holy motherfucking shit," Robin says with a relieved sigh.

I drop the wrench onto the kitchenette table and push my hair from my forehead, fanning away my nervous sweat. "Christ on a cracker, Marmee, you nearly gave me a heart attack," I say to the fat gray cat, who's ignoring me and reaching a whole leg into the mouse's hole. Is this the same cat that didn't even flinch when a mouse ran by her nose in New Orleans? I guess returning to the home of her kittenhood really has given her some youthful energy.

Robin checks the closet and bathroom, flipping on lights to make sure we're all clear. Once satisfied, she says, "I guess I'd rather have mice than a ghost infestation."

"Agreed," I say, recognizing that this will be funny one day when my heart isn't racing.

Robin points to a chair lying on its side, toppled from when Marmee jumped from it. "That must have been the bang."

The cat's tail flicks, knocking the string hanging from a nearby window's blinds into the metal radiator. "The tapping sound," I say.

Robin nods, then rubs her eyes. "Now that's settled, I should probably go back to bed."

"Me too," I say. "I'll patch that hole tomorrow and pick up some humane traps."

I grab Marmee, who meows in annoyance, as Robin turns off the lights and closes the door behind us. At the third floor, I drop the cat, who considers sneaking back upstairs before changing her mind and wandering toward the main level, presumably for a snack.

I pause at my doorway, tugging my robe closed. "What do you say we officially call off the pranks?" I suggest. "I don't think my nerves can take another surprise."

"Deal." Robin shakes my hand, our touch lingering longer than necessary. "You can totally say no, but . . . what if I slept in your bed tonight? Or you can sleep in mine. Like when we slept in the dining room after Dot told us about the ghosts in the penthouse. I'm still spooked, I don't know if I'll be able to sle—"

I must be making a face, because Robin backtracks immediately. "Never mind. Forget it. I'll leave a lamp on."

"It's an emphatic no from me," I say as Robin turns to head downstairs. I'm shocked that she's chicken enough to ask, and also admittedly a little smug that I'm brave enough to not say yes. "Not just a no, but a *hell* no."

"All right, you don't have to get nasty," Robin says without looking back. "I already said forget it."

"I'd rather take my chances with the ghosts."

Robin stops on the second-floor landing and puts her hands up. "Your call," she says. "But I'm definitely a better cuddler."

"And a bigger drooler," I say.

"At least *I* don't snore," Robin swats back.

"Good night!" I say, slamming the door behind me.

I crawl back into bed and try to forget the whole incident. But my brain plays dirty. I've never felt so wide awake. And every time I get anywhere close to relaxing, I hear some normal old house noise that freaks me out all over again. I can't go through another day without a good night's rest. My to-do list is way too long.

I put on a T-shirt and reluctantly head to the Zinnia Room. Sharing a bed with my ex is objectively a bad idea. But I used to sleep like a rock with Robin beside me, and after two nights of interruptions, I would give my left foot for some rest. I tap lightly on Robin's door.

"Change of heart?" I hear her say, clearly wide awake.

I find Robin tucked under the fluffy white comforter. A rerun of *Grey's Anatomy,* which we used to watch together, is playing on the TV above the dresser, volume turned down to barely a whisper. Robin looks up at me from the bed with a smirk, at least three times smugger than I was when she first asked. But it's too late to turn back now.

I cross my arms and say, "No touching. I'll stay on my side, you'll stay on yours. Agreed?"

Robin considers my proposal, then says, "Fine." She flips back the edge of the blanket nearest to me. "But no putting your cold toes on my legs."

I climb in, pull the sheets up to my chin, and say, "No promises."

22

Robin

WHEN MY ALARM GOES OFF, IT FEELS LIKE I HAVE TO SWIM
through a vat of syrup to wake up. I can't even move my arm
to reach my phone. As I crack open my eyes, I realize the
heavy feeling isn't just in my head. Molly, Ms. No Touching,
is spooning me. Her body is tucked against my back, one arm
stretched under my neck, the other wrapped around my
middle, our legs tangled together. Apparently I wasn't the
only one sleeping heavily; she's snoring so loudly I can feel
the vibrations through my pillow.

I shift to silence the alarm, and Molly's snores come to an
abrupt halt. It takes her about two seconds to realize where
she is, then another second to launch herself out of bed.

"What . . . I . . . You . . ." she slurs, squinting at me
through sleep-fogged eyes.

"Good morning, sunshine." I roll over to face her, languidly stretching as if waking up to her snuggling with me didn't throw me at all. Inwardly, I'm freaking out that we can so easily slide back together after years apart. I logically want this to mean nothing, yet I've got some kind of uncontrollable oxytocin rush making me feel ridiculously cheerful. But playing it cool gives me the upper hand. And besides, it's pretty clear who instigated the spooning.

Molly looks down, seeming to just now realize that she's not wearing pants. Tugging at her shirt, she says, "I didn't . . . we said we . . ."

"I never could understand you before your morning coffee," I say, enjoying making Molly squirm. "Why don't you get back under the covers and I'll make a pot?" I point to the coffee maker on my dresser.

I see her internal battle through the shifting expression on her face. She desperately wants the coffee, but she's also trying to be mad at me for something that clearly wasn't my fault. There's embarrassment in there too, and maybe a tiny yearning to crawl back into bed and snuggle a little longer. She's trying to hate me right now, but she's just as well rested as I am, and it's hard to be angry when you're so freshly cuddled. I'm tickled that all of this is as easy for me to read as a recipe. Even after years apart, I'm still fluent in Molly.

"I have to go," she blurts out before turning tail and running.

Feeling a little guilty for toying with her for breaking her own rules, I call out, "I'll bring you a cup of coffee when it's ready!"

I'VE GOT THE DAY OFF from Counterculture, and the weather
is gorgeous, so I focus on gardening. The quicker I can spruce
up the yards and move on to the rest of the inn, the sooner
we can sell it and I can get out of here and back on my feet
somewhere else. Not the Pacific Northwest. I've worn out
my welcome there. I can try somewhere safer, closer to Arkansas but still with a decent culinary scene. Nashville. At-
lanta. Chicago, maybe, if I can stand the winters.

The couple at the garden store loaded me up with seedlings for the flowers, fruits, and veggies I want to replant.
When it comes to produce, I want fast-growing stuff I can
sell to Jesse: leafy greens, radishes, strawberries, cucumbers,
tomatoes. Ozark tomatoes really are special. It's the rocky
soil, the mountain minerality. I'm not a geologist, but I *am*
something of a tomato connoisseur, and those big, juicy
beauties are unbeatable.

It takes a few hours to get my new plants situated and
labeled, then another hour to pick ripe blackberries and
raspberries and shallots and herbs. I'm weeding the flower-
beds when I get a phone call from my mom.

"Birdie!" she says. "Glad I caught you. Are you still in
Eureka, or have you jetted off to Timbuktu without seeing
your adoring parents first?"

"Hi, Mom," I say, my patience already thin from the
nickname. "I'm still in Eureka."

"So you've gone a whole month without visiting us, even
though we're only a few hours away?"

I rub tiny, firm circles on my temple. "I've been busy. I'll
come down soon, I promise."

"You'll be here for your nephew's first birthday party next
weekend, then?"

"I . . . next weekend? I'm not sure, I think I may be work-ing."

"Take some time off," Mom says, as if it's that easy. "It'll be good for you. Details are in the email I sent yesterday."

I deleted the email without opening it because my mom's fancy e-vites instantly make my blood pressure rise. They're a whole production, almost as overly complicated as the ac-tual parties she throws. "I'll look at my schedule and get back to you," I say.

Mom's hum sounds like she's unconvinced. "Bradford is turning one, and he hasn't even met his Aunt Robin yet," she says. "Annalise hasn't seen you since two Christmases ago. Gabriel would never say as much, he's far too stoic, but it wounds him that his only sibling isn't more involved in his children's lives. Or *his* life. Have you congratulated him on his promotion at the insurance company yet?"

Gabe and I weren't that close growing up; he was always deep in a video game or a book, and I spent as much time as possible away from home, trying all kinds of sports teams and clubs, spending whole summers away at camp. We only got further apart after I left for college. But I *want* to be a good sister to Gabe, and even though I never thought much about being an aunt, his oldest, Annalise, is cool as hell. I'm racked with guilt by my mom's words, but also irritated that she'd pull all these cards on me at once. "Okay, Mom," I say with a sigh. "I'll come to Bradford's birthday party."

"Oh, I'm so glad, dear," she says, her tone immediately lighter. "Gabriel will be delighted. What do you think of bringing a cake?"

I wipe my sweaty forehead and feel the trail of dirt my hand leaves behind. "Sure, yeah. I can make a cake," I say.

"Wonderful. Something citrusy would go well with the menu. Decorated with little frosting balloons. Balloons are the theme. We hired a balloon artist to decorate the house and a clown to make balloon animals for the children. Maybe you could also make one of those darling cakes for the baby to make a mess with for the pictures. What do they call it?"

"A smash cake," I say, gritting my teeth. Not only has she strong-armed me into going to the party, now I'm baking not one but two cakes. But it's not really about Mom. I want to do this for Gabe. "I'm on it."

"Splendid. See you Sunday, then?"

"Sunday. I'll be there."

We say our goodbyes and I tuck my phone back into my pocket, my mood dampened. Spying the basket of berries and herbs I picked, I realize exactly what I need.

Fifteen minutes later, I knock on the door of the shed.

"Come in," Molly calls out.

I stick my head in far enough to spot her hunched over her worktable, scrubbing at something with a dirty rag. "Interested in happy hour?" I hold up a glass pitcher. "Blackberry mojitos, super fresh. I literally just picked the berries and mint."

"Actually, yeah, that sounds nice." Molly gives whatever is on her table a final wipe, then steps back to examine it with her hands on her hips. "Perfect timing. I just finished buffing this. What do you think?"

I can't help but note how different things feel between us now than they did when Molly first showed up. A few weeks ago, Molly would have sooner punched me in the nose than ask my opinion on anything. I put the pitcher down on a stool and walk closer to see what she's been up to.

When I see the enormous stained-glass window, I gasp. Bright shades of red and blue and green, a playful mix of shapes, whimsical yet tasteful, a unique geometric design. I can't believe Molly made this with her own hands. Then again, of course I can. Haven't I seen her prove over and over again that she can make something remarkable out of nothing?

"Molly, it's . . . it's phenomenal." I lean closer to see the colorful dice, the winding trail of squares around the edges, the shiny copper lines pulling everything together. "You made this?"

"I did," she says, pride shining through her smile. "For the new board-game shop on Spring Street."

"It's incredible, Moll. Every business in town is going to beg you for one." I look between my ex and the brilliant work in front of me. "I knew you could make stained glass, but this . . . this is beyond. It should be in a museum."

"Oh, stop, it's not that good," she says, blushing behind her freckles.

"It is." I grab Molly's shoulder and look her directly in the eye. "You should be really fucking proud of this."

She tries to hold back a smile. "I am," Molly says softly. "I'm proud of it."

"Good." I grab the pitcher. "Let's have a drink. To celebrate."

"Give me a minute to clean up and I'll meet you on the back porch?"

"Deal."

WE SAVOR THE PORCH'S SHADE on two rocking chairs, toasting
Molly's brilliance as we watch a few hummingbirds flit
around their feeder. It feels good, being normal with Molly.
Enjoying a cold drink. Chatting about our days. Not fighting
or giving the silent treatment or trying to scare each other
off. Between agreeing to work together on the inn and the
mouse-in-the-attic fiasco and a little platonic cuddling, I
think we've leveled up from enemies to . . . friends? Or
maybe just functional roommates?

"I needed this," I say as I top off my glass. "My mom
called a bit ago."

I can feel Molly's gaze on me. "How's Sharon doing?" she
asks.

"Oh, same as always. Splitting her time between planning events at the country club, shopping, and making me
feel like I've disappointed my whole family."

"They can't be disappointed by you," Molly says. "You're
literally famous. You have fans. You have restaurants. Plural."

"*Had*," I correct her, my voice strained.

Molly's rocking chair creaks to a stop. "Oh."

I can't bring myself to look at her. Does she really not
know? "The pandemic was rough on the whole industry, but
it hit at exactly the worst time for me," I admit. "I'd just made
a lot of big investments in new spaces, expecting them to pay
off quickly, but they never had a chance. So I took the hit,
shut my restaurants, and put all my eggs in one risky, experimental basket that I thought was perfect for the moment, an
outdoor dining experience with campfires where customers

cooked their own food. By the time I got it off the ground, the moment had passed. It couldn't survive."

Molly is quiet for a moment. I'm grateful, because it gives me a chance to swallow back any embarrassing emotions. "That's why you're here?" she asks eventually.

I nod. It still hurts, but saying it out loud makes the burden a little lighter to carry.

"I'm sorry, Rob," she says gently. "I heard about that new show getting canceled, but I had no idea about the restaurants." I wince at Molly's words, and she says, "Sorry, that's probably a sore subject too."

"You Can Take It with You." I shake my head. "A series about the best takeout in the country seemed like a great idea in 2020. But by the time it aired, no one wanted to relive the worst of the lockdown days. I probably should have learned my lesson from that, but I still went full steam ahead with Kindling. Foolish." I grip the arm of my rocking chair to keep my free hand from shaking. "Anyway, what was I saying? Right, my mom. She's making me drive down to Little Rock next weekend for my nephew's birthday. I'm supposed to bring cakes."

"Holy smokes, Gabe's a dad? That's hard to picture."

"Right? Two kids, actually," I add. It feels good to talk to someone who knows my family dynamics. I've drifted away from everyone who knew the old me. "I haven't met the youngest one yet. Annalise probably thinks I'm just the stranger who sends gifts."

"They'll like you for more than the presents," Molly says. "You've always been good with kids. Weren't you the most popular counselor at Girl Scout camp?"

"Kids are easier to talk to than my parents. That's for sure." I take a long sip of my cocktail. "I'm dreading seeing them, to be honest. I've kind of been avoiding them since my career fell apart. They always told me the restaurant industry was too volatile. That I should have followed in my dad's footsteps and been a dermatologist."

Molly takes a deep breath, then says, "Do you want me to go with you?"

I turn to look at her for the first time since the confession of my various failures, stunned by the offer. "You would do that?"

"If it would help you, yeah, I would."

"Why? They've been terrible to you," I say. I'm still haunted by the first time I brought Molly home. We'd already bought the inn together, and instead of trying to get to know her at all, after I bragged about her DIY skills, my dad asked her to fix the garbage disposal like she was some random handyman, then told me afterward she wasn't in my league. I was so angry I didn't speak to them for six months, the longest I'd gone at the time. But I'm not faultless either. I could have done more to defend her back then. And I probably should have apologized for leaving her and the inn high and dry instead of jumping to the defensive when we both landed here at the same time a month ago. I should have made it clear when we first started talking about selling the inn that she's so much more than a handyman. She's brilliant. "*I've* been terrible to you. Lately, at least," I admit.

"Not always," Molly says, more generous than I expected. "I don't mind being a buffer. And I haven't been to Little Rock in a while. I bet you'll buy me a milkshake from the Purple Cow if I ask nicely."

"I'll buy you a million milkshakes," I say. Molly's offer is more than I expected from her, more than I deserve after all the ghost nonsense. More than I deserve for letting my parents belittle her for years. "I'll absolutely take you up on it, if you mean it."

"I mean it." Molly seems to surprise herself with her words as much as me. "Besides, we're wives, and wives look out for each other."

"Wives." I laugh at how weird the word feels in my mouth now. "I guess we still are."

23

MOLLY

IN TRUTH, WHILE I THINK OF ROBIN AS MY "EX-WIFE," IT'S MORE in spirit than in legal standing.

As I ride in her car to visit the people who are technically still my in-laws, it's harder than usual to push that fact to the back of my brain. Neither of us has ever been a fan of paper-work. Or lawyers. When we got married, I didn't even con-sider how messy it would be to divide our home and our business. Divorce wasn't the first thing on my mind on our wedding day; I'd assume most happy couples feel the same way. And when the split happened, I wasn't going to take responsibility for making it official when breaking up wasn't even my idea. If we were too annoyed with each other to talk about what to do with the inn, there was no way we could rally the energy for divorce proceedings.

Robin was the one with a new girlfriend and business partner. Surely she'd get around to filing the paperwork when things got serious, I figured. I wasn't in much of a hurry. I wasn't seriously dating anyone. And at first, the inn was still bringing in good money under the management company's watch. I cashed those checks without sending a cent to Robin, figuring she'd gotten rich enough off her celebrity-chef status. I feel a little guilty about that now, watching her operate the same green Honda CR-V she used to leave the inn in 2018 instead of some fancy new sports car, knowing she's now in dire straits.

Ever since we agreed to sell the inn, or since we reached a truce on our ghost and doll antics, or maybe since we kissed at One More Round, it's been harder to leave our past in the past. Maybe that's why I offered to go to Little Rock with her. Even as the words came out of my mouth, I couldn't believe I was saying them. Me being around the Lasko family has never ended well. But I guess I felt bad for Robin, seeing her so bummed at the very idea of going home to her family. Her parents are far from perfect, but they love her, something I've seen plenty of evidence of, even if she can't recognize it. I'm actually a little excited to see Gabe, who eventually welcomed me into the family in his own quiet way. And there is cake involved.

"Robin, dear, so glad you could make it," Mrs. Lasko says when we reach the Laskos' home. It's just as dramatic and impressive as I remember, with three stories of ivy-draped white-painted brick and a grand arched entryway beneath a Juliet balcony, except now it's decorated with a riot of color-ful balloons. Mrs. Lasko wraps Robin in a hug, and I'm surprised when she turns to me with almost as much enthusiasm.

"Molly. Wonderful to see you and Robin back together. I've always thought you had a way of grounding her."

"Mom!" Robin interrupts. "We're not together. Molly's here as a . . . friend," she finishes awkwardly.

"Oh, well." Mrs. Lasko recovers quickly. "Friends are nice too. Come in, I'll show you the crystal serving ware I've set up for the cakes."

Robin and I make eye contact, her apologetic, me shrugging it off. I'm not sure what Robin told her parents about me coming with her, but I'm guessing she was too busy trying to get them off the phone quickly to share many details. We grab the boxed cakes and follow Mrs. Lasko through the front hall, passing a string quartet and a crowd of decorators with armfuls of balloons.

"They went all out, huh?" I say under my breath to Robin while Mrs. Lasko directs a sound technician to the nearest outlet.

"As if Bradford will even remember his first birthday party," Robin mutters back.

I look at the elaborate balloon sculpture of a dolphin leaping from waves constructed by the fireplace. "Maybe Bradford won't, but everyone else will."

Mrs. Lasko reappears in front of us with Mr. Lasko at her side. "My favorite daughter!" he says to Robin, clapping her on the back so hard I worry she'll drop the cake in her hands. I'm thrown off when he does the same to me, saying, "And Molly! It's been too long since we've seen your face."

After brief greetings, Mrs. Lasko waves us toward the kitchen. "The caterers are using the island for setup, but you can use the breakfast nook. We've got to figure out where the clowns are. I'll be right back."

They leave, and Robin and I get to work moving the cakes to their stands. They look gorgeous, of course. The small cake has a smooth coating of light blue buttercream and a colorful hot-air balloon piped on top. The larger cake for serving the crowd has the same base color with a variety of fondant hot-air balloons floating up and around the sides. Robin pulls out an offset spatula to fix any imperfections as I watch, hands on my hips, fresh out of ways to make myself useful.

"Maybe I should see if your parents' garbage disposal is still working," I joke.

"No way," Robin says as she smooths a bit of frosting at the base of the larger cake. "You're doing more than enough by keeping me sane."

"Yeah, well, I don't know that your parents are thrilled to have me mixing and mingling with their friends."

"What do you mean?" Robin says sarcastically. "Didn't my mom just say you keep me grounded?"

"I think that was a polite way of saying I keep you stuck in the mud."

We hear the sound of an upset child outside the kitchen door, plaintive cries about some kind of bogeyman getting closer. Then a tiny torpedo with blond ringlets and light-up sneakers hurtles across the kitchen and crashes into Robin's legs.

"Guncle Robbie!" the little girl says, her arms wrapped around Robin's knees.

"My favorite niece!"

"Guncle?" I say to Robin, raising my eyebrows. Clearly she was wrong when she said last week that Annalise had probably forgotten her.

"I told her to call me that Christmas before last," Robin says, grabbing the girl under the armpits and hauling her up onto her hip. "And you remembered because you're a genius, didn't you, Annalise? Guncle Robbie's favorite future astronaut?"

"I don't wanna be an astronaut anymore," Annalise says, rubbing her face against the soft cotton of Robin's T-shirt. "I wanna be a zoologist."

"A zoologist, huh?"

"A person who makes friends with all the animals at the zoo," Annalise says.

"That sounds cool." Robin uses her sleeve to wipe away the tears still glistening on Annalise's cheeks. "What was all that about the bogeyman?"

"The Oogie Boogie," Annalise says, her eyes widened with fear. "I think he's here. I saw a creepy bug under the back porch."

Robin squints thoughtfully. "The Oogie Boogie from *The Nightmare Before Christmas*?"

Annalise grips Robin's arm harder as she nods.

"I heard the Oogie Boogie never leaves Halloween Town," Robin says confidently. She sets her niece back on the ground and produces a plastic astronaut figurine from her pocket. "But just in case, how about I give you this space explorer to keep you safe? She may be tiny, but she's *very* tough. Even the Oogie Boogie is scared of her."

Annalise squeals with delight as she snatches the toy from Robin's hand. She runs around the kitchen, holding the astronaut aloft as if it's zooming through the galaxy, then jets out of the room. "Thanks, Guncle Robbie!" she calls over her shoulder.

My heart has turned from concrete to Jell-O. And I'm not even a kid person. If all the thirsty lesbians in Robin's DMs saw this, they'd probably break down her door.

Robin is wiping off the edges of the crystal cake stand when her mom returns.

"Hot-air balloons? I said *regular* balloons were the theme," Mrs. Lasko says.

I see the tension in Robin's shoulders, but before she can retort, Gabe appears behind Mrs. Lasko. "Whoa, Robin, you *made* those?" he says, getting between Robin and their mother for a closer look. "You're a magician. Heather, come look at these!"

Gabe's wife, Heather, enters the kitchen with a baby, presumably Bradford, on her hip. "They're gorgeous!" she says upon seeing the cakes. "Thank you so much, Robin. The smash-cake pictures are going to be adorable."

We exchange a round of hugs and introduce ourselves to the baby while Mrs. Lasko inspects the cakes, seeming to warm to them after Gabe and Heather's praise. "What flavor?" she asks.

"The smash cake is vanilla," Robin says. "The big cake is vanilla and chocolate swirl on the bottom for picky eaters, lemon-pistachio with blackberry filling on top for the more adventurous."

Mrs. Lasko nods, seemingly satisfied, before being called away by decorators carting even more balloons. All four of the remaining adults seem to relax an inch once she's out of the room.

"We're so glad y'all came," Heather says, bouncing Bradford. I think I've only met Heather four times, the first of which was at her wedding to Gabe, but she seems genuine.

"Lasko parties are always better with you two here. Especially you, Molly. We're glad you two have worked some things out."

"We're not actually back together," I rush to say, surprising myself with my apologetic tone. "Romantically, I mean."

Gabe shrugs. "But you're here, right? That's because you're still family."

Gabe and Heather have to run off shortly afterward for pictures, and Robin and I busy ourselves greeting an endless parade of Robin's family members, old neighbors, and acquaintances. It's surprising how easily I slip back into being at Robin's side: making knowing eye contact when someone says something passive-aggressive about Robin's career, resting an arm across the back of her chair, cooing at the birthday baby when he gets passed our way. Clinging to each other at this party where we both feel somewhat out of place, it's like we're on the same team for the first time in years.

Once we're well into the party and the Laskos have had a chance to greet all of their guests, I'm surprised when Mr. Lasko calls us over to where they're holding court in the dining room.

"Molly!" he says as if I'm an old friend, not someone he never saw as good enough for his daughter. "Pull up a chair."

This time *I'm* the one making pleading eyes at Robin to not leave me alone, but it turns out I don't need to; she's already taking the chair right beside me, placing a fortifying hand on my knee under the table.

"We're so glad you made it," Mrs. Lasko says, lifting her champagne flute in my direction.

"It's always a pleasure to be Robin's plus-one," I say.

"Plus-one?" Mrs. Lasko says, laughing. "If we'd known you were in town, we'd have extended an invitation. It's an honor to have a highly respected artist at Bradford's party."

I nearly fall off my chair at that.

Mr. Lasko leans forward, seeming to really look me in the eye for the first time. Ever. "We saw your profile in the *Arkansas Times*. And your installation at Crystal Bridges. Very impressive. It's a pleasure to say we knew you when."

I pick my jaw up off the floor enough to thank them.

"Do you have any other media planned? I can give you a discount on Botox treatments before your next photo shoot," he offers.

I feel Robin's grip on my knee tighten. "Um, that's all right," I manage to mumble.

"You have to start early if you want to maintain a natural look," he says. I know this is just standard conversation for him, but wow is it uncomfortable for me. "Robin, have you been letting yours lapse? Between the brows there? You've got to stay camera-ready for when your next opportunity comes along, especially since your restaurant flopped."

Robin opens her mouth to respond, but I beat her to it. "I certainly wouldn't call a business named a best new restaurant of the year in *Food & Wine* magazine a flop," I say, imitating his casual-party-chatter tone. I googled Robin's restaurants after our heart-to-heart on the porch last week, and I'm fully prepared to put my knowledge to use. "Plus Kindling got a two-page review in *Bon Appétit*, and Robin was a finalist for a James Beard Award for Best Chef of the Northwest and Pacific."

I turn to Robin with an encouraging grin on my face. She looks like I just started speaking fluent Hungarian. "Um, yeah," she manages to say.

I turn back to Mr. Lasko, who's examining me with a combination of irritation and curiosity. "Of course, we're very proud of Birdie. I'm sure whatever comes next for her will be huge." He leans forward to look at Robin. "What *is* coming next for you?"

Robin clears her throat. "Nothing official yet."

A departing party guest calls Mr. Lasko away. Mrs. Lasko, Robin, and I all stand, understanding our conversation to be over. But before she leaves, Mrs. Lasko fondly cups Robin's cheek with her palm and says, "We know you'll land on your feet."

Once we're alone—albeit in the middle of a bustling party—Robin and I look at each other and take a deep breath in and out in unison.

"I owe you at least three Purple Cow milkshakes after this," Robin says.

"With extra whipped cream?"

"Absolutely."

We weave through the partygoers to the back porch for a little air, where we find Gabe with the birthday boy, playing with a set of colorful wooden blocks.

"Oh, hey, guys," Gabe says when he spots us. "Come on over."

We settle onto the ground next to them and help Bradford stack the blocks in a tower. Gabe seems different now that he's a father. Chattier. Softer. More comfortable in his own skin. He plays Godzilla and knocks the tower over, sending Bradford into peals of giggles.

"Thanks again for coming," he says as the baby begins rebuilding. "It's nice to have people here I enjoy talking to."

In the old days, Gabe hardly talked to me beyond short conversations about books or movies. He never seemed that close to Robin either, even though they're only a couple years apart in age. But maybe that's changing now that they're both older.

"You and the kids are the whole reason we came," Robin says. "Even makes it worth Mom and Dad needling me about not being good enough for them," she adds grimly.

"Of course you're good enough for them," Gabe says, sounding confused by Robin's comment. "They brag about you all the time to their friends. I always used to feel like a failure in comparison."

I sit in wide-eyed silence. I've never seen Robin and Gabe have a conversation like this. Are they actually talking about their *feelings*?

"No way," Robin says. "They're so proud of you and your perfect kids and your promotion at the insurance company. Maybe I was flashy for a second, but now there's no question who's the more impressive child."

Gabe laughs in a way that could be bitter, but I think sounds more genuine. "My new job—it's not a promotion. It's kind of a demotion. I'm going to half-time so I can be home more with Annalise and Brad. Heather's been killing it at her law firm. She's up for partner next summer, and if she gets it, we're talking about me becoming a stay-at-home dad."

Bradford spits up a little, and I lean closer to wipe it with his bib, not wanting anything to interrupt this conversation. Gabe? Who couldn't be bothered to look away from his phone during every family occasion I ever attended? A loving, attentive, full-time dad? Honestly, I love it for him.

"Good for you, dude," Robin says, impressed. "How . . . how are Mom and Dad taking it?"

"Shockingly well," Gabe says, leaning back on his elbows. "Not at first. But we talked it out. I told them how much I enjoy being a dad. And would you believe, under all the weird ways they have of expressing it, they really want us to be happy and safe and taken care of? They always figured I'd be the breadwinner, which is hella sexist. But if staying home with the kids while Heather goes boss mode brings me joy, they say they support me. And I believe them."

Robin can't seem to find the words to respond, so I say, "I'm proud of you, Gabe. Those couldn't have been easy conversations to have with your parents."

"They weren't," he agrees. "But since we had them, things between us have been easier than ever. We're pretty chill these days."

The back door opens and Annalise comes bounding out, followed by Heather.

"Daddy, Daddy, play bears with me!" Annalise says, running in a loop around the porch.

Gabe excuses himself with a wonderfully earnest grin, then starts chasing Annalise around the yard, growling playfully with his arms outstretched.

"Come here, little bear cub," Heather says, then grabs Bradford, lifts him onto her shoulders, and follows them into the grass.

Robin looks at me, confused and maybe a little bit hopeful. "That was . . . huh."

"Yeah," I say, gently patting her shoulder. "Lots to talk about on the drive home. But first . . . want to play bears?"

Robin grins, then stands and pulls me up beside her. We run off, paws clasped together, following the sound of giggles and roars.

24

Robin

"A SMALL PURPLE VANILLA SHAKE, A SMALL PB&J SHAKE, and . . ." I turn to Molly. "What flavor for the third, Moll?"

Molly scans the menu. "A small butterscotch caramel, please."

I frown at her. "Are you ordering that one because it's my favorite?"

"Not *just* because of that."

"I'm supposed to be treating you," I say.

"And I can't drink three milkshakes by myself. So if we're sharing, it might as well be something you love," Molly says, her mind clearly made up. "Besides, I like butterscotch too. My grandma always ordered it."

"Fine." I turn back to the server. "And a small butterscotch caramel milkshake."

"Anything else?" the server asks, smacking her gum.

I try to hold myself back, but this is the Purple Cow. There are some things you just can't leave without. "Can we also get a small cheese dip and chips, please?"

"How are you going to eat cheese dip while driving?" Molly says as I hand over my credit card, grateful my first check from Counterculture already cleared.

"Very carefully," I say. "You're on napkin duty."

I would have loved to stick around for the works—a juicy cheeseburger topped with grilled onions and mushrooms, perfectly crispy onion rings, a coloring sheet of a cheerful cow that's meant for kids but nostalgic fun for adults like us who grew up eating here. It's funny to think that Molly and I could have been sitting in neighboring booths in this very same restaurant back in the nineties, eating our kiddie meals, not knowing what we'd someday mean to each other. But today, we need to hit the road if we want to make it home by midnight.

Once we're on the highway, Molly feeds me chips dunked into the salty, creamy cheese dip. It's an Arkansas state treasure, seemingly simple but surprisingly difficult to get right in terms of flavor and texture. There are whole festivals and competitions dedicated to it. Families have been broken by disagreements over whether it's better with tortilla or potato chips. (Team tortilla chip all the way.) It's one of the things I missed the most while I lived in the Pacific Northwest. I make a passable version myself, but things always taste better when they come from your favorite diner.

Once the dip is gone, we start on the milkshakes, taking sips and comparing notes. The purple vanilla is their signature: simple in flavor but a stylish shade of lavender. The

PB&J isn't bad. It's pleasantly salty and sweet, if a bit cloying. The butterscotch caramel, though, has been my first choice since I was a teenager and decided I was too old for the purple one. I'm surprised when Molly also ranks it first.

"I guess my taste buds have matured," she admits. "The others are sweeter than I remember. The butterscotch is more balanced."

"Or maybe your taste buds changed after years of eating my food."

"Maybe."

I spot Molly's grin in the glow of passing streetlights. I want to look at it a little longer, but it's dangerous to take my eyes off the mountainous road. "So you looked up my restaurants," I say finally.

Molly switches Styrofoam cups and takes a noisy slurp of the PB&J shake, then says, "I did."

"What did you think?" I'm weirdly nervous for her reply, as if her opinion could ruin my businesses a second time.

"They looked amazing," she says, and I feel my shoulders drop a couple inches. "Robin's Egg seems like the stuff you were making at the inn. Breakfast and brunch. The menu used fancier words to describe the dishes, but I recognized a lot of them. So I get why it was a success."

"'Success' is a strong word."

"Didn't you open a second location on the Google campus?" Molly says, surprising me again with the depth of her research. "That's huge. They wouldn't have chosen Robin's Egg if you hadn't already proved yourself."

I can't help but feel a little proud, even knowing how it ended. "Yeah, well, the pandemic had other plans," I say, trying to sound cavalier.

"Kindling, though." Molly turns to the darkened landscape racing past the passenger-side window. "It sounds wild. In a good way, I mean. I've never heard of anything like it."

"Too wild, I suppose." I drum my thumbs against the steering wheel to the beat of the song on the radio, wishing I could be more chill about that whole situation. "I tried to break the mold, and instead the mold broke me."

"You aren't broken," Molly says firmly, facing me again. "The world wasn't ready for your idea yet. But like I said to your dad, there are a lot of ways to measure a restaurant besides how long it stays open and how much money it makes."

I feel like Molly is looking right into the most hidden parts of me. It's always been like this with her, ever since that first day we met at Home Depot. She doesn't look through me, or only see what I want people to see. She sees all of me: the good, the bad, the weird, the soft bits I try to hide.

"Thank you for standing up to him like that," I say. "I never know how to respond when he criticizes me. I either want to scream or get out of there as fast as possible. But you stood your ground. *My* ground, actually. It meant a lot."

"You don't have to thank me." Molly holds up a cup. "You already repaid me in milkshakes. And besides, your dad doesn't always mean things as harsh as they sound. From what Gabe said, it sounds like your parents are having a real self-growth journey."

"Can you believe that?" I say, suddenly energized. "Gabe's going to be a stay-at-home dad and our parents are just *cool* with it? Have they been replaced by clones?"

"I don't think it was *that* easy," Molly says, shifting in her seat. "Your parents, they have this very specific vision of what success means for their kids. Seems like Gabe had to help break that down for them before they understood."

I groan theatrically. "So you're saying I have to *talk* to my parents for them to understand me? This is a scam."

Molly laughs, but I notice it sounds a little sad. I suddenly remember that she's never had a chance to negotiate adult child/parent relationships and feel a rush of guilt at how flippant I've been about mine. I briefly consider apologizing, but don't know if we're at discussing-our-childhood-trauma levels of comfort with each other these days, so I change the subject. "Anyway, how's the window design for the cupcake shop going?" I ask.

"Donut shop," Molly corrects me, already more at ease. "And it's going. I just need to figure out how to make it look like sprinkles without having to deal with tiny pieces of glass. Otherwise I'll shred the bejesus out of my fingertips."

We chat a little longer before Molly dozes off on the winding roads up the mountains. When she wakes, I think she's forgotten what year it is, because she reaches across the console, running her fingers gently through the hair at the nape of my neck. Her touch sends goosebumps down my arms. It's bananas how quickly we went from resentful exes to friends. More than friends. Somewhere in the gray area between friends and enemies and . . . lovers? Surely not. But I'd be lying if I said I don't feel some kind of way when her skin touches mine.

"Thanks for driving," she says in a sweet, sleepy voice as we pull into the inn's driveway.

"No problem," I reply. We stay there, Molly playing with my hair, me unwilling to move because I know it will break the moment.

Eventually she stops, I open the car door, and we make our way into the front hallway. Marmalade comes running, meowing furiously that we haven't served her dinner yet even though we fed her extra before we left. Molly and I say good night and retreat to separate floors.

I've barely gotten myself under the sheets when I hear a soft knock at the door. "Come in," I say.

Molly enters and stands meekly at the corner of the dresser, her hair a messy pouf on top of her head. She's in boy-short undies and a thin blue tank top I bought for her years ago at a gas station on a day trip to Beaver Lake, the name printed on the shirt too funny to pass up. Considering we didn't speak for seven years, I can't believe how many of the gifts I gave her she's held on to.

"What's up?" I ask.

Molly bites her lower lip, clearly working up some courage, then asks, "Can I sleep here again tonight?"

"Still afraid of the ghosts?" I tease.

"Maybe a little," she says toward her bare feet. "It's just that, last week when I slept in your bed was the best rest I've had in months. Years. I've, um, had some insomnia issues. But if it's weird, I can go—"

She's already halfway to the door before I stop her. "No, stay. Please." My cheeks feel hot as I realize how much I want her to stay. How strange it's been sleeping alone. Flipping back the comforter on her side of the bed, I admit, "I slept great that night too. Like a rock."

Molly relaxes into a grin. She slides into the bed next to me, her cold toes brushing against my calf as she adjusts.

"It must be your snoring," I say. "It's perfect white noise."

Molly frowns. "I don't snore."

"Sure. And I don't have daddy issues."

Settling on her side, Molly lays her head on her pillow and blinks at me. "Thank you," she says. "For this."

I pull the sheet up to her chin and run my thumb down her cheek, across the curve of her jaw. "My pleasure."

I turn over to click off the bedside lamp, and this time she doesn't wait until we're unconscious to cuddle up against my back. I fall asleep with a smile on my face.

25

MOLLY

BEFORE I OPEN MY EYES, I THINK I'M IN OUR OLD BED IN THE attic. The sounds and smells of the inn combined with the warmth of Robin's sleeping body confuse my sense of time. Sometime in the past few weeks, I let my guard down, and now I can't seem to remember all the things I hated about her for so long. I'm not sure what's going on between us now, but it feels like we're slipping back in time to how we used to be. So much has changed, but with the scent of Robin's lemon verbena shampoo on my pillow, it feels like some things between us will always be the same.

My hips, though, are older than they used to be. My right one aches from lying on it for too long. I shift onto my back, opening my eyes, and Robin groans awake from my movement. She rolls over, rests her head on my shoulder, and mumbles, "Hi."

How did we get here, from avoiding each other like the plague to casually waking up together, in just a few weeks? We haven't had sex, but somehow this moment feels even more intimate. I tuck an arm around her shoulder and run my fingers through her hair. The platinum-blond highlights are more than half grown out now. It feels like Celebrity Chef Robin is fading away, and the Robin I fell in love with is reappearing.

"How long've you been awake?" Robin slurs into my sleep shirt.

"Not long. Just staring at that ugly beach painting and wishing it was Key's zinnia mural."

"I wish that every day." Robin tucks her hand under the bottom hem of my shirt, resting it against my hip bone. "The whole place is . . . do the kids these days still say cheugy?"

"What's 'cheugy'?"

"Boring, basic, outdated, lacking personality," Robin says. "For home design, basically shopping the IKEA and Target sale bins."

"I loved Key's mural in here," I say, staring at the now dull gray wall. "The bright pinks and reds and yellows and oranges. It was one of my favorites."

"Mine too."

"Do you think she'll paint them again? If we ask?"

Robin stretches her legs, and her knees pop. "You know better than I do," she says.

"I bet she will," I say, remembering how insistent she was that restoring the inn was the right thing to do. "Maybe *after* we close with Clint, when we have the money."

"Hey, remember that reading nook we always talked about building in the front bay window, under the hummingbird? What if we finally did it?" Robin asks.

I wiggle my toes against the insole of her foot, where I know she's ticklish. "Oh, are you going to learn to build custom bookshelves?"

"Maybe I will," Robin says, shivering from my touch. "Got a good YouTube video for that?"

"I think we should start with something easy, like flathead versus Phillips-head screwdrivers," I say. "And we probably shouldn't start adding on projects before we even really get started. We're thirteen years older now than last time we did this. It's going to be tougher on our bodies. I'm still sore from painting the kitchen two days ago."

Marmalade hops onto the bed with a chirp, and the mattress bounces from her considerable weight. "See?" Robin says, reaching to scratch the cat's soft gray chin. "Marmee thinks the reading nook is a great idea. Picture her all curled up on an armchair, refusing to let any guests sit there because it's her favorite nap spot."

I pull back my foot. "Um, Marmee won't be here. Because we're selling it."

"Oh," Robin says, her voice lower. "Right. Duh. It's just a cute mental picture, is all."

So I'm not the only one forgetting where we are. *When* we are.

Even if it was simply a mistake, Robin's comment shakes me to my core. The whole reason I agreed to renovating the inn was for closure. To move on with my life. Yet here I am, in bed with my ex, sharing pillow talk, torturing myself by reliving the best days, when we'd just bought the inn and our future felt limitless. *Fuck me.* I walked right into a pit trap.

I edge out from under Robin's arm and stand up, suddenly self-conscious about my tank top and underwear. "Can we talk about plans later? I really need to get some work done in my studio."

Robin seems to notice something's off. "Oh. Yeah, we can talk later. Do you want breakfast first? I can whip up some—"

"Nope, I'm all good. Got to go." I walk out of the room, trying to stop my hands from shaking.

26

Robin

I KNOW MOLLY WELL ENOUGH TO RECOGNIZE WHEN HER "I'M all good" is not, in fact, all good. Based on how she practically sprinted out of my room yesterday and has been hiding in her shed since, I know she's upset about something. But as I busy myself with reorganizing the basement and taking stock of what's down there, I decide Molly's mood swings aren't really my problem anymore. Or at least they won't be once we sell the inn and I get that sweet six-figure check for my half. Seven figures, if we do this thing right. My life is going to be so much easier. I can invest in a project *I* want to work on. Produce my own show. Open a new restaurant. The world will be my oyster, ready to be shucked and savored.

If only I knew what I wanted to do next.

As I pause to wipe the sweat from my forehead after digging through old documents we might need for our meeting with Clint, I think about what's been bringing me joy lately: working in Jesse's kitchen. After all the TV shoots and big fancy restaurant concepts, it's a breath of fresh air to focus on making a good dish and watching someone enjoy it. It reminds me why I started cooking in the first place. And I didn't realize how much my soul needed this time to catch up with old friends.

Molly included.

I like being here with her, I admit to myself as I peek into some boxes of old holiday decorations, bits and pieces of past Christmases and Thanksgivings and Valentine's Days. I feel like myself in Eureka. The real me, instead of the version of me I bring to sound stages and Instagram. So if I want to keep exploring where this path is taking me, I need to stay on Molly's good side. Show her I'm serious about putting in my fair share of work in the renovations. I've got to soothe whatever panic she's feeling.

I spent yesterday power washing the inn's exterior, lingering outside to try to catch Molly to learn what's been freaking her out, but every time she left her shed, she all but ran in the other direction. She didn't come to the Zinnia Room last night. But all this stuff in the basement has given me a different idea to break down the wall she's built around herself.

It's easy to clear the old dining room. I'd mostly emptied it when I used the hallway outside of it as a cooking space. I consider trying to sell the cheap mass-produced furniture on eBay, but a quick search turns up thousands of people selling the exact same things, so I just throw them on the street corner with a FREE sign.

Bringing the old furniture up from the basement is a bigger challenge; it's quality stuff made with real hardwood. I heave the four-person tables up the stairs first, and after that, the two-person tables and the chairs. The buffet tables where we used to display breakfast and coffee take what feels like forever, hoisted up one stair at a time until my lower back is screaming. Then I turn to the most crucial part of my plan.

After staying up late watching YouTube tutorials on power drills, I'm ready to put my new skills to use. I've been eyeing these horrible light fixtures the management company mounted on the dining-room walls: white plastic hands holding these big round bulbs that coordinate with the ugly thing in the middle of the ceiling, hanging where the chandelier used to be, that looks like a subway map with lights on the ends. Taking that monster down is definitely beyond me, but I'm going to take a shot at the smaller ones.

I grab Molly's drill from its charging spot in the kitchen and start with a little pep talk. "Hi, drill," I say quietly. "I'm Robin. We're going to be friends today, yeah? I'll be gentle, and you'll behave. No surprises."

I squeeze the trigger a couple times and imagine the buzz is the drill agreeing.

"Okay," I say as I pull a bit from the little yellow plastic case. "Try this on for size, drill." I turn the part I've learned is called the chuck and watch the space in front widen. So far, so good. I place the bit in the hole, pushing it in as far as it will go, then tighten the chuck. When I try the trigger again, the bit turns just like it did in the video. "Nice," I say to my drill friend, feeling pretty damn good. "All right, let's do this."

A LITTLE AFTER FIVE P.M., when I spot Molly leaving her shed through the kitchen window, I run into the dining room for the big reveal. A moment later, I hear the back door creak open and slam shut. Then Molly appears in the doorway and freezes, speechless.

"Surprise!" I gesture at the rearranged room. "I thought I'd get a head start."

I watch Molly adjust to the change, her guarded expression melting away. She smiles as she catches a glimpse of our favorite of Miss Addy's antique paintings, a regal portrait of a basset hound posed on a velvet armchair. "Colonel Wagsworth," she says, the name I'd forgotten we made up for the dog. "I missed him."

"Me too."

She finally notices what I really wanted her to see: the blank spaces and holes in the walls. "You took down those creepy hands?"

"I did!" I say, bouncing a little with excitement. "Guess how."

Molly's lips tilt up just a hint at the corners. "With a butcher knife?"

"No."

"With a butane torch?"

"No!"

"With the help of a handyman you found in the phone book?"

I blow a raspberry. "I don't even know where to find a phone book in the year 2025." I pull out the drill and make a big show of putting in the drill bit and giving it a squeeze.

"Wow!" Molly says, a full smile cracking across her face. "Congratulations! Now you're as competent at home repairs as I was by the age of eight."

"Hey!" I put the drill down and put my hands on my hips. "Give me a little credit. Eight-year-old Molly could never have reached that high on the wall without a stool."

"You're right. Great job being tall. But really, I'm proud of you." Molly walks over to pat me on the back and notices the table behind me. "What's all that?" she asks.

"I made a cake to celebrate," I say, stepping aside. "A little one."

Molly gets closer to the six-inch round cake covered in buttercream and topped with honeycomb candy and fresh berries. Her smile disappears. "Is it . . . *the* cake?"

"Earl Grey honey cake with lemon and blackberries," I say, knowing full well the weight of my dessert choice. I invented it by combining Molly's favorite flavors to mark the first anniversary of when we bought the inn, when we were still working ourselves sick. No days off, no other employees to lean on, and struggling to get guests in the door. But that was when we needed a celebration the most. "I've tweaked the recipe a little over the years, but yeah."

I cut the cake and serve two slices. When I hand Molly hers, she hesitates to take it. Seems like whatever freaked her out yesterday morning is still rattling her.

"Look, I know being here together is weird as hell," I say. "But isn't it also kind of nice? We've got plenty of bad memories here, but we have good ones too. I've been remembering the good ones more lately, and I'm starting to think . . . I mean, what are the fucking odds that we'd both show up within a few days of each other, after seven years away? And of Clint showing up, offering to buy the inn from us? Of us getting this chance to make things right after doing the Hummingbird so dirty? Maybe the universe pulled us both back here at the same time for a reason. It put our lives on hold so we'd get a shot at saying a real goodbye to the inn and Eureka. To each other, even."

Molly puts her plate down on the table and collapses into a chair. "Yeah," she sighs. "It does feel uncanny."

I sit down across from Molly. "I want to leave this place on the right foot this time," I say softly. "Not while the inn's future is murky. Not while we're fighting. I want to relive the good parts, and burn some sage or something to let the bad parts go. I want to do this as a team, both all in to make it look as good as new. Or, well, as good as old. Like it used to be."

Molly searches my face for a moment. "And what about us?" she says. "Will we be like we used to be too, while we're here?"

I notice how she's leaning toward me in her seat, how she keeps looking down at my lips, a pink glow beneath her freckles. Her words might be vague, but I know exactly what she's asking. Of *course* that's what's been weighing on her. We've definitely crossed some lines together. It makes sense that she wants clarity on what we're doing here.

My eyes dip to the tattooed blooms on her chest, peeking out from the neck of her tank top. I think of how my body still fits perfectly against hers, how just looking at her makes me hotter than a wood-fired pizza oven. Truthfully, I've spent a fair amount of time thinking about that kiss at One More

Round. Maybe we can relive our good days at the inn in more ways than one. "I'm open to that," I say carefully, hoping we're on the same wavelength. "You know, while we're here. The inn could be a place where we don't have to follow the normal rules."

"Like on boats," Molly says, nodding. "Crimes don't count on international waters or whatever."

I let out a short, giddy laugh, surprised but totally into where this conversation has led. "I don't think that's how maritime law works," I say. "But yeah, like that."

Molly looks toward the hummingbird window, glowing in the afternoon sun. "And then, when we're finished and we hand over the keys to Clint and say goodbye to each other, we'll have no regrets."

"Exactly."

She looks back at me, her green eyes sparkling just like the window. "Okay. I'm in."

I take a bite of cake on my fork and hold it up. Molly does the same, clinking her fork against mine like a flute of champagne. A divine expression crosses her face with her first taste. I try it too. The tart lemon hits first, the honeyed sweetness right behind, the complexity of the tea lingering on the tongue. The same flavors as when I created the recipe, but even better with what I've learned since.

27

MOLLY

DO I *WANT* TO SELL THE INN? HONESTLY? NO.

As Robin and I sit around a table at Clint's realtor's office working through details of our plan, I have to admit that I've grown attached to the place. I've got a soft spot for things with lots of history and character, especially those in need of a little love. It's why I enjoy combing antique shops for old colored glass to reclaim into my artwork, why I first bought this inn, why I felt so immediately at home in Eureka Springs.

And now the Hummingbird's history includes me. As we flip through pictures of the bed-and-breakfast after my first time renovating it, I realize I grew up here, in a way. I learned what I can do when I put my mind to it. I fell in love and got married here. I helped the Hummingbird grow into a new identity in the modern era. When everything fell apart, I never really got a chance to say goodbye. I handed off the keys and ran. Nowhere has really felt like home since, and I'm not sure anywhere else ever will.

But the lesson I've been learning since childhood, reinforced by my marriage and my time in Eureka Springs, is that everything in this life is temporary. I can repair and restore and reminisce about better days all I want, but that won't protect me from losing the things and people and places I love. That's why I embrace life on the road, hopping from project to project. I can give my all to one stained-glass design at a time, one city at a time, then move along before I get attached enough to have my heart broken. It sounds grim, but it's better this way.

So my time here at the Hummingbird with Robin? I'm going to give it my all, right the wrongs I left behind, get the closure I didn't get seven years ago, and then move on. I haven't gotten a lot of meaningful, intentional goodbyes in my life. They've mostly happened before I had time to realize what I was going to miss. My dad. My mom. Gram. This once, I get to end things on my own terms.

"Keyana's murals are a must," Clint says as we flip through digital photos of the guest rooms circa 2018. "Didn't you use her designs for merch in the gift shop?"

"Yes, on shirts and tea towels and mugs," Robin says, adjusting the collar of her blazer. "Guests loved bringing home stuff with the same floral design as the room they stayed in."

I've been fairly quiet at this meeting, letting the realtor take the lead, but here I lean forward. "We had a deal with Keyana. She got five percent of merch sales, paid out quarterly. Would you still be willing to honor that?" I ask.

The realtor, a friendly but somewhat intense fortysomething gay man, looks like he's about to object, but Clint speaks first. "Of course," he says with an unconcerned wave of his hand. "Remember when I went through my pottery phase? Since then, I always pay artists for their work."

I smile fondly, remembering Clint in clay-splattered aprons flirting with tourists at local art fairs. His creations had a certain rustic appeal, but it was Clint's charm that really sold them.

Clint takes a sip of his coffee. "Now, about branding. I'm talking the name, logo, website, social media accounts—would that all convey?"

We talk through more details, giving Clint tentative approval to take over everything associated with the inn and establishing a timeline to close the sale in late October or early November. I feel strangely outside of my body, talking about handing over the keys like this. But I reengage when we approach the topic we've all been waiting to discuss: money.

Robin and I did some math ahead of time, comparing the sale prices of similar historic properties in Eureka in recent years, calculating how much we spent in 2012, inflation, and how much we'll likely spend on materials while sprucing it up. We came to an agreement on the lowest price we'd accept. I fidget in my seat, hoping we won't have to do much negotiating.

"After much discussion, Clint has settled on a generous initial offer," the realtor says, then takes a sheet of paper from his leather folio and slides it across the table to us.

At first, I think my eyes are having trouble focusing on all those zeros. But when I look up at Robin, she's just as shocked, eyes glazed, mouth hanging open. Clint's offer is more than double the number we agreed we'd accept. "That's . . . wow," Robin says, mesmerized.

The realtor clears his throat. "I told Clint that this is significantly higher than any comparable property has sold for in the past five years, but—"

"I'm buying more than a building. I'm buying a legacy," Clint says, clasping his hands on the table in front of him. "Have you looked at the comments on your website lately? Checked the hashtag on social? People are still talking about what you built, and they desperately want it to make a comeback. There's plenty of cool Victorian architecture in Eureka. But there's only one Hummingbird Inn."

STILL FLABBERGASTED BY CLINT'S OFFER, Robin and I spend the afternoon creating an ever-growing checklist of projects we need to tackle before finalizing the deal. "We'll need to touch up the paint on the detail work, but we won't have to repaint the whole exterior," I say to Robin, who's standing next to me on the sidewalk in front of the inn. I jot down a note on my clipboard.

Robin points to the left corner of the porch. "And there are a couple missing doodads."

"Cornice brackets," I say, writing it down. "I can whittle those."

"Maybe I could learn to whittle?" Robin suggests. "For what Clint's offering, I'll learn anything."

"Maybe stick with the power drill for now," I tease. "You can practice by tightening up the porch handrails."

Our list grows as we circle the building. *Wood stain the gazebo. Repair cracked window shutters. Replace broken bal-*

usters. Once we're satisfied that we've marked down everything outside, we move to the much lengthier catalog of
tasks inside. *Get rid of cheap furniture. Paint walls. Pull up
laminate. Restore original wood floors. Change light fixtures.*

By the time we're satisfied, we've got five front-and-back
pages of tasks to complete. "How long do you think all this
will take?" Robin asks, leaning back in a rocking chair on the
front porch with a glass of iced tea in hand. The summer
heat reminds me that it's now July; we've spent a full month
cohabitating without killing each other.

"I'm not sure," I answer. "It took us, what, six months the
first time around?"

"And that was with twenty-two-year-old energy," Robin
says. "Thirty-five-year-old me will probably need more naps."

"Plus we've both got other jobs to balance now." I wipe
the sweat from my forehead with the bottom of my shirt. "In
good news, it will be easier than last time. The cleaners kept
it from falling into total disrepair. We have the right furniture
and finishings, once we get them from the storage unit. No
major structural issues or leaky pipes."

"At least since you fixed the pipe in the kitchen," Robin
adds.

"Right," I say weakly. "Which is all wrapped up."

"The kitchen's in great shape now, especially with that
new backsplash." Robin's chair creaks as she rocks.

"Thanks." A cool breeze wafts by, and we enjoy it in silence. Once it's passed, I ask, "Where will you go when we're
done? Back to Seattle or Portland?"

Robin scratches the back of her neck, contemplating.
"No, I don't think so. There's nothing for me up there anymore."

I can't help but ask, "Not even Georgina?"

Robin laughs, but not in a joyful way. "Definitely not Georgina. That's been over for a while." She's quiet long enough for me to think that's all she has to say on the matter, but then adds, "She gave me an ultimatum. During the pandemic."

My heart is tugged in a dozen directions. Relief Georgina is out of the picture. Curiosity about what happened. Sympathy for Robin. Jealousy, always jealousy, whenever I think of Georgina. As much as I've tried to let it go, she's grown into the big bad wolf who broke my marriage.

Curiosity wins out. "She wanted to get married?" I ask.

"Kind of. Not really." A stream of air escapes Robin's lips. "It was about you, actually."

"Me?" New emotions pile onto the mishmash inside me. Satisfaction, guilt, a disorienting dash of pride.

"Yeah," Robin says. "She was really bothered by us still being legally married. It wasn't that she wanted me to marry her so much as she wanted me to divorce you. She thought I was still hung up on you, that I didn't take her seriously."

"Did you?" I ask, knowing I'm wading into dangerous waters. "Take her seriously?"

"Of course! We were business partners. Our restaurants shared kitchen and dining space. Robin's Egg for breakfast and lunch, her concept for dinner and late-night bites. I wouldn't have signed up for that if I wasn't serious."

A taste of bitterness hits the back of my tongue. "But we were business partners too."

"Yeah, that's exactly what Georgina said."

Marmalade strolls around the corner of the porch from the backyard and collapses into a sleepy pile of fur between our chairs. Our fingers touch when we both reach over to pet her. I pull back first.

"Why didn't you divorce me?" I ask. If I want closure, I have to know.

"You know I hate paperwork." Robin looks up at me with a crooked grin that makes it clear we both know that's not the full answer. She straightens, leaving Marmee purring beneath us. "And I guess I never liked how we ended things," she adds. "It felt so sudden. And hostile. You deserved better than some manila envelope in the mail. *We* deserved better."

"We could do it together," I say, admitting out loud what I've been quietly thinking for a while: It's the natural conclusion to the agreement we've made. "File for divorce. It could be a two-birds-one-stone situation with selling the inn. Maybe we could get one lawyer to help us with both."

Robin turns to look at me, and something in her eyes reminds me of my own inner turmoil. This thing between us has gotten so messy. Won't we both feel better once we've cleaned it up? "I . . . I guess that would make the most sense," she says.

"Key has some lawyer friends in the area," I offer. "I can ask her for a recommendation."

"Great," Robin says, entirely lacking enthusiasm. Either she really does hate paperwork, or she's feeling a little bittersweet nostalgia from the thought of saying goodbye too.

We agree to discuss next steps on redecorating tomorrow, and I retreat to my shed. This is all exactly what I wanted. Answers, open lines of communication, moving on with my life.

So why do I feel sad?

28

Robin

IT'S A GREAT DAY TO BE IN THE KITCHEN AT COUNTERCULTURE. We're testing seasonal appetizers for July and August. Nothing sparks my love of cooking more than experimentation, and Jesse's vegan restaurant is pushing me out of my comfort zone in the best way. Until now, my flavor philosophy has been "There's no such thing as too much butter or cheese."

Caro arrives to join the taste test just as we're plating up our experiments. Being in a relationship with a chef has excellent benefits. Caro may not have graduated from culinary school, like Jesse did after he left the Hummingbird Inn, or gotten a crash course in culinary television like me. But they've developed their palate beyond your average diner. The first two dishes we tasted were no-goes: underwhelming avocado-radish gazpacho and off-puttingly slimy seaweed-wrapped enoki mushrooms. Fortunately, we saved the best possibilities for last.

"I love that it's fresh and bright and vegetable-forward," Caro says after trying one of Jesse's ratatouille sliders, a stack of thinly sliced grilled eggplant, tomato, and zucchini seasoned and drizzled with an herby tomato sauce, served between two tiny buns. "But the squish factor is high," they say, wiping their fingers on a cloth napkin.

"Yeah, I think without the toothpick, all the components would slip right out," Jesse says, turning his creation to examine it from all sides. He takes a bite and adds, "And it could use a crunch."

"What if instead of sliders, you served it on a toasted baguette slice?" I suggest. "You can fan the veggies out so they're less likely to slide. Or you could roll them into a rosette."

Jesse snaps his fingers. "Carb genius Lasko strikes again."

"What did you make?" Caro asks, turning to me.

"Jesse's got me turned on to jackfruit, so . . ." I present a plate of golden-brown orbs and a bright pink sauce. "Jackfruit croquettes with a roasted beet coulis."

We each grab a ball, drag them through the swirl of beet purée, and pop them into our mouths.

"I like it," Caro says. "And the beet sauce is pretty. 'Eighties bad bitch in a power suit' vibes."

"Could take a little more garlic," Jesse suggests. "But it's got great texture and a good punch of flavor in the sauce. Different from the other appetizers we have on the menu right now."

"Would a little heat balance the sweetness better?" I ask. "Roasted habanero, maybe?"

Jesse nods. "Could work."

"I'll see what the line cooks and servers think after the lunch rush." I pull back the croquette plate and swap it for a loaded serving board. "Okay, this last one is a collaboration," I say. "Maitake pâté."

"Maitake is a mushroom," Jesse clarifies for Caro.

"It went through a few iterations before we got to a flavor and texture we both liked," I say. "Jesse made the seeded crackers and the crostini. I made the cornichons, marinated olives, and fig compote."

We take a moment to build our perfect first bites and give them a taste.

"I'm not big on mushrooms or pâté," Caro says after swallowing, "but that's actually really tasty. Savory and creamy. I like it with the crunch of the cracker."

"I knew you'd be our toughest audience on this one," Jesse says proudly. "If you like it, I think we got it right."

"And all the other stuff makes the presentation feel fancy. Celebratory." Caro pops an olive in their mouth. "Oh, Robin, those are delicious. Is there citrus in the marinade?"

"Orange and lemon peel."

"This is definitely going on the menu," Jesse says, loading up another cracker with fig compote and pâté. "It'll be our late-summer bestseller, I can already tell."

We continue snacking as Caro tells us about the upcoming wine tasting they're planning at their hotel. "I'm really going to focus on delegating this year," they say after running down a head-spinning to-do list, almost as long as the one Molly and I made for the inn yesterday.

"That's what you said last year," Jesse says wryly. "And the year before that. And before that . . ."

"Yeah, but for real this time." Caro gestures to me as if I've already taken their side. "Robin knows how it is in hospitality. You've got to build trust in someone before you can hand over responsibility for guest experiences. Especially when it's one of your biggest moneymakers of the year. Speaking of, how's the reno going at the Hummingbird?"

"It's great!" I say, my chest puffing up with pride. "I learned how to use a power drill."

Caro seems duly impressed, but Jesse says, "Just now? You're telling me you knew how to use a sous vide machine before a drill? What kind of lesbian are you?"

"One with a wife who can build furniture in her sleep," I volley back. "Er, ex, I mean."

Caro eyes me through their curly bangs. "So you and Molly are getting along all right?"

"Now, yes," I say. "At first I thought being there together was going to end with at least one of us dead, but we've reached an understanding." I don't add that our "understanding" left a door open for more than redecorating. I've been waiting for Molly to come back to the Zinnia Room to test our boundaries for the past two nights, but I think we're both waiting for the right moment to see how far this reunion will go.

"Well, I'm glad to hear it," Caro says, looking at me like they read between the lines anyway. "It was hard watching what went down between y'all."

"Almost as hard as dealing with the management company when y'all left," Jesse grumbles. But before I can apologize again, he says, "It's not on you, dude. Molly offered Caro and me the opportunity to manage the place, but we didn't feel ready for that responsibility."

"But whew, did we regret turning her down. We *hated* that management company," Caro says with a dramatic sigh. "We tried to talk them out of 'modernizing' everything, but they basically told us we weren't paid to have opinions."

Jesse nods, frowning. "Switching to mass-produced heat-it-and-eat-it breakfasts was the last straw. If that's all the experience I was going to get, I could have worked at McDonald's."

"And they shot down a dozen ideas I had for holiday celebrations and collaborations with other businesses in town," Caro added. "They just wanted me to check people in and out, no big ideas. When I quit, they replaced me with an automated kiosk."

Guilt is crawling all over my skin. I hate that I abandoned Jesse and Caro like that. And Molly. And now I'm thinking about all the restaurant employees that ended up jobless when my other businesses failed. Why did I ever let anyone rely on me for their livelihood?

Then I remember what started this conversation. The inn. That's one thing I can still fix. "When we're done with the renovations, we'll leave it in good hands with Clint," I promise.

"He'll be great," Caro says, patting my shoulder. "He always loved the Hummingbird."

"And he's got some serious business chops," Jesse adds. "You saw what he did with One More Round. He gave me some tips before I opened Counterculture too. Helped me pick out the paint colors and furniture and brass decorations at the bar. Suggested handing out free samples during some local festivals before I opened to build hype. A real hometown hero."

An idea strikes me like lightning, and I nearly drop the pâté-topped cracker I'm holding. I put it down and say, "Would y'all ever consider going back to run it with him?"

"Us?" Jesse says, clearly surprised by the suggestion. "Go back to the Hummingbird?"

"It could be killer," I say, the gears in my brain turning. "Clint can't run it alone, not when he's still got the bar. Caro, you could be in charge of guests and property management. And Jesse, you obviously know how to run the kitchen better than I ever did. You could make it just like our glory days, after our feature on *Inn for a Treat*." I still remember that life-changing appearance on a travel show hosted by a gay comedian and his interior designer husband. They visited and rated bed-and-breakfasts across the country. Ours got their first ever ten out of ten mimosas rating. The whole town turned out to celebrate with us at our watch party at One More Round. "Remember our regulars?" I ask. "Our waitlist? How all the reviews talked about our amazing queer team? You two helped make the Hummingbird magical."

"We loved the inn, but it was you and Molly who made the magic happen," Jesse says. "Besides, what about the restaurant? And Caro's job?"

"Part-time, maybe," I say, realizing that Jesse and Caro aren't leaping at this opportunity. "Consulting, even. Training the new team, finally making use of those suggestions the management company refused."

Caro trades a look with Jesse before saying, "I don't think we can go back that easily."

"I'm sorry to throw this at you so suddenly. It would be a big decision," I say, trying to let go of the sparkling vision I just had of the inn's future. It feels so good to picture the bed-and-breakfast back in action with two people at the helm who I'd trust with my life. Part of me wants to give them the hard sell, convince them, refuse to take no for an answer. The other part of me has to admit that they both look pretty skeptical about the idea. If it was to work, it would have to be their dream, not mine. And even if they did want the roles, Clint would have to be the one to offer them, not me. "I know you have your own career paths and lives separate from the Hummingbird now. But I can't imagine a better team to run the Hummingbird than you two and Clint. I hope you'll consider it," I say finally.

"We'll think about it," Caro says gently, tucking their unruly curls behind their ears. "Later. For now, I've got to get to work." They lean over to kiss Jesse goodbye, grab another jackfruit croquette for the road, and leave through the back kitchen door.

I'll also have to table the idea for now. The other line cooks are arriving, and hungry customers will be here soon. I turn my attention to the lunch-shift mise en place.

29

MOLLY

"SO LET ME GET THIS STRAIGHT," KEY SAYS, LOOKING AT ME like my head is made of cheese. "You and your ex have essentially made a sex pact, agreeing to bang as much as you want while renovating the inn, and when you're done, you'll get divorced and walk away, no strings."

"It's not a sex pact!" I say, nearly spitting my coffee onto the floor of Key's studio. "We haven't even had sex."

"Yet," Key says, one eyebrow raised. "But you've already kissed and slept in the same bed and, let me guess, you've been intentionally wearing your sexiest underwear because every time you make eye contact it feels like it could go down at any moment."

I don't say a word, especially not about the lacy black French-cut panties under my denim shorts right now.

"And you don't foresee this becoming emotional torture for you," Key says, correctly interpreting my silence. "Even though you're a Pisces, and romanticizing the past is your drug of choice and you don't know how to set boundaries."

I gulp. She's not wrong. "You're the one who said to do this the lesbian way."

Key bites into a vegan scone I brought. "Yeah, but the lesbian way means figuring out how to be friends and then *moving on,* not falling back in love with your ex and potentially getting your heart broken again," she says through the crumbs.

"I'm not falling back in love!" I say, indignant. "I just want to get laid. Is that such a crime? Besides, you're the one who said renovating and selling the inn was a good idea."

"It is," Key says. "It's the cuddling and kissing and sex and acting like you're back together before signing the dotted line on your divorce papers that sets off alarm bells for me."

"It's not like that," I say, fidgeting with my napkin. "We're not back together. But being a *tiny* bit romantic can be part of the closure. A last hurrah."

Key takes a long sip of her iced coffee as I anxiously await her response. "Honestly, I like Robin," she says, weighing her words. "I still consider her a friend, although I obviously took your side in the non-divorce. I don't think she's a bad person. I don't even think she's necessarily a bad match for you. But Moll, you were so young when you met. Neither of you had much figured out. And astrologically speaking, Pisces are mutable signs—followers—and Capricorns like Robin are cardinal signs, people who prefer to be in charge. You used to let her take the lead a lot, until you didn't follow her to Portland. And then you felt so adrift because you weren't used to making decisions alone. But now you know yourself better. You know what matters to you and how you want to live your life. So if you want to go back to Robin, short-term or long-term, I'll support you. I just hope you'll be honest with yourself about what you're doing. And remember what you've learned about yourself to find more balance."

Keyana got me into the zodiac stuff, and now I check my favorite astrologer's website daily. But it's less fun when she uses the stars to point out my flaws. "I don't think Robin's interested in long-term," I say, frowning. "She'll move on to her next big thing soon."

"What do *you* want?"

It feels like Key just turned a spotlight on me, and the heat burns my skin. "I . . . um . . ."

Key sighs. "Just try not to get hurt, okay?"

"Okay," I say meekly. "So, about those murals . . ."

"Of course I'm in," Key says, grabbing a second scone. "I loved painting them the first time, and I bet I can make them even better this time around."

"Thank you," I say, relaxing. "Do you want to be involved when we pick the paint colors for the other walls in the rooms? We're going to the hardware store this afternoon."

"Nah, y'all can do all that and then I'll plan my designs to fit your color schemes."

"Sounds good." I twist the hem of my tank top as I ask, "And that lawyer you know?"

"I'll introduce you," Key says. "I'm not sure if she's the right person for both real-estate dealings and divorce, but she can at least point you in the right direction."

"You're the best," I say. "I owe you, for real."

"I still want that window for the studio," Key says, faux chiding me. "You better not bail on me because you're back on your HGTV bullshit."

"Of course I won't," I promise. "Robin's working at Jesse's restaurant Thursdays through Sundays, so I'm spending that time in my studio. The Drizzled Donuts piece is really close, and you're up next."

"Good." Finished with her scone, Key wipes her mouth with a napkin, stands up, and starts pulling out various oil paints from her storage cabinet. "Speaking of, I saw the window at Wild Card yesterday. It looks gorgeous. Have you taken pictures for your website and socials?"

I cringe. "I forgot."

"You know, Roxie's coming back from parental leave next week." Key points at me with a tube of cobalt-blue paint. "And she's going to be pissed if you haven't promoted any of your work from the past four months."

Dammit. I'd completely forgotten to update my platforms with what I've been working on since Roxie, the art agent who represents both me and Keyana, had twins. She's going to be peeved. Not even the very expensive double stroller I sent as a gift is going to keep her off my back. Don't get me wrong; Roxie is incredibly lovely and our biggest advocate. But she's also the queen of chewing me out with a cheerful smile—all in my own best interests, of course.

"I'll take pictures of the Wild Card window on my way home," I say sheepishly.

"Good. I've got to get to work," Key says, shuffling through her collection of brushes before selecting one. "Thanks for breakfast."

"Of course. See you for drinks on Thursday?"

"Duh. And Molly?"

I pause halfway to the door to Key's front showroom. "Yeah?"

"Even if I have my reservations about the reno, and even if Roxie's going to try to get you booked and back on the road soon, I'm glad you're sticking around Eureka a little longer."

I smile at Key over my shoulder. "Me too."

30
Robin

"TOO BLUE," MOLLY SAYS FIRMLY.

I point to another paint sample on a square of cardstock taped to the dining-room wall. "How about this one?"

Molly shakes her head. "Too green."

"So something in between? Teal-ish? Basically whatever color you dye your hair?"

Molly looks toward the hummingbird window that faces the front porch. "The walls used to match that blue green on the hummingbird's feathers," she says. "God, why didn't we write down the paint colors back then?"

"Even if we had, who knows if they make them thirteen years later?" I shuffle through the thick stack of samples we picked up at the hardware store yesterday and hold a new one up against the wall. "How about this?"

"Better, but it's a tad dark. Don't you think?"

"We don't have anything like that but lighter." I look between the walls and the window, trying to picture how it used to be. I served hundreds, *thousands* of breakfasts in this room, yet I can't remember the walls. "Let's sleep on it. We picked colors for all the other rooms, so we're making good progress."

I've been trying to take some initiative over the past week to prove I'm not dead weight in this project. So far, I'd say it's going all right. Molly's clearly more knowledgeable, but I picked up a thing or two while overseeing the design of my restaurants. I place the stack of paint samples on a table and look at my watch. "Want to move some more furniture before I start dinner?"

I found some guy online who owns multiple vacation rental homes in the area and jumped at the chance to buy all our bed frames, dressers, and nightstands for a low price. He's picking them up tomorrow. I'll be at the restaurant, but I'm doing my best to get everything down on the main floor and ready to go beforehand so it will be easier for Molly. And I'm staying on her good side by keeping her well fed.

We've already cleared the new furniture on the second floor, besides the Zinnia Room where I've been sleeping, so we start with the third floor. Luckily, the fact that it's all cheaply mass-produced means it's fairly light. Moving the antique furniture from the basement and the storage unit will be way harder. Still, my back aches from yesterday. I savor the break from the stairs as we wrap plastic covers around the mattresses, which we decided to keep. The management company bought them shortly before the inn closed, so they're practically good as new. At least *one* thing they bought was an improvement instead of tragically hideous.

When we've finished emptying the unoccupied bedrooms on the third floor, we stand in silence by the pile of furniture, wiping our dusty hands on our shorts and deciding how to address the thing we've both been pretending hasn't occurred to us.

"So, um, the last two bedroom sets," I say as if it's a brand-new thought. "We could leave the Zinnia Room mattress on the floor and I could—"

"We should both move to the penthouse," Molly says quickly, as if she's been working up the nerve to suggest it. "It makes the most sense. Right?"

"The penthouse . . ." I say, trying to hide my surprise.

"I'd rather not sleep on a mattress on the floor and live out of a suitcase," Molly says. "And fixing up the guest rooms will be easier if we're not living in them."

She has a point. But I also remember the freaky sensation of seeing the penthouse again when I considered it for a cooking space. Molly and I have shared a bed a few times without things getting too heated—in a sexy or a murdery kind of way. But living together in our old apartment feels like a much bigger deal. "It won't be . . . weird? Being there together again?" I ask.

Molly blinks. "Not if we don't want it to be weird."

"Okay." I nod, realizing that this is it: the moment I've been waiting for since that chat over cake nine days ago, when we agreed to maritime law for our relationship inside the inn. I can't stop thinking about that time we kissed at One More Round, and the mornings we woke up snuggled together. Could those things happen again? Could *more* happen? Because I'll admit it: I really fucking want more. Based on the way Molly's looking at me right now, I'm pretty sure she feels the same. "I can move my things upstairs real quick," I offer.

Molly nods. "I'll do the same."

"All right, then." I push my sweat-dampened hair off my forehead, feeling as bubbly as a schoolgirl with a crush. I grin at Molly and say, "See you in the attic."

WE DROP OUR BAGS IN the penthouse, and Molly and I empty the furniture from the rooms we've been sleeping in for the past month. For dinner, I whip up a quick pasta with veggies from the garden and a white-wine butter sauce, which we both devour, starved after all that physical labor.

Then, both of us acting as if it's completely normal and not at all like we've somehow traveled back in time to our twenty-two-year-old selves, we go to the attic.

I light a couple candles to freshen the stuffy attic air, then unpack my things into my old half of the closet and double dresser while Molly takes a shower. When she comes out, a towel wrapped around her torso, her hair wet, the scent of her favorite tea tree and mint shampoo wafting off of her, I catch myself right before kissing her out of sheer muscle memory. Instead, I gulp, look away, and lock myself in the bathroom for my own shower.

Molly's in bed when I finish, reading some serious-looking novel in a pair of green reading glasses. I've never seen her in glasses before. They make her look older. In a good way. Like, I can see how mid-thirties Molly will age into forties Molly and fifties Molly and even sixties Molly. And she's going to look hot as hell.

When I slide into bed next to her, Molly inhales sharply and adjusts her posture.

"Something wrong?" I ask.

"It's just my shoulders and neck," she admits. "Not as resilient as they used to be."

"I feel you," I say. "My knees have been creaking louder than that fifteenth stair. Would a massage help?"

I doubted she'd take me up on the offer, but she immediately says, "God, yes, please."

She ties her damp hair in a bun on top of her head, whips off her loose sleep shirt to reveal a black sports bra, and sits up, turning her back to me. As soon as I make contact with her skin, there's a tiny shock.

"Static electricity," I say. Secretly, I think it was the ghost of all the energy we've expended in this bed before.

As I get to work on Molly's muscles, she groans, melting into the palms of my hands. All the bread and pasta dough I've kneaded over the years has made me a pretty good masseuse. It's all about feeling the give-and-take of what you're working with, stretching to the limit before easing back, making sure no kinks get left behind.

She leans back into my chest the moment I stop, resting the back of her head on my shoulder. "That was so good," she sighs. "I feel reborn."

"Glad I could help," I say, my heart rate increasing as I take in the view directly down her sternum into the V of her low-cut sports bra.

Molly sits up straight, swiveling toward me. "Your turn?"

"You don't have to."

"You moved heavy stuff around all day," she says. "You're going to feel it tomorrow."

God, Molly looks so good. It's hard to imagine a massage feeling better than simply staring at the tattoos wrapping around her ribs, water droplets sliding down her neck, the way she bites her pouty bottom lip while looking back at me.

"Yeah. Thanks," I say, pulling my eyes away and turning my back to her.

"Don't you want to take your shirt off?" Molly says, sitting up on her folded legs.

"I'm, uh, not wearing a bra."

Molly says a breathy "oh," then starts rubbing her thumbs into the muscles of my shoulders. She's right; I didn't realize how sore I was until she starts working out the knots. Molly's got strong hands too, from hours cutting glass and soldering and whatever else goes into the windows she creates. It can't be light work.

I also, admittedly, wish I didn't have a shirt on. I want to feel Molly's hands on my bare skin. But going nips-out on our first night in the penthouse together seems a bit forward. During the massage, for just a moment, I let myself truly wonder what it would be like to make love to Molly now. It's a thought I've been holding back for a month. For years, actually. But it's a hell of a lot harder to block out when she's in the same room.

When Molly trails her nails down my spine and creeps them up under the hem of my shirt, I wonder if I'm dreaming. She glides her fingertips over my lower back, and all of my skin responds with goosebumps. The room is so silent that I don't think either of us is breathing. Her hands move upward, pulling my top along with them. I feel the heat of her torso, leaning in, her knees on either side of my hips. My shirt is pulled all the way up when Molly's palms reach my shoulder blades. The vibe has shifted; however casually this started, it's gone somewhere else now, and I wouldn't dream of going back. I feel the soft pressure of Molly's lips against the back of my neck, and this is it, we're at the top of the roller coaster, ready for the plunge.

And then there's a meow and the squeak of bedsprings as Marmalade hops onto the mattress.

Startled, Molly and I jump away from each other like teens whose parents just caught them making out. Part of me wants to shoo the cat out of the room and keep things going. The other part of me thinks it's a sign we needed to pump the brakes.

Molly makes the decision for us. She clears her throat, puts her shirt back on, and turns off her bedside lamp. "Good night," she says, her voice tight, pulling the quilt all the way up to her chin.

"Good night," I reply, my pulse racing. I'm certain I'll never fall asleep with this whirlwind of emotions. But with the sound of Molly's steady breathing, the scent of her shampoo on my pillow, and the warmth radiating from her body, I fall into a deep slumber and dream of green eyes gleaming like colored glass.

31

MOLLY

FIVE NIGHTS. THAT'S HOW MANY TIMES WE'VE SLEPT IN THE
same old bed, in the same old room, in the same old attic,
testing the boundaries of our old/new relationship without
having sex. Without even kissing, if that moment my lips
touched her neck before Marmee interrupted doesn't count.

Five mornings we've woken up together, our bodies en-
tangled, forgetting for a moment upon waking that all this
isn't normal. That we aren't *really* together. That it's all an
extended farewell. Seven mornings, if you count those two in
the Zinnia Room.

Between all that? Four times we've brushed our teeth
side by side at the bathroom sink. Three times we've ex-
changed massages at the end of long days. Six times I've
caught Robin staring at me when she thought I wasn't look-

ing. Infinite times I've stared at her and hoped she wouldn't notice.

All this intimacy math is making my head spin. Or maybe it's the paint fumes.

This morning, we had an ambitious plan to finish all the guest rooms on the third floor. But now it's six P.M. and we have to admit that we're only going to get halfway to our goal. The bathrooms are more challenging than I remembered, taping around the tubs and toilets and cabinets and mirrors and whatnot. And they're a tight space for two people. Robin and I ended up pressed against each other more than once while trying to reach the farthest corners. And neither of us chose the obvious solution of stepping away to paint somewhere else.

But now the Sunflower Room is a warm golden yellow and the Lily Room is the same pink as the Stargazers in the garden. Having just finished the last corner, I throw my roller brush into a paint pan and collapse onto the plastic tarp on the floor. I close my eyes and pray for a breeze through the open windows.

I sense the shadow Robin casts over me. "Is it cooler down there?" she asks.

Cracking open one eye, I see the paint splattered across her basketball shorts, her skin-tight white tank, the backward Razorbacks cap holding her hair out of her face. "Not really," I admit. "But lying down feels nice. Muscles I didn't even know I *had* hurt."

"Mind if I join you?"

I fling out a hand next to me on the tarp. "Be my guest."

Robin sprawls out on the floor and sighs. "Was painting this hard when we were twenty-two?"

"I'm pretty sure back then we turned on some music, had a little dance party, and the walls painted themselves."

"That's how I remember it too." Robin rolls to her side and rests her head on her fist, examining me. "Hey, are those the overalls you used to wear back then when we painted?"

I look at my denim-clad torso. "Oh yeah. I forgot I've had them that long."

Robin leans in for a closer look. "There's some of the paint from the Lilac Room," she says, pointing to a spot near my waistband. "And orange from the Zinnia Room. Is that the teal from the dining room? Maybe we should have taken these to the hardware store when we were picking samples."

"Nah, that would have made it too easy."

Robin frowns. "Wait, why aren't you covered in paint from today? I look like I got attacked by a group of finger-painting preschoolers and the only paint on you is a decade old."

"You were always a messy painter," I say. "I think most of this on my overalls is from you touching me with your painty hands."

"Is that so?" Robin tosses away her hat with a mischievous gleam in her eye that reminds me so much of her younger self that it takes my breath away. "Well, maybe I should get some of this paint on them in case we need it for reference in the future."

I realize what she's up to just as her hand reaches the tray of paint past our heads. "No no no no—" I protest, trying to escape, but it's too late. Robin dips into the pool of pink and splays her fingers across the denim above my belly button, leaving a full handprint of Frosted Fuchsia. But she's not done. She comes at me again as I wriggle away, squealing and giggling, playful sounds I can't remember the last time I made.

"Gotta get the back too, for good measure," Robin says, swiping another palmful from the tray. We twist and turn together, her fighting to grab my ass, me trying to catch the wrist of her paint-covered hand. She manages to catch the bare skin of my side under my overalls and below my black bandeau bra, leaving a cool smear of pink.

I roll over and pin her down by the wrists with her back against the tarp and my knees on either side of her hips. "Hey, just because *you're* messy doesn't mean the rest of us have to get on your level," I tease.

"Okay, I'm sorry," Robin says. "I promise I'll be good."

I loosen my grip on Robin's wrist, and she immediately makes me regret it by smearing paint across my left cheek. I gasp and narrow my eyes at her. "Oh, now it's on," I say in a low voice before dunking my own hand in the tray. I make a line down her jaw, then manage to place a full handprint on her tank right between her breasts before she pushes me off to reload her own colorful ammo. We tussle for a few minutes, streaking each other with glossy pink, slipping on the tarp until we collapse in a pile of laughter, our limbs tangled, both slick with sweat.

We stare into each other's eyes as we catch our breath. There's something more between us now, a sizzling tension both old and new.

Robin's gaze trails from my eyes to my lips to my heaving chest. She reaches for the tray and dunks one finger in paint. "One last mark?"

I nod.

Robin unhooks the left strap of my overalls and stretches down the top of my bandeau. She traces the outline of a heart right over where my own heart is beating faster than a hummingbird's wings. Her fingertip against my skin sets my whole body on fire. Before I can parse who started it, our lips are pressed together in the kind of kiss that stops time and shifts the entire planet on its axis. It's different from the kiss we shared at One More Round, without the anger or jealousy. It's also different from any of the kisses in the before times; it feels richer, colored with new shades and shadows. We're not the same people we were back then, but whatever magic was between us has been lying in wait, growing even more powerful.

My hands find their way under Robin's tank, and I pull it over her head, revealing a light blue bra. She unclips the other strap of my overalls and pulls them down my torso. Our lips stay locked together as I pull off Robin's basketball shorts and she shimmies my overalls over my hips. Suddenly, we're in nothing but our underthings on an abstract mural of half-dried paint. All the tension between us is finally coming to a head, picking up speed, ready to vault over the edge of the cliff.

But as Robin reaches under the hem of my underwear, stroking the outside of my thigh and moving inward, I pause.

"Wait," I say breathlessly, despite everything in my body begging me to keep going.

Robin immediately pulls away, panting, pushing her bangs from her forehead. "Is . . . is this a bad idea?"

I soften at her shaky uncertainty. In truth, I've been struggling to get Key's concerns about the arrangement out of my head. But kissing Robin only confirmed for me how badly I want this. "No, not bad." I crawl closer to her across the plastic tarp and stroke her arm from shoulder to wrist. "I'm *very* into it." I twist her hand palm up and press my lips to a clear patch of skin on the inside of her forearm. "But your hands are covered in paint, which is, uh, probably not safe for sensitive areas."

Robin looks at her bright pink palm. "Oh. You're right," she says, realization dawning.

"But," I say, nestling myself between Robin's spread thighs, wrapping my legs around her middle, looping my arms around her neck, "after a shower . . ." I trail my lips over a paint-free strip of her neck below her left ear, and she pulls me closer with a sharp intake of breath. If I said I hadn't been thinking about this every second since we agreed to new rules, I'd be a liar. "I think we should see where this goes," I whisper.

Robin ducks her head and kisses me again. When I open my eyes after our lips part, I swear I still see stars. She rests her forehead against mine and says, "I'll shower in the Zinnia bathroom. You take the penthouse."

"Now?"

"We've already waited almost seven years," Robin says. "Isn't that long enough?"

I nod, then untangle myself from Robin's embrace and stand. I reach down and pull her up next to me. Hands still pressed together, I say, "I'll be fast."

Robin tucks a loose strand of my hair behind my ear, one I can see out of the corner of my eye is streaked with pink paint. With fiery intensity, she says, "I'll be faster."

32

Robin

I GRAB A WASHCLOTH, TOWEL, AND SOAP FROM A STORAGE closet on the second floor and hop in the shower before the first droplets even hit the tile. I spent my first few weeks here telling myself I didn't *really* want to have sex with Molly. It was just my brain repeating old patterns. Then, after the kiss at One More Round, I couldn't lie to myself anymore.

But now, with what just happened in the Lily Room, knowing Molly wants this as much as I do, I've never been so ready. I shower with furious speed, scrubbing at dried paint until my skin is its own shade of irritated pink. Then, buck-ass naked because I forgot a change of clothes, I race upstairs to the attic.

True to my word, I beat Molly. I hear the water running

in the penthouse bathroom. I'm left alone long enough to wonder whether I should crawl into bed naked or put something on. Which is less weird? Or is it weird either way, sleeping with my ex-wife who isn't my ex-wife, with whom I've been sharing a bed for almost a week?

I'm still indecisively standing at the door of the closet when Molly emerges from the bathroom, wrapped in a teal silk robe that matches the streaks in her damp hair. We both turn and lock eyes, and all my awkward feelings melt away. There it is again, that indescribable energy pulling us together, the one I've been trying so hard to ignore.

I watch Molly watch me, feel her gaze like a caress moving from my dripping hair to my parted lips to the hollow at the base of my throat to my heaving chest to where my thighs meet to where my feet are planted on the wooden floor, then back up again. She strides over to me and runs a hand down the center of my chest. Her touch is so gentle that I could almost be convinced I'm daydreaming. Her fingers pause at a crooked scar to the right of my navel.

"What's this?" she asks.

"Old burn. Knocked a saucepan off the stove and caught it with my stomach."

Molly winces. "Ouch."

"I survived. And saved the sauce." I brush my thumb across Molly's jaw, then trail my hand down to the sash tying her robe closed. She's had the chance to see how my body has changed in the last seven years, how I've settled into my own skin. I'm dying for the same opportunity. "Can I?"

She nods, and with one tug, the robe slips off of her dewy body and pools like water around her feet. I stare for a moment, frozen by the perfect shape of her, not quite the same as it was before, but still the most beautiful thing I've ever seen.

"What?"

I shake my head. "You're breathtaking, Molly."

A blush rises behind her constellations of freckles. I trace the edges of flower petals tattooed below her clavicle. "The peonies and wisteria—you didn't have those before, right?"

"I got them while I was living in Birmingham."

My fingers venture around the sides of her breasts to find the familiar sunflowers on her rib cage, her nipples responding to my touch by coming to irresistible peaks. I follow the honeycomb and bees across her hips and down to the stained-glass pattern on her upper thighs. "And these?"

"Started them in Memphis. Added more in St. Louis and New Orleans."

I get down on my knees to better inspect them, following the geometric lines with my thumb. "From windows you created?"

"Yes." Her legs quiver as my fingers travel to her inner thighs. Eager to make her tremble again, I press a little farther, following her tattoos with my pinkie so that my other fingers graze the tuft above them. Her legs part just enough to invite me to continue. I tease her open with one gentle stroke and find her warm, wet, and hyperresponsive to my touch.

Molly gasps, leaning against the frame of the closet door. Still kneeling, I pull one of her legs over my shoulder. As soon as my tongue touches her, I'm a goner. It feels silly to say it's like riding a bike, but my body really does remember what to do. Her racing pulse, hitched breath, and fingers in my hair are better than any five-star review I've ever gotten. Something deep inside me roars to life. I've never wanted to make someone come as badly as I do right now.

It doesn't take her long. Sharing a bed for the past five nights has been the longest, most tortuous form of foreplay. I'm on the edge before she even touches me.

And touch me she does. Molly pulls me up from the ground and kisses me passionately. I almost peak simply knowing she can taste herself on my lips. She guides me to the foot of the bed and pushes me down on the mattress with my legs hanging off the side. I want the weight of her naked body on top of me forever. But then she works her mouth down the side of my neck, across my chest, below my navel, and I happily trade the warmth of her against my upper body for a different kind of heat.

I wonder if it's like riding a bike for her too. If it's like belting along to a favorite song after thinking she'd forgotten the lyrics. If she's found a lost part of herself in me like I have in her.

But there's not much room for thinking. Not with all the other sensations my body is processing. I've awakened under her touch, as if the past seven years were a bad dream. I come with a quake that probably registers on nearby seismographs. Thank god there's no one else in the inn, because I couldn't have controlled the sounds I made if I'd tried.

I don't pause before tugging Molly onto the bed beside

me and going for the next round. The second time is almost as swift as the first, and we climax together, riding the waves in a sweaty embrace. For the third, we take our time, reacquainting ourselves with old favorite spots, lingering over the subtle changes in how our bodies respond to each other. The fourth time is another delicious fast-paced frenzy, ending with both of us panting in a tangle of sheets.

It's never been like this with anyone else. The one-night stands with fans, the short-lived relationships, even the bond I had with Georgina was flavorless and stale compared to this. It's not just the best sex I've had since Molly and I split; it's the best, full stop. I remember our first visit to the Hummingbird during the honeymoon period, how we couldn't keep our hands off each other. Not even that can compare to us now. So much of being with Molly is like I remember it, but she's also got some surprises up her sleeve, a confidence to her movements, a new rhythm that brings me right to the precipice, gives me a moment of breathless suspense, and then sends me careening into the unknown.

But my body needs more than Molly's touch. As we catch our breath for a quiet moment, me stretched diagonally across the bed, Molly's head on my chest and her arms draped around me, my stomach interrupts with a loud growl.

"We never ate dinner," I realize, looking down at her unruly brown and teal waves.

As I start to sit up, Molly tightens her grasp and murmurs, "Don't go" into my sternum.

"Aren't you hungry?"

"Starving."

"I'll grab something from the kitchen." I kiss the top of Molly's head and promise, "I'll be so fast, you'll hardly notice I'm gone."

Molly allows me to escape, then sprawls across the mattress with a relaxed smile. I pull her silk robe from the floor and wrap it around myself. "This is nice," I say, admiring how it swishes against my thighs, more femme than my usual style. I strike a pose with one hand on my hip and the other behind my head. "How do I look?"

"Better naked," Molly says from the bed. "But still pretty damn good."

I jog down the stairs and dig through the refrigerator, grabbing leftover hunks of cheese, prosciutto, sourdough, and pickles I brought home from Counterculture, plus fresh berries I picked a few days ago from the garden. Marmee rounds the corner into the room with an annoyed meow, mad at me for locking her out of our bedroom for the evening. She forgives me in exchange for a teeny bit of Brie. I arrange the charcuterie on a wooden cutting board, grab a bottle of pinot noir and two glasses, and return to Molly.

We sit at the small table in the kitchenette, me in Molly's robe and Molly wrapped in a quilt, quickly devouring the cheese plate. Between mouthfuls, we reminisce about the places we used to frequent in Eureka Springs, the shops we hope to revisit, the neighbors we'd still like to catch up with.

"Do you think we can snag an invite to Dorothy and Eleanor's for dinner?" Molly asks, plucking a raspberry from the board. "I'd kill for Eleanor's chicken potpie."

"I bet, especially if I bring Dot's favorite French silk tart for dessert." I scrape up the last bit of soft cheese with a piece of bread and say, "We've got another three months to make it happen. After that, the inn will be in Clint's hands, and we'll be who knows where."

Molly watches me take a bite, a pensive look on her face. "Dot and Eleanor thought we were together, when I ran into them at One More Round," she says. "Everyone did. And it didn't help that we made out on the patio."

I shrug. "Let them think what they want."

Molly shifts in her seat, tightening the blanket wrapped around her naked body. "They'll be confused when we make the divorce official, then."

The *d* word looms over me unexpectedly like a storm cloud. But that's the plan, and I should get used to discussing it. I swallow, then say, "Tonight. Was it . . . okay?"

I hold my breath, waiting as Molly slowly, agonizingly pulls apart a piece of prosciutto. "Much better than 'okay.' I don't want this to stop," she says.

"Me neither," I say on an exhale.

Molly reaches across the table to lace our fingers together. "We've spent enough time dwelling on the bad stuff that happened between us. This is our last chance to remember the good. And tonight was *really* good."

I'm glad to hear it, because my hands are already itching to touch her again. I stand, come around the table, and straddle Molly's legs. She opens her arms and wraps the ends of the blanket around me too, enclosing me against her skin within the cocoon. "So maritime law is still in effect aboard the SS *Hummingbird*," I say.

"Definitely."

I take the lobe of her left ear between my lips as my hand creeps between her thighs. "Which means we can do this again later." Molly gasps as I suck at a tender spot on her neck, certain to leave a mark. "Or right now," I suggest.

Molly arches her back, pushing into my touch. "Right now, please."

I grin into her freckled and tattooed shoulder. My stay in Eureka just got way more pleasurable.

33
MOLLY

AS I FIX MY HAIR IN THE COUNTERCULTURE BATHROOM BE-
tween courses, I remember my gram's favorite cure-all. Better than saltines and ginger ale and even Vicks VapoRub, it
was the motto "Live in the moment." I heard it when I
whined about things I wanted to happen sooner (like a road
trip to the beach when I was seven), when I didn't want
something to end (like leaving the arcade at age ten), when I
wanted something I didn't enjoy to be over (like the last
month of sixth grade before summer break), or when I
wanted something that clearly wasn't going to happen (like
for my mom or dad to visit at any age). Gram's answer was
always "There are many things we want but can't have. Embrace what you have now. Live in the moment." It was kind
of Zen, in retrospect.

This whole agreement I've got going with Robin? I'd say it's peak living in the moment. I'm taking advantage of where I am in my life right now, without being angry about what happened in the past or sad about going our separate ways in the future. I'm finding pleasure in my current situation. (A *lot* of pleasure.) Wouldn't Gram be proud?

Looking in the mirror at the big, goofy smile on my face now, I've got to admit it's working wonders for my mood. All the animosity between me and Robin has evaporated completely. Restoring the inn to its former glory is emotionally rewarding—and will be financially rewarding in the end. I'm sleeping better than I have in years. I feel, dare I say it, *happy*? Genuinely joyful, creative, relaxed. It's all because of the closure I'm getting with Robin. And maybe the incredible sex.

And the food. God, the food. Fresh bread. Handmade pasta. Cakes and pastries galore. Fruit and veggies straight from the garden. Considering I've spent the past few years on the road eating mostly things I could get from a drive-through, this is heaven.

Tonight's meal is the most magical yet. Jesse's starting a monthly dinner series at Counterculture. Robin says it's his opportunity to get really experimental. Since I somehow still hadn't visited his restaurant, Robin reserved a friends-and-family seat for me next to Caro. The dinner series features small-plate courses organized around a theme, today's being *Alice's Adventures in Wonderland,* Jesse's childhood favorite book. In his speech for the full room of enthusiastic diners, he said he always dreamed of a world filled with delightfully strange creatures where everything was a bit queer.

I knew Jesse could cook. I saw how quickly he picked up

new skills at the Hummingbird. But this is a whole new level. The first course was a series of brightly flavored mousses served in mismatched teacups: a vivid green avocado-herb, a purple coconut-ube, and a reddish sun-dried tomato. Next was a foraged-mushroom tartlet, a work of art for both the eyes and the taste buds. Then there was a vegan mock-turtle soup served in a sourdough bread bowl shaped like a turtle. As the Cheshire Cat would say, the chefs must be a bit mad here, because the last plate before dessert was a tea-smoked cauliflower steak that somehow tasted meaty. Who even thinks of that? Naturally, each dish came with a paired cocktail labeled DRINK ME.

I find my seat next to Caro for the final course, which I've been waiting for all evening. Robin's in charge of dessert, although she's been tight-lipped about her plans. She delivers my plate with a wink that makes my heart skip a beat. There are three tiny round cakes in front of me, each covered in a thin white glaze and topped with the words EAT ME in chocolate.

"What are they?" I ask, bending over to inspect them.

Robin gives me a cryptic grin. "Surprises."

"The last course," Jesse announces, his white chef's jacket surprisingly pristine after an intense night of cooking, "was created by my first culinary mentor, who believed in me when no one else would, who I'm lucky enough to call my friend and, for now at least, my sous-chef, Robin Lasko."

The room erupts in applause, and I'm reminded that Robin is a celebrity. C-list, maybe, but still recognizable, particularly for foodies, and this room is filled to the brim with those. As she steps to Jesse's side, people whisper and pull out their phones for pictures. A twentysomething lesbian at the table next to me looks like she might pass out from excitement. The churning feeling in my gut isn't jealousy, but it's not *not* jealousy either.

"Thank y'all so much," Robin says, projecting demure charm. "But it's Jesse who dreamed this up and made it happen. Let's hear another round of applause for Jesse!"

The crowd responds immediately.

"All right," Robin says once the room quiets. "Before you is a trio of vegan petits fours, meant to surprise and delight. I would tell you what each contains, but wouldn't that ruin the fun? All I'll say is, eat them from left to right. Enjoy."

Caro and I turn to each other with matching bewildered expressions. "That was mysterious," they say.

I nod. "Why do I feel scared?"

"Me too. But let's go for it," Caro suggests, straightening their emerald velvet smoking jacket.

We pick up the petits fours on the left of our plates and hold them up, nodding toward each other in solidarity. I pop the whole thing in my mouth.

"It's good," I say tentatively as I chew. "Sweet. Strawberry, I think? Whoa." I rear back, hit with a wave of heat. My eyes tear up as my whole face starts to tingle.

"Spicy!" Caro says, delighted. They've always been an adventurous eater and were the first to recommend Robin and Jesse start bottling the Hummingbird's signature hot sauce to sell at the gift shop. "It's, like, buzzing in my mouth somehow."

All around us, diners are exclaiming about the first cake, fanning themselves with their menus, chugging their waters. Although it was a risk for Robin to surprise everyone like this, folks seem to be enjoying it, laughing at one another's reactions. The sensation is already starting to fade into the sweet coating of the glaze, leaving behind the fresh strawberry flavor. I can't believe one bite took my taste buds on such a wild ride. What do the next two cakes have in store?

Seemingly reading my thoughts, Caro picks up the second petit four from their plate and asks, "Ready for the next surprise?"

As soon as my teeth break through the layers, I shiver. There's something cold in there, a semi-frozen layer in the middle, but there's also an unexpected tingly cooling sensation on my tongue. "Is it minty?" I ask Caro.

"I think so," they agree. "And a little coconutty. I like it."

I swallow and feel the chill travel all the way down to my stomach. "I'm cold all over," I say. "Weird."

"Refreshing after the spicy one." Caro watches the other people around us shiver and rub their arms for warmth. "What do you think the third one will do?" they ask, eyes wide.

"Only one way to find out." I pick up the third cake, grin at Caro, and give it a try. As I start to chew, I think the surprise is the small crunchy bits with bright, citrusy flavor between the layers. But the real reveal comes a moment later as the bits dissolve on my tongue with fizzy pops all across my jaw.

"Pop Rocks!" Caro says, delighted. "But also not? They're denser and more tart."

Everyone else in the room is equally tickled by the final treat. I'm surrounded by gasps and giggles, as if Robin transported us right back to our childhood selves. It's a perfect end to an evening of culinary wizardry.

Caro and I stick around chatting while the other guests

effusively praise Jesse and Robin. With a full and grateful stomach, I refuse to acknowledge any discomfort I feel about the beautiful women lining up for selfies with Robin. She's not really mine to be jealous of anymore. Even so, once we finish helping clean up the decorations, I'll be the one at Robin's side for the afterparty at One More Round. What do we do when we're having jealous feelings about our not-quite-ex-wives? We live in the moment.

34

Robin

GOD, IT FEELS GOOD TO BE BACK.

It's been a long time since I felt like myself. Not the polished, TV version of me. And definitely not the rock-bottom failed-restaurateur version of me. The real Robin. The one who's creative and playful and full of surprises. *This* is what I love about being a chef, I think as we celebrate our sold-out dinner at One More Round. Creating something new, something that gets people talking. Seeing someone's eyes light up as the food I've made rocks their taste buds. I've finally got my cooking groove back.

Maybe Molly's got something to do with it too. Watching her enjoy my work was half of tonight's magic for me. She's standing at the bar with Keyana now, looking absolutely stunning in a little black dress that shows off her tattoos. I can't believe how lucky I am to be the one going home with her after this. She's gorgeous, she's talented, she's got a huge heart under all those freckles and scowls, and she's decided to let me back into it, even if just for the time being, to make things right. She's giving me a second chance to prove myself, just like Jesse, just like this whole town that for some reason has welcomed us back with open arms. I love everything about this night. I love food, I love Eureka, and I love Molly.

Yikes. Okay, I might have taken that a bit too far. Whatever we're doing is temporary. Do I love her? Of course. But more in the way you love your childhood friends, the ones you don't necessarily see all the time but wish the best for and remember to text once a year on their birthdays. *Love* love is in the past.

Isn't it?

I feel a firm clap on my shoulder and look away from Molly's curves in that dress to find Jesse behind me, handing over a pint of beer.

"Can't believe we pulled that off," he says, still glowing. "I couldn't have done it without you, Rob. Years later, you're still inspiring me and teaching me. Cheers."

We tap our glasses together and take our first sips. "Don't be modest," I say, wiping the foam from my lips. "You're the one who owns a killer restaurant, my dude. I feel lucky to be here."

Jesse throws an arm around my shoulders and shakes me, sending a splash of beer down the front of my black tee. "We're a team," he says. "You're the Tweedledee to my Tweedledum. And for one of these dinner-series nights, you'll be in charge and I'll be *your* right-hand man. Just tell me which month. It'll be even better than this. Right, Molly?" he asks, turning to her as she approaches us with Clint and Key.

"Right what?" Molly asks.

Jesse takes his arm from my shoulders and says, "I was telling Robin that once things wrap up at the inn, she should take the lead on a dinner-series night."

"Oh. Yeah, sure," Molly says. I slide an arm around her waist and kiss her temple in greeting, still riding the high of our success and forgetting for a moment that we're not at the inn and maritime rules don't apply. Luckily, she doesn't flinch. "But it will be hard to top what you did tonight, Jesse. It was a work of art," Molly adds.

Jesse bows with a flourish. "It was an honor serving you, my lady."

"You're a magician," Clint says, clinking his martini glass against Jesse's beer. "We really need to do a collab with your restaurant and my bar."

"I can't believe I missed it," Key groans.

Molly pats her on the shoulder. "You couldn't cancel that MoMA interview. And there will be more."

"I won't miss it next time!" Key says. "Everyone's saying it changed their lives."

"Oh, I forgot." I reach into my backpack under the table. "I brought you some extra cakes, Key. And not to rush you, but they probably shouldn't be left out too long or they'll lose some of their magic."

Key grabs the box from my hands eagerly. "I'm starving. I'll eat them now."

"Okay, but they're probably more impressive when you can hear them," I say above the bumping bass of the bar's music, thinking of the audible fizzing and popping baked into the third cake. Key's head tilts in confusion.

"Go out on the patio," Molly suggests. "Robin, you go with her to watch her reactions."

"What reactions?" Key says, one eyebrow arched.

"It'll be fun," Molly says, then kisses me for a surprisingly long moment, considering all our friends are watching. Are we cool with that now? Does all of Eureka fall under inn rules? When we part, I catch Jesse, Caro, and Clint glancing at one another like they've just settled a bet. Key, meanwhile, is squinting at me with obvious skepticism.

I gesture toward the patio door and ask Key, "Shall we?"

Molly was right. Watching Key eat the cakes is a treat for my ego. She goes on about how cute and perfectly round they are, and about the delicate flavor of the first petit four— before the spice hits.

"Fire mouth! What the hell!" she exclaims once my mystery ingredient does its job, fanning her mouth with her hand. "I love spicy things, but whoa. It's, like, vibrating."

"Sichuan pepper oil," I explain. "Don't worry, it fades fast. And the antidote to the first cake lies in the second."

Key pops the second cake into her mouth. After a few chews, her eyes go wide and her lips purse. "Brrr! How does it make my mouth all cold like that?"

"There's a layer of coconut-mint cream in the middle that was frozen, but it's been out of the freezer for a minute," I say. "The natural menthol in the mint reacts with the Sichuan pepper from the first one."

"Fucking wild," Keyana says. "What does the third one do? Turn me into a billionaire?"

"When I figure out how to make a cake do that, I'll let you know."

Key's even more delighted by the third cake than the first two. "It's popping! Can you hear it?" She leans in close to my ear.

"A little bit, yeah."

"Are there Pop Rocks in it?" she asks.

"I had to make it harder for myself than that," I say, leaning against the natural stone wall at the back of the patio space. "I made little sugary bits with baking soda and citric acid to create the chemical reaction on your tongue."

"Damn. Didn't realize you'd become a kitchen chemist."

"I've picked up a few new skills," I say, just shy of bragging.

Key purses her lips and looks me up and down. "Mm-hmm. Based on the way Molly kissed you in there, I'm guessing you've got some other new skills you've been showing off too."

I purse my lips, silently waiting for her to continue. It's clear she's got a bone to pick with me, and I've got a feeling I know which one.

"This thing with Molly," Key says, all business. "What are your intentions?"

I shrug. "I don't have 'intentions.' I'm following her lead here."

"Uh-huh," Key says, clearly unconvinced. "Tell me how you see it, then."

I scratch the back of my neck, looking toward the door for someone to save me from this interrogation. "A little nostalgic fun," I reply carefully. "Molly says it's our chance to put the past behind us and end things on a good note."

"And how exactly does it end?"

At least I've got the right answer to this one. "We agreed to finish redecorating the inn, sell it to Clint, and finalize our divorce," I say. "Then say our goodbyes and move on with our lives. A clean break."

"Right." Key gives me another searching look. "You'll go back to being a hotshot celebrity chef, open some fancy conceptual restaurant, and have a whirlwind affair with one of your adoring fans. And what happens to Molly?"

"She . . . drives around doing stained glass?"

"And continues pining over you and nursing a broken heart for the rest of her life?"

"I, uh, no?" I fumble.

Keyana shifts her weight and crosses her arms before saying, "Molly thinks of herself as this independent, thick-skinned person who doesn't need anyone. Right? She tries to give off this untouchable 'I don't need you' aura. But I know, and I'm pretty sure *you* know, that she's got big emotions, even if she tries to wall them off. All she wants is to take care of the people she loves and feel loved by them in return."

I tuck my hands in my pockets, the stone wall against my back keeping me steady as I wait for Key to make whatever point she's working her way toward. It's bizarre having her explain Molly to me. Key has obviously seen a different side of Molly than I have these past seven years. Even though all three of us used to be close, I get why Key chose Molly's side in the breakup. I know leaving Eureka made me the bad guy. But does she really think she knows Molly that much better than I do now? Is it that hard for her to imagine there are parts of Molly I see that she doesn't?

"But honestly, it's no wonder she tries not to get attached

to anyone," Key continues. "Every person in Molly's life she's ever cared about has left her. Maybe not by choice. But her parents. Her childhood friends after she came out. Her grandmother. You."

My stomach sinks, knowing she's right. I was too caught up in my big dreams for Portland to realize it at the time, but the guilt sank in later when I thought about why Molly took my leaving so hard. Why, when I asked her to come with me, to abandon the town that was the only home she had left, to move across the country when she'd never even been on an airplane before, she refused and then accused me of abandoning her. Because I was just one in a long line of people who failed Molly. "But you never left her," I say to Key, wanting a happier ending for Molly, even if she is my ex. "You're her best friend."

"She's mine too, and I try to be there for her," Key says heavily. "But I can't always, especially when our work sends us in different directions. There have certainly been periods when we grew apart and had to nurse our friendship back to health. I basically fell off the map when my dad was sick. Still, she was there for me at the funeral and picked me up off the floor. I owe it to her to look out for her."

I soften, realizing that's why Key's being so hard on me now. I can take the heat. I deserve it.

Key looks through the window into the bar, watching Molly straighten the collar of Caro's shirt. "You leaving back then, it broke something in her. Her faith that she could truly rely on someone. She got way more independent for it, became a better artist, learned to set boundaries. She glued herself back together, but she lost a lot of faith in people along the way, and I don't know if that's something that will ever heal."

I follow Key's gaze to where Clint is handing out a fresh round of drinks to our group. Molly hugs him, and he lifts her up, spinning her in a circle before putting her back down. "She doesn't seem very broken to me," I say, hoping it's true. Even at my angriest and most frustrated, I never wanted bad things for Molly.

"Since you two entered this 'agreement,' she's started acting like the old Molly. She laughs more. Gets out of the studio. Lets herself care about things other than her art." When Key looks from the window to me, I see fear in her eyes. "But what if, when it ends, she's worse off? What if it confirms what she's seen her whole life, that no one ever stays?"

The thought of causing Molly more pain than I already have is excruciating. Being together again has reminded me how deeply I care about her, even if we can never be to each other what we were before. And isn't that why we agreed to do this in the first place? To feel good, to celebrate what we used to have before we leave it behind? Aren't we supposed to be healing, not hurting? "This was just as much her idea as mine," I say, defensive to mask my fear.

Key sighs. "I like you, Robin. But if you and Molly are going to hook up again, it can't be a flippant, short-term thing that leaves her crushed. You may be able to throw yourself into your career and move on, but Molly's heart will hold on to that pain forever."

My instinct is to fight, to say I know Molly best and she's obviously enjoying herself. But everything Key says rings true. I've been living a dream for the past week. Is the dream now worth a potential nightmare for Molly when it's over? Have I been the bad guy all along, when I was always so completely convinced I was doing the right thing? "What should I do?" I ask, my cracking voice betraying me.

"You have to make a choice," Key says firmly, her eyes locked on mine to make sure I hear every word. "Either you're getting back together or you're not. You're staying or you're leaving. This gray area you've been living in is unsustainable. Molly needs clarity. You don't have to make a lifetime commitment, but you can't be all lovey-dovey for a few weeks and then disappear. If you're doing this with her, do it for real or draw firm boundaries around your friendship. She can handle the truth. Just . . . be gentle with her, all right? Molly is special. A brilliant artist and one of the most loyal, caring people I've ever met. She may look tough, but she's softer than she seems. Softer than she'll ever admit."

Key's words are still crashing over me when we're interrupted by a burst of noise. Molly walks through the glass door onto the patio and comes toward me with a drink, followed by the rest of our rowdy group. Keyana gives me one last look before she slips back into the bar. But as the night goes on, her voice never leaves the back of my brain. *She's softer than she seems.*

35
MOLLY

AT FIRST, I ASSUMED ROBIN WAS JUST TIRED. SHE HARDLY SAID a word on our walk home from the celebration at the bar, then crawled into bed and went to sleep without even giving me a kiss good night. Then she was already working in the garden before I awoke Saturday morning, and I was passed out when she arrived home late after her dinner shift, so I chalked up our missing each other to how hard we've been working to get the inn ready. But after a third night of little communication and absolutely no romance, I was certain something was up.

I intended to ask what was wrong when tensions were low and she was in a good mood. Maybe right after a meal, or a nap. Certainly not here and now, when we're both sweaty, frustrated, and holding power tools. But here we are, halfway through tearing out a crappy built-in closet in the Lilac Room that the management company inexplicably chose to install with a gallon of liquid nails, when I press against Robin to help her tug at a stuck piece of particleboard and she jumps away like I'm a rabid possum. I can't hold back any longer, so I demand she tell me why she's been acting so weird.

"Key told you to shut this down?" I say, holding back a wave of shock and anger at Robin's confession. With all this hot-and-cold nonsense, I've been having terrible flashbacks to that last year at the Hummingbird. My fight-or-flight instincts are telling me to raise hell or shut down and get out before I get hurt again. But my heart doesn't want this to be over, so I'm trying to hear her out.

"Key's worried about you," Robin says, watching my reaction like I might catch flame. "About how you'll feel when this is over."

I put down my drill and ball my fists, trying to control my gut reaction of rage and hurt. "I didn't realize the two of you were holding forums on my mental well-being," I say.

"We weren't trying to go behind your back," Robin says, kicking away scrap pieces of wood on the floor between us. "It just came up. Please don't be mad at Key. This is what best friends do. Put their noses in your business."

"I'll deal with Key later," I say. "But instead of making unilateral decisions about our relationship based on conversations I wasn't involved in, could you talk to me first?"

"You're right. I'm sorry." Robin puts down the putty knife she was using to pry the built-in from the wall and looks at me fully for the first time. "But Key did have a point. How does this end? Can we really live in this fuzzy gray area of sleeping together and being all lovey-dovey and then, bam, it's over? Don't we need boundaries, clarity?"

"We *have* clarity. We're doing this because we agreed it makes sense for us, and I've never felt clearer-headed in my life," I say, trying to convince myself it's true, even though the past few days *do* make me question how I'm really going to feel when this is over. Until Robin got all broody after the Alice in Wonderland dinner, I was having the time of my life, and I desperately want that to continue. I walk closer, tucking my hands into my coveralls' pockets, and say gently, "This ending will be easier. Mutual. And we'll both have something else to focus on next in our lives."

"Sure," Robin says skeptically. "In theory."

"If it doesn't go like we're hoping, if it's harder than it seems . . . well, at least we'll have been happy for a while," I say. "I know it's not forever. We've both got careers and lives outside of this place. My agent emailed a couple days ago and she's itching to get me back on the road. But for right now, this inn is where I want to be. What do *you* want?"

"I want that too," Robin says, her voice tender. She cups my face with her hand, running her thumb along my cheekbone. "Being together here again has been unbelievably wonderful, against all odds. But I've already hurt you too much. What if I do it again?"

I place my hand over hers, holding on to her touch. "We can never guarantee we won't hurt each other. We're imperfect people in a messy, complicated situation." I pull Robin's hand to my mouth and kiss the pad of her thumb. "But we can promise to try. We can do our best to take care of each other and ourselves for the time being. Don't you think that will make it easier to say goodbye?"

The worry in Robin's brow fades a little as she looks at me. "I hope so."

I never thought I'd be the one making this argument. When we first met, I was so closed off to love, to trusting someone. Robin, with her goofy sense of humor and thirst for life, cracked my shell wide open and talked me into trying things I never thought I'd do. And now here I am, fighting for this risky opportunity to be the person I was again, to feel the passion and purpose and possibility I once felt. I lean closer to Robin, so close that I can see every eyelash framing her big, golden-brown, trusting eyes. "So we can keep doing this?"

"Please, god." Robin grabs me by the hips and pulls me to her for a passionate kiss, one that feels like fresh air after a weekend of holding my breath.

THE NEXT DAY, I STORM into Key to Happiness Art Studio and march straight to the back room.

"You told Robin to break up with me?" I ask the moment I spot Key at her easel.

She turns to look at me, brush aloft. "Um, no. Not exactly."

I cross my arms. "So what *did* you tell her?"

"The same thing I told you. That I think it's a dangerous idea. That you'll get your heart broken again when it's over."

"And *I* told *you* that it's my decision to make, yet you went to Robin anyway."

Key sighs and sets her paintbrush on a side table. "Aren't you setting yourself up for pain later for the sake of a little comfort now? Do you really believe this can end well?"

"Yes," I reply immediately. "This isn't some elaborate act of self-sabotage. I've thought it through, a lot more than you have. I'm happy, Key. Can't you see that? For once, I actually feel like I'm in the right place at the right time and doing the right thing. And even if it is a mistake, it's my right to make it."

"It is," Key says, hands on her hips. "And I'm glad you're happy now. But it's really hard watching your best friend wind up to punch herself in the face without stopping her."

I want to scoff, but a tiny voice in the back of my head stops me, asking if maybe she's right. If maybe I *am* sabotaging my own chance at moving on. If I thought this arrangement was a relaxing nap in the sun, but I've actually been lying on railroad tracks and now the train's a-coming.

"I shouldn't have gone to Robin like that," Key says, guard lowering. "But I did it because I love you and don't want to see you get hurt. You get that, right?"

"I understand why you did it," I admit. "And even though I'm ninety percent annoyed, I'm also ten percent grateful that you care about me enough to be honest, even if it's not something I want to hear. Well, I'm a hundred percent grateful for you all the time. I'm just also annoyed right now."

Key pulls off her smock and wraps me in a hug. "Fine, I'll let you punch yourself in the face," she says, her words muffled by my shoulder. "I'm sorry for inserting myself in your weird situationship with Robin. How can I make it up to you?"

I pull back, holding Key by the elbows. "Are you done painting for the day?"

"I can be."

"Good." I pull my keys out of my pocket and shake them. "I know just what you can do."

A COUPLE HOURS LATER, KEY and I admire our handiwork, standing with Thembi in front of Drizzled Donuts.

"What do you think?" I ask.

"I'm stunned!" Thembi says, ecstatic. "When Key first told me about your windows, I knew it would be a nice face-lift, but this is beyond my wildest dreams. It already feels like the heart of the shop." She beams at the stained-glass window stretching above the storefront. It's a pattern of colorful circles that don't immediately read as donuts but become recognizable when you spot the sprinkles and drizzles. It has a sense of playfulness and joy that isn't always found in a medium associated with stodgy old churches, but it's also modern and geometric enough to not look childish or corny.

"It's really one of your best," Key agrees. "Maybe you should use food as your inspiration more often."

I pull out my phone to photograph the finished product of weeks of work. I can almost always find something to improve upon in my windows, but with this one, I wouldn't change a single pane. Even though I nearly lost my fingerprints from all the cuts and burns working on those sprinkles. "It'll look great with the morning light," I say, closer than I'd usually come to bragging out loud. "You'll have to send me pictures, Thembi."

"I will," she promises. "And I can't believe you did it for such a low rate. As a small business owner, I could kiss you for that. Thank you so much."

"And what do I get?" Key says in a playfully chiding tone. "I learned to install a window. Don't I at least get a pat on the back?"

"You learned to assist me while *I* install a window." I the-atrically clap Key's shoulder. "But there you go."

"I can do better than that." Thembi opens the door to her shop, jingling the attached bell. "Can I send y'all home with some donuts?"

Key and I happily agree. As we wait for Thembi to box up the day's leftovers, Key turns to me. "I'm next, right? I've tried to be patient, but I'm dying to see what magic you're working for me."

I smile, picturing the fresh design I've sketched out for Key's studio. "Don't worry," I say. "I saved the best for last."

36

Robin

ON WEDNESDAY, WE TAKE ADVANTAGE OF THE SURPRISINGLY pleasant weather—usually Eureka feels like one big sweaty foot in late July—to work on outdoor projects. We've been getting a fair amount of rain, and flowers, produce, and weeds alike are springing up in the garden at a breakneck pace. I spend the morning picking and watering and pruning while Molly knocks a few things off our exterior to-do list nearby.

In the afternoon, we refinish the gazebo. Molly teaches me to inspect the wooden boards, hammer in loose nails, and paint the stain evenly across the planks for a consistent color. When we're done, I stand back to inspect our work. The structure looks as good as new. Well, maybe not *new*, but pretty damn good for being decades old.

Her job done, Molly throws herself on a shady patch of freshly mowed grass, arms and legs spread like she's about to make snow angels. When she hasn't moved a few minutes later, I walk over to make sure she's still breathing. "Everything all right down there?" I ask, wiping the sweat from my face with my T-shirt.

"Yep. Fine. Just going to lie here until my bones crumble to dust and absorb into the earth."

"That doesn't sound very fine to me."

Molly cracks her eyes open. "When did we get so old?" she asks. "I swear I used to get three times as much done in a day and wake up limber, energized, and ready to go again. Now I feel like I've been mauled by a bear."

"Only you could get mauled by a bear and still look this cute," I say, eyeing her messy-chic bun, sun-pinkened cheeks, and the tantalizing strip of skin between her yellow crop top and denim shorts.

Molly's mouth twitches with a smile. "I'd trade my cuteness for less sore joints in a heartbeat."

"I have something that might help," I say, remembering what I tucked away in a kitchen drawer last week. "Be right back."

I return a minute later, plop down on the grass beside Molly, and hold out an offering.

"A joint?" Molly says, sitting up. "That hasn't been hiding in the inn since 2018, has it?"

"It's fresh. A line cook gave it to me. You're not a snitch, are you?"

"Hell no." Molly grabs the joint from my hand, and I pass her a lighter. She puffs to get it going, then exhales a cloud of smoke. "Ahh. Wow. I haven't smoked since New Orleans."

She passes it to me. I take a hit and hand it back. This time, she does a fancy French inhale, releasing a puff from her mouth and breathing it back in through her nose.

"Damn," I say. "Looks like you've practiced since I last smoked with you."

Molly brings the joint to her mouth and blows out a series of smoke rings. "I'm an *artiste* now. It comes with the territory," she says, then holds out the roll to me.

"We in the restaurant industry are more no-nonsense about it." I take a big breath in, then try to hold back a cough but fail spectacularly.

When I recover, Molly has an amused look on her face. "Should I shotgun you like you did for me when I was a little newbie stoner?"

I laugh, remembering when I first got Molly high by blowing smoke into her mouth. Weed was never hard to find in this town. Eureka kind of loophole legalized it in 2006, a good ten years before Arkansas passed a medical marijuana law. That's what happens when retired hippies have a strong majority on the city council. "I still can't believe you'd never smoked before we met," I say.

"Where was I supposed to get drugs?" Molly says. "I never went to college, had no friends, and lived with my grandma."

"Fair point."

Molly takes a big hit, then leans into me, lips to lips, and blows the smoke into my mouth. I breathe it in and hold it. I get momentarily lost in the thought that the air in my lungs came directly out of Molly's, that there's a pocket of space inside of me that was once inside of her. I release the smoke in a thin stream, never breaking eye contact.

"It's kind of fun being on this side of the shotgun," Molly says.

"You never shotgunned any hot lesbians on your art tours of the Southeast?"

Molly smirks with red, narrowed eyes. "Never," she says. "No matter how much they begged and pleaded."

"You must have left a trail of broken sober hearts in your wake."

"What about you? I imagine you blew weed smoke into the mouth of every girl who asked for your autograph."

I grin. "You know me. Always a giver."

"Did you shotgun Georgina?"

I watch Molly for signs of animosity. Georgina's name used to be an instant fight-starter between us. It still seemed like a sticking point last month, when we talked about Georgina on the porch. Maybe it's the chill of being high, but now she just seems curious.

"Not that I remember," I answer, relaxing. "Georgina wasn't into PDA, and we did most of our smoking in the alley behind Robin's Egg and Stargazer with our employees nearby."

Molly tilts her head. "Your shared restaurant building?"

"Yeah, in Portland," I reply, finding it less painful to talk about than expected. "It honestly was a bad idea, trying to share a kitchen and dining space between two restaurateurs. It only lasted as long as it did because I left her in charge while I opened the second Robin's Egg location in Silicon Valley and the Hatch in Seattle. We were broken up by then. Just trying to make it work as business partners."

Passing back the joint, Molly says, "Tell me about your

restaurants. What were they like inside? What would I have ordered if I'd visited?"

I raise my eyebrows in surprise. "Didn't you already google them?"

"I did," Molly says, running her fingers through a thick patch of grass. "But that's not the same as seeing them through your eyes."

I'd typically dive off one of Eureka's rocky cliffs before reliving my restaurant failures, but Molly's looking at me like she really believes they were special. So I give in and start with my first, Robin's Egg in downtown Portland. I describe the Instagrammable patio space with ivy-covered walls and punny neon signs and the airy interior, full of mismatched furniture painted in bright colors. The design was similar at the short-lived Google HQ Robin's Egg location, which had the misfortune of opening five months ahead of March 2020. When I tell her about the miniature quiche cups that came in a million seasonal flavors, the ones I later turned into a mass-produced frozen product that saved me from going completely broke during the pandemic, she nods in recognition.

"I bought them once," Molly admits shyly. "The first time I saw them at the grocery store, I couldn't resist. I fully intended to hate them out of spite, but they actually tasted pretty good. Not as good as the quiches you made at the inn, but still."

She ashes the joint as I move on to the Hatch, my higher-priced farm-to-table restaurant in Seattle. With Robin's Egg thriving on early buzz and a big check in my pocket from Google, I decided to open a dinner concept just under a year after cutting the ribbon on my first place. Oh, the ignorant audacity. Guests picked their own garnishes from herbs grown in pots and window boxes around the restaurant, and they could grab fruits and veggies from the garden out back for the cooks to add to omelets or flatbreads. Finally, I reach my favorite child and biggest disappointment, Kindling. I map out the restaurant in the air, how guests walked down a forest trail from the parking lot to a clearing in the trees where chairs circled ten firepits, with the kitchen hidden in a cabin built off the clearing. After watching each of my restaurants shutter in 2020, all that open air felt like a safe bet, even if the concept itself was risky. I tell Molly about the gourmet skewers and steaks and seafood guests grilled themselves over fires, the flame-cooked side dishes in cast-iron pans, the s'mores made with gourmet marshmallows, cookies, crackers, and drizzles.

Over the course of our conversation, we've sunk down in the grass, staring up at the clouds with my head on Molly's stomach. Sharing what I loved about my restaurants with her feels surprisingly healthy. Picturing them at their peaks instead of when I turned the OPEN signs to CLOSED for the last time.

"Do you miss it?" Molly asks when I'm finished. "Running a restaurant?"

"Which part?" I say sarcastically. "The long-ass days with no sleep? The cruel Yelp reviews? The constant fear of not breaking even and worrying about making payroll?"

"Not those," Molly says, her fingers combing through my hair. "The good parts."

I close my eyes, enjoying the gentle scalp massage, and picture the look on my first Robin's Egg customer's face when she took a bite of my bananas Foster French toast. The enthusiasm with which the Hatch's front-of-house manager

guided customers through the pick-your-own fresh herb garnishes. The family dinners I'd eat with my team around the
last campfire at Kindling after close.

"Yeah," I say, barely loud enough for Molly to hear over
the wind in the trees above us. "I do miss it."

"As much as you miss being on TV?" Molly asks.

"TV's fun sometimes," I say, noticing how my head rises
and falls against Molly's stomach as she breathes. "Winning
competitions. Meeting some of my heroes. Cooking and eating things out of my comfort zone. But it's a lot of waiting. I
couldn't even talk about anything until it aired, and half the
time, when I watched the shows, the producers edited them
so much that they looked nothing like when we filmed. Restaurants are real-time. I get to watch people eat what I make
as soon as it hits the plate."

Molly's fingers graze my neck and come to rest on my
chest, right above my heart. "It sounds like your heart is in
restaurants," she says, voice hoarse, probably from smoking.
"And once we sell the inn, you'll have the capital to open a
new one."

I open my mouth to respond, but can't find a single word.
When Molly says it like that, my decision sounds so easy.
But is it how I really feel? How do I give up the fame and
clout of TV? And if a new restaurant is the answer, what?
Where? With whom? And why does the idea of leaving the
inn to start something new sound so scary?

Molly, seeming to understand my conflicted silence,
says, "All this food talk has made me realize I'm starving. I
could eat a whole hog, snout to tail."

I grin at the phrase, another of her gram's Southernisms.
"Same. But getting up to cook sounds so hard," I whine.

Molly crawls a few feet to grab the end of the water hose I used earlier. "Good thing we've got a whole farmers market's worth of produce right here," she says, waving the hose toward the garden.

We pick berries and beets and radishes and spinach, then clean them off and snack while Molly tells me how she spent our years apart. Between bites, she explains how, after teaching herself to repair the inn's windows and creating the smaller original designs for the guest rooms, she started restoring old stained glass at churches and historic buildings around Arkansas. Then she worked her way up, making bigger original pieces, thinking more outside the box in terms of style. She tells me about the first commission she ever made, a high-impact design of colorful triangles for an art museum in northwest Arkansas. That's how her agent found her, and from there, things took off quickly. Molly took a welding class and used her new skills to make freestanding steel-and-glass works, which caught the eye of a Route 66 restoration committee and led her to a multistate job that paid more than she'd expected to make in a lifetime.

"Wait," I say through a mouthful of radish. "You're rich?"

Molly's cheeks turn pink. "Not, like, idiot-billionaire-who-rockets-himself-into-space rich," she says. "But rich as in having more money than I know what to do with, yes."

"This whole time, I thought we were both broke," I say, stunned. "During that first-month standoff, you could have rented somewhere else to live?"

Molly bites her bottom lip. "I could have bought a whole other inn."

I can't help it. I laugh. I laugh so hard that I snort, which sets Molly off, and then we're those stereotypical high teenagers, giggling and rolling around on the grass, cracking up at the other cracking up, tears running down our faces. It takes us minutes to recover. When we do, Molly picks up a blueberry and starts moving her mouth weirdly like she's talking to it.

"What are you doing?" I ask.

Molly looks up at me like she'd almost forgotten I was here. "I was just thinking about how blueberries are the happiest fruits," she says. "Saying their name makes you smile. Blueberries. Bluuueberrieees. Try it."

I follow her lead, and the corners of my mouth do curve up at the word. "It works for all berries," I say. "Strawberrieees. Raspberrieees. Blackberrieees."

She tests out the words while I stare, mesmerized by her lips, and then we both realize how silly we look and sound, and then we're off on another fit of laughter. I watch as Molly calms, her face settling into a relaxed grin, observing the clouds passing overhead. I don't think I've ever seen her this at peace, walls down, beaming brighter than the sun. Our time together at the inn has brought out a new Molly. It's changed me too, I think. I'm starting to see the world, and what I want from it, differently these days. Will I still be this Robin when I go back to real life, to the cameras and investors and food critics? Will Molly still be the same gorgeous, confident woman she is beside me right now? Will we even stay in touch enough to find out?

37

MOLLY

"YOU MUST BE MOLLY," THE LAWYER SAYS, WELCOMING US INTO her office. "I've heard so much about you from Key. Nice to finally meet you. I'm Danica."

"Thanks for meeting with us, Danica," I say, shaking her hand. Danica is intimidatingly tall, fashionable, and put together. Or I *would* be intimidated by her, if I hadn't heard all of Key's messy and dramatic stories about their college friend group. Now she's got a successful legal practice in Fayetteville with a waitlist for new clients, but Key helped us jump the line. "This is my . . . um, wife for now, Robin."

"You look familiar," Danica says while shaking Robin's hand. "Have we met before? Are you from Conway?"

"Close. Little Rock," Robin says.

"You might know her from TV," I say, jumping to the inevitable. "*Let's Do Brunch* Season One, or *You Can Take It with You* on Foodie TV."

"Right!" Danica says, eyes lighting up. "The chef! You made those frozen quiche cups too, right? My kids love those."

Robin's smile is a practiced mix of confidence and modesty. "It's an honor. Kids are usually my toughest audience."

We settle into the chairs at Danica's broad marble-topped desk. "So what can I help you with today?" she asks, pulling out a leather-bound journal and uncapping a pen.

Robin and I dive right in, explaining how we bought the bed-and-breakfast, got married, split, and are preparing to say goodbye to the Hummingbird and our marriage. We've been working on our renovation checklist for three months; the walls are painted, the floors refinished, the fixtures replaced, and the old furniture restored. Keyana's completed half of the guest-room murals. Everything's coming together right on schedule, but it feels like a whirlwind. One minute we're making a to-do list, the next it's October, Clint's realtor is preparing the closing documents, and we've got to get a move on the divorce paperwork. Between reno projects and catching up on the sex Robin and I didn't have during our seven years apart, our time together slipped away faster than either of us expected.

"Selling the property shouldn't complicate things much," Danica says once we reach the end of our explanation. "You already have a buyer, your initial investments were fifty-fifty, and you've put roughly equal work into it, so I don't foresee any problems handling that."

"That's good," I say, looking to Robin, who smiles back.

"The divorce, however," Danica continues, "might be a little more complicated."

"It's a no-fault situation," Robin says quickly. "Friendly. Neither of us wants alimony or anything, and the inn is our only shared asset. Open and shut."

"Not quite." Danica purses her lips as she passes us a thick printed booklet. "The state of Arkansas has . . . uniquely stringent requirements to obtain a divorce."

Robin and I make eye contact, and I'm guessing my face looks just as confused as hers.

"No-fault divorces are allowed," Danica continues. "But only if the couple has lived separately for at least eighteen continuous months."

"A year and a half?" I exclaim.

"That's right."

"We did live apart," Robin says. "For seven years. Does that count?"

"Living together for the past four months complicates things," Danica says. "Could either of you prove residency elsewhere in recent years?"

"Well, yeah, but no permanent address," Robin says. "I've still been using the inn when I have to list my residence for taxes and renewing my driver's license and whatever."

Danica looks from Robin to me and I meekly admit, "Same." It's strange to realize that, on paper, Robin and I have theoretically been living together at the inn all this time.

Danica scribbles something in her journal, then turns her attention back to us. "So your first option is to move apart for eighteen months. In Arkansas, that is. Or to another state where you can legally file for divorce once you've established a period of residency."

"We've waited long enough," I say firmly. "What's plan B?"

"Your other alternative is fault-based divorce," Danica says. "It's not as combative as it sounds, but you will have to qualify for one of Arkansas's official grounds for divorce with evidence and third-party testimony."

Robin removes her arm from the back of my chair to fiddle with the collar of her navy button-down shirt as she asks, "And those grounds are?"

"A separation of three years due to incurable insanity," Danica lists. "Violence that puts the other's life at risk. Willful failure of one spouse to provide basic necessities for the other, which would be hard to prove considering you've both earned enough to support yourselves for the past few years."

"Any other options?" I ask, beginning to realize the hurdle we're facing.

"General indignities making life together intolerable is the most popular," Danica says, shifting to cross her legs.

When Robin and I make eye contact this time, I can tell we're both thinking of our peaceful breakfast together this morning, our afternoons drinking tea on the front porch, our off-key sing-alongs while polishing furniture. Everyone in Eureka Springs who didn't immediately assume we were back together has seen us walking around arm in arm over the past couple months. Life together has been thoroughly tolerable lately.

"'Intolerable' is a strong word," I say carefully. "But we could play it up for the judge."

"Legally, I can't suggest lying. It could get you in a stickier situation. Besides, you'll need evidence. Do you have some kind of physical proof of how one of you has made the other's life hell?" We blink at Danica, and, sensing our answer, she moves on. "Adultery is another frequent option. But evidence is required. Does either of you have a significant other who could testify?"

I look to Robin, the thought of Georgina a relief for once, but she mumbles no in the direction of the floor. I shake my head, cutting off that option.

"The remaining grounds for fault-based divorce, then," Danica says, "are impotence, conviction of a felony, or habitual drunkenness for one year."

"You're joking," Robin says. "I can only get divorced if I have some kind of provable sexual dysfunction, commit a felony, or stay drunk for a year? What the hell?"

"Technically you can't just commit a felony. You'd also have to get caught. And I could look into an argument for how impotence applies to same-sex relationships, but I'm not optimistic." Danica shrugs apologetically. "Arkansas has some of the most antiquated divorce laws. It's a 'conservative family values' issue."

"But we're lesbians!" I say, nearly shouting. "Shouldn't we get a free pass? They didn't believe we should get married in the first place!"

"It *is* a ridiculous situation," Danica admits. "So let's talk about what you can do."

"We can pick one of the grounds and make it true, right?" I suggest. "I mean, getting drunk every day for a year probably isn't great. And obviously we shouldn't beat each other up or commit a crime."

"So what, then?" Robin says, turning to me. "Are you going to test out the incurable insanity option?"

"Adultery!" I say like I've just won bingo. "One of us sleeps with someone willing to declare it in court."

"Is there a Tinder setting for that?" Robin asks.

Danica looks physically pained by her own words when she says, "Unfortunately, Arkansas law prohibits agreeing to an act specifically to procure a divorce."

Robin leans forward, her elbows on the desk in front of her. "Danica, tell us the truth. Are you pranking us? Did Keyana convince you to make all this stuff up?"

Danica laughs grimly. "I wish. I have to go through this with couples way more than I'd like. But most of them have court-recognized reasons to hate each other, at least more so than the two of you."

Even through my frustration, that feels a bit like a teacher telling me I'm a pleasure to have in class. "So what do you suggest?" I ask, sitting up straight.

"Waiting might be your best option," Danica says. "Eighteen months living apart in Arkansas, or move to another state with more lenient divorce laws and establish residency."

"And if we want all this finished by the time we sell the inn in a couple months?" I say, praying for some divorce-granting genie to pop out of Danica's metal water bottle. That kind of delay was not in our plans, even if where each of us goes next is still up in the air.

"If one of you finds a new romantic partner—a physically intimate partner, according to the code—that's the fastest option I see." She taps the divorce booklet in front of us with a shiny, pointed purple nail. "But read through this in case there are any other conditions you might meet without lying or falsifying evidence."

Robin and I thank Danica for her time, then spend the drive home in stunned silence. Planning a wedding was tough. But who knew planning a divorce would be so much more complicated?

38

Robin

IT'S EIGHTY-FIVE DEGREES TODAY, A TREAT IN EARLY OCTOBER.
Molly and I would be fools not to take advantage of it. So
we're putting off regrouting the bathroom tile and soaking up
some sun at our favorite swimming hole.

They're a real thing. Even though this one, Hogscald
Hollow, sounds like it was made up by J.R.R. Tolkien.
Looks like it too. Tucked into the stacked limestone mountains of the Ozarks, it's a gorgeous turquoise color, dotted
with waterfalls and surrounded by trees, currently vivid
shades of orange and yellow and red. It's a secret spot
known pretty much only by locals, surprising considering
the centuries-old legends of its healing properties. Everyone in town flocks to it in the summers, and the old Eureka
hippies used to skinny-dip there, I hear from Dot and Elea-

nor. But today's a quiet autumn Tuesday, so we get it all to ourselves.

You can't drive right up to Hogscald Hollow. There are no parking lots or formal hiking trails. Instead, you drive as close as you can get before the gravel roads are swallowed up by trees, then follow your instincts toward the water. Molly and I do it while balancing our old kayak and paddles on our heads.

We peel off our hiking boots and shorts and T-shirts as soon as we reach the lake, throw them in a bag, and tie it to a tree branch away from bugs and critters. I've got on some swim trunks and a blue bikini top. Molly's wearing a simple black one-piece with a plunging back that reveals a swath of tattoos. I could spend all day staring at her, but we've got other plans. We jump right in. It's pleasantly chilly, and, even more refreshing, there's not another soul in sight.

After splashing around for a few minutes, we climb into our kayak and paddle toward our favorite spot, just a little farther down Beaver Lake (a name that still makes me giggle like a teenage boy). It's a quiet cove tucked away in a corner, surrounded by magnificent rock formations and lush green-ery, with a brilliant blue waterfall that looks too beautiful to be real. The cliff a good fifty or sixty feet above it is known as Lover's Leap.

When our kayak makes the turn into the cove, Molly and I stop paddling to appreciate the view.

"Is today the day we finally brave it?" Molly asks, looking up at the zenith of the waterfall.

I used to be the one trying to convince Molly to take the leap, but it looks like the tables have turned, and now I'm the chicken. "I'll stick to the ten-foot jumps," I say.

We tie our kayak to a tree trunk and dip back in the minerally water. Molly floats on her back, a look of pure bliss on her face. "I know I've never been farther from home than I can get in a car," she says, barely audible over the rushing bellow of the waterfall. "But you can't convince me there's a more beautiful place on earth than right here."

I tilt back to join her, my eyes closed against the glare of the sun. "Remember when we came here after our wedding?" I ask. "After everyone left, we rented that cabin and spent a full day out here, sunrise to sunset, swimming and picnicking on the cliff?"

"Of course I remember," Molly says, her voice dreamy, hair floating in a watery halo. "It was our honeymoon. We ate the leftover cake and split the last bottle of champagne. It was perfect. I kind of wished we could have skipped the wedding and just hung out here instead."

"Oh, come on," I say, kicking to propel myself closer to Molly's side. "You wouldn't really have skipped the wedding."

"I absolutely would have."

"Probably would have saved us this whole divorce nightmare."

Molly turns, dipping below the water, then resurfaces. "I wouldn't have skipped out on the marriage part," she says, staring at the waterfall across the swimming hole. "Even now. But the wedding . . . it took me a long time to look back at it without it hurting."

"Hurting?" I say, shaking water out of my ears. Our wedding wasn't perfect. Since it was at the inn, we had to handle a lot of logistics ourselves. And same-sex marriage wasn't allowed in Arkansas until a couple months after our wedding, so the ceremony was legally meaningless. We used our celebration as a test for future weddings (which became a huge moneymaker for us). And our vows were interrupted by a thunderstorm that came out of nowhere. But in the end, even though I was exhausted, it was a good day. My family and friends had a great time. The cake I made was killer. We even got a stunning rainbow out of the weather delay, and the pictures of us kissing under it made it into a bunch of queer magazines and blogs. Talk about free advertising.

Molly pushes her wet bangs from her face. "I'd never been so confronted by how lonely my life was until our wedding," she admits. "No family, no old friends. Only Key trying to hold me together with hair spray, safety pins, and pep talks. That day never felt like mine. It felt more like a marketing ploy."

I'm shocked by Molly's candor, and shattered to know this has been hanging over her for all these years. "Why didn't you tell me?" I say, my voice raw. "I never wanted you to feel that way. I would have done things differently."

"Like what?" Molly asks, surprisingly calm. "Canceled the wedding on all of your family and our team? Made my parents less estranged? There's nothing you could have done."

"I could have involved you in more of the decisions," I say. "You were so checked out of all of it. I was annoyed that so much of it became my problem. Maybe we'd both have been happier if we'd actually talked about how we were feeling." I chuckle grimly. "Imagine that. A relationship that could have been improved with better communication."

Molly dances her fingers across the surface of the water, a trail of rings expanding around her. "I blamed you unfairly for a while. Especially after our marriage fell apart. I convinced myself you were using me to advance your business, planning the whole event as a photo op where I was just a prop. But eventually—recently, actually—I realized *I* was the one who disappointed me. I couldn't control what happened with my parents, or keep Gram from dying, or make my childhood friends less homophobic. But when I ran out of people to trust, I could have focused on building trust in myself, gotten comfortable being alone. Instead, I put all of my energy into us and our love for each other. And that was too much pressure for any one relationship to take."

I push my hair straight back, thinking about what Key said about Molly being softer than she seems. "That's not fair. To you, I mean. You've had a lot of shit thrown at you in your life. It makes sense that you have trouble opening up to folks. But there *are* people you trust. Keyana, for one."

"Yes, and I'm grateful for her every day. But her life is bigger than me. She's got her whole family, her sisters, nieces and nephews, all her artist friends and college buddies. I've just got Key."

"You've got me," I say, pulling a leaf from Molly's shoulder. "I know you didn't for a while. But I don't want it to be like that again. I want to be someone worthy of your trust. Someone who sticks around, even if it's just through phone calls and occasional dinners when we're in the same city."

"So you want to be those stereotypical lesbians who are besties with their ex-wives?" Molly says, smirking.

"Maybe they're on to something."

Molly holds a hand above her eyes to block the sun as she says, "Well, we have to get divorced before we can be ex-wives."

I groan and dramatically throw myself under the stream of the waterfall. Then I duck under the water, grab Molly around the waist, and pull her with me. We laugh and splash each other, which turns into kissing for a while. Afterward, we climb into a cave-like gap in the rocks behind the cascade and sit on the edge, dangling our feet above the lake.

"You know, I wasn't totally satisfied with our wedding either," I admit, still thinking about Molly's confession.

"You weren't?"

I shake my head. "I spent so much of it trying to please my family and worrying about how the pictures would look for the website. You're right. It didn't really feel like it was about us."

We absorb my words in silence, and I wonder if every couple feels that way, if weddings always leave a bittersweet aftertaste.

"So how are we going to end it?" Molly asks. "Do we wait another year and a half for a divorce?"

"It would have to be eighteen months living apart, if at least one of us can establish residency at another address in Arkansas," I say, remembering the pamphlet Danica gave us. "Or we have to establish residency in another state and figure out their divorce laws, and neither of us really has a plan to live anywhere long-term. So realistically, it could take years to figure out if we don't find another way now."

Molly rubs a hand along the edge of the rock platform, smoothed by centuries of water. "It seems like adultery might be our quickest option. Do you want to find a girlfriend, or should I?" she asks.

I sigh. "This is so stupid. I hate this fucking state."

"You could call Georgina," Molly suggests. "She would at least understand the situation."

"No way," I say immediately. "Things got messy between us at the end. At this point, I don't think she'd throw me a rope if I was drowning."

"That's probably what you would have said about me too before this summer," Molly says, her fingers sliding from the rocks to my thigh, tracing patterns that give me goosebumps.

"I don't think so. I always knew, or at least hoped, that we would make things right again." I look at Molly and draw my thumb slowly across her bottom lip, then kiss her. "I just didn't realize it would be this good when we did."

"Me either. But one of us will have to find someone else," Molly ventures softly, my hand cupping her jaw.

I stare at Molly for a moment, taking stock of each freckle and dimple, before I ask, "Can I be honest?"

"Always."

I shift to face Molly and she mirrors me, our legs crossing and knees pressing together. I tuck her half-dried hair behind her ears and rest my hands where her neck meets her shoulders. "Even though the plan is to split up and move on, even though there are probably other people out there for both of us in the future, maybe the near future . . . you're the only person I want right now. While we're still under maritime law, I don't want to go looking for someone else."

The corners of Molly's lips tilt up, and I swear the sun starts shining brighter. "I feel that way too," she says.

"If other people have the most success with the . . . what did Danica say? The one about making each other's lives miserable? It must be the easiest to prove," I reason.

"Sounds logical," Molly says. "What should be our main point of conflict?"

"Probably," I say somberly, "how you always put your cold toes on me when you first crawl into bed."

"Hey!" Molly shifts to playfully dig her toes under my thighs. "How about how you sing in the shower before I've woken up? Off-key, I might add."

"You're lucky," I say. "It's a very exclusive concert. And *you* take long-ass showers that use up all the penthouse's hot water, so I have to get in early."

Molly loops her arms over my shoulders, her fingers toying with the tie of my bikini top. "Easy solution," she says, her eyes glittering. "Get in the shower with me next time."

My body temperature spikes. God, this woman is going to kill me. I can't resist tucking my hands into the low back of her swimsuit, cupping her ass, pulling her closer until her legs are wrapped around my waist. A moment ago we were talking divorce proceedings, but that's firmly out of mind by the time I catch her lower lip between my teeth. Suddenly her fingers are tangled in my hair, and we're rolling our bodies against each other, breathing fast.

My right hand slides under the stretchy fabric of her suit between Molly's legs, and she grinds herself against my palm, moaning. I kiss my way down her neck, then pull the front of her one-piece down with my teeth and circle my tongue around her nipple. I want to make her scream louder than the rushing water hiding us from view. I insert one finger, then two, my other hand under her thigh, guiding her rhythm as she bucks against me, faster and faster until she comes, her head thrown back, swimsuit askew, loud enough to echo across our hidden paradise.

I don't notice she's untied my top until I feel mist from the waterfall hit my chest. Apparently Molly doesn't need a moment to recover, because suddenly she's pushing me back against the smooth rock, throwing my bikini aside, running her hands and her lips over my torso. She shimmies my trunks over my hips and licks a path down my ribs, below my navel, and I only briefly wonder if she can taste the minerals from the lake water before I'm gasping for air, arching my back against the ground, begging Molly to keep going, yes, right there.

Moments later, we're laid out side by side, panting for breath. I turn to look at Molly, and we both realize what just happened before we could think better of it.

Molly swallows. "Did we just . . ."

"Have lesbian sex under Lover's Leap on Beaver Lake?" I say. "Yeah. We did."

"Wow." Molly lets out a laugh-sigh. "I think that's officially the gayest thing I've ever done."

I shift to my side, resting my head on my fist, and use my free hand to trace the outline of Molly's swimsuit, finding my way to the nipple still visible above the stretched neckline. "You know what would be even gayer?" I ask with a devilish grin. "If we did it again."

39

MOLLY

THE WEEK AFTER OUR VISIT TO HOGSCALD HOLLOW, ROBIN AND I can't seem to stop bickering on and off. Nothing serious; tiffs about stupid things, like which curtains should go on which windows and how much WD-40 to use on a squeaky hinge and how many pillows is too many in our bed. Blissful as our day at the lake was, I have to wonder if it was the peak of our long goodbye. The best it could possibly get. And now we're barreling toward an ending that, even though we both know it's for the best, neither of us is really prepared for.

As our reno draws to an end, I feel myself growing more irritable and uncertain. I don't know where I'm headed next, what I'll be working on, or for how long. I mostly enjoy life on the road. It keeps my creative muscles in shape, and I don't have to worry about anyone letting me down because I'm off to the next place before they have the chance. But it's been nice putting down roots in Eureka again for a little while. Almost nice enough to make me want to stay.

In quiet moments, I find myself wondering what would happen if we made this temporary arrangement permanent. If Robin and I didn't get a divorce. If we reopened the Hummingbird ourselves. Then I remember that we're not the same people we were when we ran the inn. The only reason we're working together so well right now is because we know how it ends. Neither of us is meant to stay in one place. We can't last here together without going stale or sour. After this, I want to figure out how to visit Eureka more regularly. Being around old friends—*having* old friends—is good for the soul. Either that or there's really something to all those claims about healing waters.

WHILE TRYING TO GIVE ROBIN some space to avoid spats, I've been catching up on Key's stained-glass window. It's slow going; lots of tiny pieces and details. I want it to be absolutely perfect.

I'm deep in a section of golden hexagons when I hear a knock on the shed door.

"It's me!" Key's voice calls out when I turn off my sander.

I remove my goggles and open the door. "Hey," I say, sliding off my gloves. "What's up?"

"I'm finished," Key says proudly, paint-covered hands on her hips.

"Already?"

Key nods. "Want to come see?"

I follow Key into the inn and up the stairs to the Snap-dragon Room, where I'm greeted by her freshly painted mural of towering blossoms with billowing petals in vibrant shades of pink, orange, yellow, and red.

"It's even better than the first time," I say, smiling from ear to ear.

"I would hope so. I've been painting for a decade longer," Key says.

"They're all brilliant, and you did them in, what, half the time?" I hug Key, both of us unbothered by her paint or my glass-cutting oil. We've been covered in worse. "I can't thank you enough. It's not the Hummingbird Inn without your paintings," I say, misty-eyed.

Key waves my compliments away. "It was fun revisiting my old stuff. It'll be weird for them to be here with Clint in charge, though. They were, like, the genesis of our friend-ship."

"He'll take good care of them," I promise. "And Clint's a lifer. He'll actually stick around."

"I still wish it could be *you*," Key says with a sigh. "Or, really, I wish you'd stay. I want my bestie to be a part of the new Eureka I'm trying to build."

I shake my head, a sad smile on my lips. "I'm turning the page. Besides, I hated running the inn without Robin. It doesn't feel right with just me. This whole project is a chance to end it like we began it: together."

Before Key can respond, my phone starts blaring Nelly Furtado's "Maneater," my ringtone for my agent.

"Roxie?" Key asks. "You better answer. She's extra scary now that she's a mom. She's already got the 'I'm not mad, just disappointed' thing on lock."

I accept the call. "Hey, Roxie! I've been meaning to call you," I lie. I've been dodging her for a week.

"Molly!" Roxie's strident New York accent booms through the phone. "Glad I finally caught you. You must be very busy in your studio lately."

"I have been," I reply truthfully. "And you must be busy with the twins. How are they?"

"Just started teething. Not a thing in my apartment is safe. And the diapers. Oh my god, the diapers."

I keep her talking about the babies for a few more minutes while I watch Key pack up her supplies. But I can't distract Roxie for long.

"So that guy with the mansion in Memphis," she says, her voice shifting into business mode. "He wants that stained-glass triptych as soon as possible. When can I tell him you'll arrive? A week? Two?"

"I'm sorry, but I don't think I'll be able to leave here until next month," I say. "I've still got to wrap up the sale of my property in Eureka and handle some other . . . legal matters."

"And finish *my* window!" Key says, jokingly stern.

"Is that Keyana?" Roxie asks. "Put me on speaker."

I comply. "Okay, she's here."

"Hi, Roxie," Key says toward the phone while frowning at me like I've betrayed her.

"Key! That buyer in Austin has been blowing up my inbox. When will you have a sketch for him?"

"Soon. Nearly done," Key promises while shaking her head at me and making a zero with her hand, I'm guessing to convey she hasn't started yet.

"That's what I like to hear! So, Molly," Roxie says, turning her attention back to me. "Memphis. What can I tell Mr. Rydell? First week of November?"

"Second week?" I say meekly. "Tentatively."

"All right. He won't be thrilled. But some draft design concepts would tide him over, if you can draw something up."

"I'll see what I can do," I hedge. Working on the windows here in Eureka, with full creative freedom and in support of cool small business owners instead of rich jerks who always want the most boring stuff, has been a treat I'm not ready to give up yet.

"I know he's a pushy guy. The richest ones always are," Roxie says like she's reading my mind through the phone. "But might as well knock it out, collect the check, and move on to the next one. You'll love what I have cooking up. A resort in Cancún. Huge project early next year. Almost as big as the Route 66 deal. And if I play my cards right, you'll get to live on-site in one of the suites. You could use a beach vacation. A *working* vacation."

"Sure," I say, visions of palm trees and clear blue ocean less enticing than Roxie thinks, especially if they require me getting on a plane. "You're the best, Rox."

"When's *my* working beach vacation?" Keyana asks loudly. "Does that resort need some murals?"

"You told me you weren't available for travel for the next year," Roxie says, clearly pleased by the question. "But say the word and I'll see what I can do."

"I've got to run," I say, thinking of all I still have to finish here before I can leave town. "Thanks for the updates, Roxie."

"Of course. I'm here when you need me," Roxie says.

I say goodbye and hang up. Key must see the stress on my face, because she comes over and pats my shoulder. "Memphis, huh?" she says. "That'll be nice. Only a five-hour drive from here. You can visit me for Thanksgiving. And Cancún, wow. The refreshing start to a new year you'll need after all this . . . reminiscing."

"Mansions and fancy resorts," I mumble, shaking my head. "I always feel so out of place working on them."

"I get that," Key says sympathetically. "I've painted more than enough murals for gentrifiers. But think of all the fun projects you can take on once you fill your bank account."

"Hey, do you want to see how your window is coming?" I say, changing the subject. "I've got it laid out in my studio."

"Obviously yes, but no." Key throws her bag of paint and brushes over her shoulder. "I want to be surprised."

I shrug. "Okay, then. How about java-chip cheesecake? Robin made it yesterday."

Key's eyes light up. "Now, *that* I want to check out."

40
Robin

"RIESLING OR SANGIOVESE?" JESSE ASKS, HOLDING UP TWO half-full wine bottles. I point to the red. "Good choice," he says, then splits it between two glasses.

"Cheers," I say, clinking mine against his. Sunday nights are my favorite shifts at Counterculture. Jesse and I polish off the unfinished wines while we plan the specials and order supplies for the upcoming week. It's a nice escape from the tension brewing at the inn. "Busy few days, huh?" I say, smacking my lips to savor the bold, herby Sangiovese.

"Great," Jesse agrees, setting his wineglass on the metal prep station between us. "Since we started the dinner series, we've been booking up more frequently. Lots of repeat customers. Higher tabs too, and more tables ordering the chef's tasting menu."

We brainstorm seasonal dishes for the coming week based on what we've got a surplus of in the walk-in, but I'm interrupted by a buzzing from the pocket of my chef's coat.

"Sorry, Jesse, I've got to take this. It's my dad."

"No problem."

"Hey, Dad," I say into my phone, stepping behind a storage rack. "What's wrong?"

"Why's something got to be wrong?" Dad says, chuckling. "I can't just call my favorite daughter to check in?"

You can, but you don't, I think.

"Sorry," I reply. "It's late. What's up?"

Dad spends a few minutes catching me up on the new resident he hired at his practice and his trip to the zoo with the grandkids last weekend. He really must be changing. He *never* took Gabe and me to the zoo. Afterward, he asks, "How's the inn? Closed on it yet?"

"Soon," I say. "We're almost done with renovations. We've got a walk-through with the buyer next week."

"Glad to hear it," Dad says. "Getting a good return on the investment of your trust fund money, just like I taught you. And great timing, because I've got a job opportunity for you."

I freeze, unsure where this is headed. "You do?"

"A buddy of mine was tapped as director of dermatology for a new medical spa resort in the Sonoran Desert. You know, the kind of place where celebrities go to get plastic surgery and recover in private. They're looking for a head chef. Your name could be a real draw, and it pays almost as much as being a physician." He laughs at his own non-joke. "What do you say? Can I connect you?"

The gig reminds me of my Robin's Egg location at Google

HQ, which got shut down by Covid before it really got off the ground. But before that, I was already frustrated by the limitations that came with being one small part of a big campus. Too many higher-ups telling me what I could and couldn't do. "It doesn't sound like my kind of thing," I say.

"Psh. Living in the lap of luxury at a five-star resort is *everyone's* kind of thing."

"Thanks for thinking of me, but I don't think it's the right next step," I say, picturing myself making brothy soups for actors with fresh lip filler to sip through straws. A medical spa resort sounds like where culinary inspiration goes to die.

"I didn't realize you were in a position to turn down a good opportunity," Dad says. "You got something else brewing I don't know about?"

"I'm working on it," I say noncommittally.

"Sure. Well, if you want something more low-key while you figure things out, our country club is looking for a chef. Nothing as fancy as a spa resort, but you'd be closer to home."

"I'm not going to work at your country club, Dad." I realize as the words come out of my mouth how ungrateful I sound. There's nothing wrong with the jobs my dad is offering, and as recently as a few months ago, I couldn't afford to be this picky. I look toward Jesse, who's pretending not to listen but has been examining the same bag of rice for a suspicious amount of time.

"Sorry, that was harsh," I say quietly to Dad. I rub my eyes and take a deep breath, trying not to take my own anxiety about the future out on him. "Your country club is great, and it's thoughtful of you to suggest it. I just want something that . . . feels like mine, I guess. After being in charge of my own restaurants, it's hard to go back to cooking for a boss." *Besides you,* I mouth to Jesse.

"Makes perfect sense, Birdie," Dad says. "I'd feel the same way if someone asked me to leave my practice and go back to a hospital setting. So you'll do more TV, then?"

Memories of four A.M. call times, infinite reshoots, and styling screen-ready entrées with tweezers pop into my head. "I'm not sure," I say honestly.

"Well, Birdie, tell me what you want," my dad says, his frustration beginning to show. "Whatever it is, I'll help you however I can."

"Whatever it is?" I say skeptically. "Even if it's not a Michelin-starred restaurant or an award-winning TV series or something else that will impress your friends at the club?"

"To hell with my friends," my dad says, nearly knocking me over. "You're my daughter. I want you to be happy. Even if that means running the deep fryer at a catfish shack."

Those are words I never once expected to come out of my father's mouth. I look at my phone like I'm being Punk'd, then return it to my ear and say, "That's . . . surprising to hear."

My dad sighs. "You and I have had our differences. But I've always been proud of you, no matter what."

Thinking of all the times he's made me the butt of stupid jokes, how he talked me out of going to culinary school and pushed me toward a business degree, his belittling my success with the inn and pushing me to aim higher, I can't help but say, "You've had some weird ways of showing it."

There's a pause before my dad speaks again. "You're right. So I'll say it again. I'm proud of you. Of what you built in

Eureka, in your restaurants, on TV. But also of where you are now, figuring things out. It takes a lot of guts to step back from big opportunities and think about what you really want," he says, serious, not a punch line in sight. "I haven't always been the most supportive parent. But I've learned a lot from watching Gabriel with Annalise and Bradford. Life's funny like that. Sometimes you learn the most about parenting from your kids and grandkids. Gabriel helped me realize that you two being happy and healthy is what really matters. So what would make you happy, and how can I help you get there?"

I'm at a loss for words. If my conservative, status-driven, patriarchy-born-and-bred dad can have such an open mind, I guess it's my turn to grow up. "That means a lot to me, Dad," I say, my voice cracking a little. "I'll let you know as soon as I know. Maybe I can come down to Little Rock soon and we can talk about it. I'll cook dinner."

"Tell me when and I'll clear my schedule, Birdie."

I almost tell him to stop calling me that stupid nickname, but before I do, I realize it's growing on me. "Okay, Dad. Thanks. I love you."

"Love you too," he says before hanging up.

"Your dad's trying to find you a job?" Jesse asks as I take a seat at the prep station.

"Apparently," I say, still processing what just happened. I take off my backward ball cap and run my fingers through my hair. Molly trimmed off the bleached ends for me last week, and now it's completely back to my natural dirty blond. "It's nice of him, I guess. If only I knew what I wanted my next job to be. That's the whole reason I came to Eureka. To figure it out," I say.

Jesse sits on a stool next to me, dropping his clipboard next to the sink. "I know what might help." I look at him curiously, hoping for a magic answer. "What do you say to leading the dinner-series night next month? Whatever theme you want. It can be your culinary goodbye before you sell the inn and leave town. And maybe it will spark an idea for what comes next."

I think about how Jesse's dinner series gets my creativity flowing, how I always leave them on a high, reminded of why I love what I do. Part of me wants to pass, not wanting to take up too much space in his kitchen, but I also recognize the honor it is to be invited to do something like this. I decide I want to live up to the person he thinks I am. "I'd love to," I say.

Jesse's face lights up. "Dope! Just tell me what you need. I'm here for you one hundred percent, like you've been for me."

"I know you are, dude." As I pat Jesse's shoulder, I remember how I asked him and Caro to consider returning to the Hummingbird. I see now that I shouldn't bring it up again. They have their own legacies to build in Eureka. Leaving that vision for the future behind, I say, "Thank you for the opportunity. Really. I don't think I could have survived these last few months without you."

Jesse smirks at me. "I don't know about that. Seems like Molly's had something to do with it too."

My cheeks turn warm. "Maybe. But truly, I'm grateful."

"Don't mention it," Jesse says. "We're in this together. And we're gonna make a dinner they'll never forget."

41

MOLLY

"MOLLY!"

I jump at Robin's yell and bang my head on the brick front of the fireplace. I'm still seeing stars when she bursts into the dining room.

"Molly, I need you!"

"I'm busy," I say irritably as I push the goggles from my eyes and rub the growing lump on my forehead. Clint and his posse of advisers and assistants are scheduled to arrive at eleven, and we must be cursed, because things keep going wrong. After we polished the dining room's centerpiece chandelier and changed out the bulbs two weeks ago, it wouldn't light up, so we had to take it to the electrician to fix whatever was wrong with the wiring. They didn't finish it until this morning, and Robin has to pick it up so we can rehang it before Clint arrives. And now the fireplace damper, which was working fine when we tested it last week, won't stay open. Clint's realtor specifically requested we have a fire going when they arrive to prove it's in working order, so I'm teaching myself to repair it under duress.

"It's an emergency," Robin says, frantic. "I must've run over a nail or something yesterday and now I have a flat tire. I need to get to the electrician fast if we're going to get the chandelier hung before Clint gets here."

Seriously? Is the universe playing another prank on us? It's a cruel reminder of the morning in 2018 when Robin abandoned the inn. She loaded her suitcases and boxes into her car, only to realize the front passenger-side wheel was flat as a day-old Coke. I refused to make it easier for her to leave me. Instead, I watched her struggle from the porch, getting some perverted kind of satisfaction from her frustration.

Now I pull my hand from my forehead, my fingers smeared with soot. "I'm dealing with my own emergency at the moment," I say, reaching for a can of WD-40. "Just take my car."

"The chandelier's too big. It won't fit in your car."

"Then change the tire yourself," I say, sliding my goggles into place and leaning back into the fireplace. "You've done it before."

"But you can do it so much faster," Robin whines. I know she's right; I've changed about a million flat tires since learning how on Gram's clunker before I was old enough to drive it myself. "Without the chandelier, the dining room will look dark and sad. Please?"

I take a deep breath in and out, staring up at the accumulated ash and rust above me. The stressful lead-up to our walk-through with Clint and his team has made for a tense week at the Hummingbird. We've been fighting almost as much as when we first arrived at the inn in June. I keep telling myself it will be better once we've gotten past this step. I hope I'm right, or else we're going to end this thing the same way as last time: hating each other's guts.

"Fine," I say, emerging from the fireplace. "But you're helping me."

We bicker our way through putting on the spare, an activity sure to escalate an argument between any couple, but especially us, especially here. Robin gets annoyed at how long I spend reading the manual, which is obviously always a good idea. I yell at her for stupidly resting her leg under the jacked-up chassis, which could lose her a limb. I'm still muttering under my breath when she pulls out of the driveway and I return to freeing the jammed hinges of the damper.

I manage to finish and get a fire started just as Robin returns with the antique crystal chandelier. I wipe the muck off my hands and rush to rehang it in its place at the center of the dining-room ceiling. Robin hands me tools while unhelpfully reminding me Clint is due to arrive at any minute. Right when I connect it and the bulbs flick on, there's a knock at the door.

"Ladies! So good to see you," Clint says as soon as we answer, both breathless and high on adrenaline. He wraps Robin in a hug, then freezes before he can do the same to me. "Oh my god, are you all right?"

"What? Yeah, of course," I say with a too-big smile.

He reaches toward my face but stops short of touching it. "Are those bruises?"

I rub my face and come away with a smear of soot. "Oh. No, just some gunk from—um, car trouble," I say, deciding that admitting to fireplace issues is a bad way to sell a house. "Excuse me," I add as I run off to the hall bathroom to wipe my face.

When I return, Robin has shown Clint and his team into the entryway. I shake hands with his lawyer, his realtor, his assistant, and his financial adviser/life coach, all of whom are expensively suited gay men who make this whole ordeal feel very formal.

"It looks just like I remember it," Clint says, spinning with his arms spread like Maria in *The Sound of Music*. "Isn't it gorgeous, y'all?"

"So charming," Clint's assistant says, not looking up from his iPad.

Clint walks over to the grand staircase and strokes the banister. "I helped strip and polish all this natural wood back in 2012. Remember, Molly?"

"Of course I remember," I say, trying not to get distracted by Clint's life coach peeking into a closet we forgot to organize. "I couldn't have done it without you."

Clint's realtor leans all the way down to the bottom stair. "These look awfully tall," he says. "Is the house ADA compliant?"

"It meets all historical property requirements. We can share that paperwork with you after the tour," Robin says quickly.

Meanwhile, I silently wonder if we made the wrong choice by not hiring our own realtor. We already had a buyer in mind and didn't want to lose out on a percentage of the sale. But what if Clint's realtor hits us with a question we can't answer?

"Speaking of tour," Robin says, "shall we begin? This is the main floor, and our check-in desk is just down the hall."

The group starts walking farther into the house, and Robin and I catch sight of the tall ladder and tools still set up in the dining room at the same moment. Her eyes widen, and she tilts her head toward the room in a gesture that I'm guessing means she expects me to handle it. I know she's better with people, but why do I always get stuck with the dirty work?

"This wall here is where we used to have a gift shop with Hummingbird Inn merch," Robin says, drawing the group's attention away from the dining room.

I rush in to shove the tools under a tablecloth. But when I collapse the ladder and try to heave it toward the basement, I accidentally knock over a chair.

Clint's head appears in the doorway. "Everything all right in here?"

"Better than all right," I say, shoving the ladder in a corner and righting the chair. "Just forgot to put this ladder away after some last-minute cleaning."

"So cozy!" Clint says, spotting the roaring fire as he leads his group into the room. "I'm glad it still works."

"Good as new!" Robin says brightly. "As is our chandelier, refurbished and ready for a new generation of guests."

Robin's using her TV voice, which, considering how

much we've already been butting heads today, gets under my skin. But Clint and his posse are eating from the palm of her hand.

"Look at how shiny the crystals are!" Clint says, delighted. "So much better than that ugly modern garbage the management company put in here."

Robin stands tall. "We've worked hard to bring back the inn as you remember it. Shall we look at the kitchen?"

Even if her schmoozing is driving me bananas, I know it's what the moment calls for, so I stay quiet. The tour continues, with Clint delighted by Key's murals, his realtor and lawyer skeptical of every detail, Robin countering that the inn is a one-of-a-kind treasure, and me rolling my eyes whenever the group is looking the other way. I know I need an attitude adjustment, but I've got soot under my fingernails and I haven't eaten anything all day and, honestly, that flat tire situation has me remembering the worst day of my life. An hour later, we're back in the entryway answering final questions when I hear a suspicious clank. Everyone else politely ignores it, but I'm racking my brain to figure out what it was when I start to smell smoke.

"Shit," I mutter, running to the dining room as smoke starts billowing into the hallway.

"—fine, I'm sure, just a log readjusting—" I hear Robin saying to our guests' concerned questions before she's cut off by the fire alarm.

Coughing, I cover my mouth and nose with my shirt, then slide the handle of the damper back to open, but it won't stay put. I hold it in place with one hand and start scooping sand from a decorative bucket onto the flames.

Meanwhile, Robin escorts Clint and his team outside, presumably convincing them all that everything is totally fine,
spitting out a bunch of smoke is just something working fire-
places do sometimes.

"What the hell, Molly?" Robin says when she returns,
immediately dropping the friendly tone she'd been using for
guests. "I thought you fixed it."

"I thought so too," I say, moving to open windows. "But I
was rushed because *you* couldn't handle a flat tire on your
own."

"Well, it nearly ruined the whole tour," Robin says. "Now
Clint's realtor is on high alert. I promised him we'd get a
professional out to look at it before the inspection, but this
fiasco could lower their offer."

I honestly do feel terrible for putting the inn at risk by
lighting a fire without being completely certain the damper
was fixed. And I *know* that this time has truly been different,
that we've shared the load instead of all the messy work falling on my shoulders. But my guilt and logic are no match for
my anger, which is sparking into its own poorly contained
flame. Robin blaming me, even if it is actually my fault,
pushes me into old patterns. I can tell I'm having an outsize
reaction to carrying this responsibility, to having to frantically
google how to fix a fireplace, replace Robin's tire, hang a
chandelier, and then having all our hard work literally and
figuratively burn up in our faces.

Unfortunately, knowing I'm overreacting doesn't mean
I can stop it. If I open my mouth to respond, I'm afraid I'll
either scream or cry. So instead, I stomp out of the room
toward the stairs.

"Where are you going?" Robin says, following me.

"To lie down," I grumble, knowing my exhaustion is clouding my judgment.

"Now?" Robin scoffs. "What about all this smoke and mess?"

"You clean it up," I reply, halfway up the first flight. "I've done enough."

42

Robin

BY THE TIME I FINISH AIRING OUT THE DINING ROOM AND sweeping up the sand and ash spilling out of the fireplace, I'm covered in grime and fucking fuming.

"What was that?" I say, bursting into the penthouse apartment to find Molly freshly showered and wrapped in a robe, reading a book in our armchair. "I thought we were in this together."

"Really?" she says, jumping back into fight mode so fast I wonder if she was even really reading. "Because it didn't seem like we were 'in this together' when you blamed *me* for the damper closing."

"And it didn't seem very 'in this together' when *I* had to lead the tour because you were too busy moping around and giving me angry looks."

"Right," Molly says, tossing her book on the footrest. "Because playing HGTV-show host is so much harder than all the manual labor I did."

"Why are we doing this?" I say, throwing my arms up. "The whole point of this stupid thing was to get back on the same team, sell the inn, and leave on a positive note. If that's not happening, why are we even here?"

"We're supposed to be fixing things between us. Sharing the burden of the reno. Moving past all the things we used to fight about." Molly's expression goes pained, then quickly guarded, gaze hardened, jaw set. "And instead we're fighting over the same old garbage. I'm still doing all the grunt work, you're still getting all the glory."

"I'm not going for glory! I'm trying to sell the inn, like we agreed, so we can both benefit. And you don't want to lead a tour anyway!" I rip off my soot-covered shirt and stomp into the bathroom. "I'm done with this argument. I need a shower."

I slam the bathroom door behind me and turn on the water. I pull off the rest of my filthy clothes and step under the cool stream, mumbling comebacks I wish I'd thought of a minute earlier. My eyes are closed when I hear the door open.

"Fine, give up," Molly says over the sound of water hitting tile. "Might as well move out now too. Leave me alone to handle the rest by myself, *again*."

Annoyed to hell, I slide back the shower curtain, not at all bothered by the fact that I'm fully naked. "I'm not leaving," I say firmly. "We're seeing this through to the end, together, like we planned."

Molly's eyes travel down my body, then drag themselves

back up to my face. I let her look. "That was the plan the first time too, yet I still found myself standing alone on the porch while you drove away," she says, her voice shaking.

I see something in Molly's expression now that I was too distracted by my own rage to notice earlier: hurt. Molly's not being logical or mature right now because her inner child is afraid of being left. These past five months have shown me so many ways she's grown, ways both of us have evolved. But maybe Key was right. I've set her up to feel that pain of being abandoned all over again. We get so caught up in our old fight patterns that I forget things are different now, that what drove us apart the last time doesn't have to this time. This arrangement is supposed to be healing, not digging deeper into old wounds. I step out of the shower and wrap Molly in a hug.

"What are you doing?" she says, tense in my arms, sooty water dripping on the floor around us.

"I'm sorry, Moll," I say into the fabric of her robe. "I shouldn't have blamed you for the fireplace. This fight? This is the old us. Not the new us. Can we take a breath and let this old shit go? Be kind to each other again?"

Molly inhales, exhales, then relaxes into me. "I'm sorry for leaving you to clean up," she says, voice cracking. "This morning, the stress, the flat tire . . . it took me back to—" She can't bring herself to say it.

"To then," I finish. "When I left you." It's the first time I've said it out loud like that. I've always tried to deny it, to insist that I asked her to come with me, that, if anything, *she* abandoned *me* by not agreeing to go to Portland, a plan I made without her input. I see now that neither of us was blameless, even if both of us felt like the victim. I rub circles on Molly's back as I say, "But until recently, we've been en-joying being here together. Haven't we?"

"That's what scares me," Molly admits, pulling back with her arms around my waist. "The longer we're here together, living in this weird nostalgia world, the harder it's going to be to leave it. Don't you see that?"

"Yeah, I do," I admit. Every day I've spent with Molly has made it harder to picture leaving, even if every day is sup-posed to take us closer to the end we planned.

"But I have to figure out how to move forward," Molly says. "So do you. Your dreams were always bigger than this inn. I'm sorry I didn't support you like I should've back then. You deserve someone who cheers you on, not someone who stands in your way."

"*Never,* Molly," I say, stunned. I grab Molly's face be-tween my hands and look at her earnestly. "I *never* felt like you were standing in my way. I could only ever dream so big because of you."

Molly's glance darts across my face, looking for truth.

"I mean it," I say. "My parents, they always pushed me to be something I wasn't. You saw me for who I was. You en-couraged me to trust myself, to learn new things, to follow what excites me instead of what impresses others. Hell, buy-ing this inn was a huge leap of faith, and it's the only reason I've built this career. I couldn't have done any of it without you."

"I tried to talk you out of opening your restaurant," Molly says, her voice wobbling. "I tried to convince you to stay here. Because I was selfish."

I move my palms from Molly's cheeks to her shoulders, then run them all the way down her arms to grab her hands.

"You weren't selfish," I say truthfully. "I was so eager to prove myself that I was willing to walk away from this beautiful thing we built without figuring out what happened to it next. I promised to be a partner to you, then I made decisions for both of us without really asking what you wanted."

"I was selfish too," Molly says, tears dropping from her eyelashes. "I was so lost in my fear that I wasn't enough for you that I looked for ways to prove myself right. So when the opportunity came up for you in Portland, I didn't fight hard enough for us. I think there was a part of me that *wanted* you to leave so I wouldn't have to keep dreading that it was coming."

"You were always enough," I say, my heart cracking wide open. "I wanted you to come with me. I wanted it to be us in Portland, starting something new. I thought you were too afraid to leave Arkansas. Too afraid we'd take a big swing and miss, and I couldn't let it keep me from taking the swing."

"I *was* afraid." Molly's voice quavers. "I'm still afraid. Afraid to choose someone, something, someplace, and put my whole heart into it only to have it not choose me back. Especially after I thought we chose each other and the Hummingbird, for better or worse. I felt like you'd changed your mind about what you wanted back then, and I desperately wanted us to stay like we were in the beginning. But we couldn't stay the same. No one can. Change is the only constant in life, and it's hard and scary and unpredictable and takes things I love from me. But I have to accept that nothing lasts forever. I have to learn to let go."

"I think I've been afraid of standing still," I say, tucking a tuft of Molly's hair behind her ear. "After our feature on *Inn for a Treat,* after all those producers came knocking, and with my dad pushing me to do something bigger, I got it in my head that the Hummingbird was just a jumping-off point. That I was meant to do more. So I chose fame. I chose to go to a bigger town where I could capitalize on my moment in the limelight. Instead of appreciating what I had, I wanted to see how far I could go."

Molly gulps. "Maybe that's not a bad thing," she says. "Maybe it's smart to look forward instead of back, like I always do. You can still go even further after this is over."

I pause, wondering if Molly's right. I've done a lot of looking back since I've been in Eureka Springs, and it's taught me a lot. This conversation alone has changed the way I look at my marriage, my life choices. I wish the answers for my future would fall out of the sky and land right on top of my head. "I . . . I don't know if I want to go further," I mumble, looking down at the puddle of water around my feet. "Not after everything I built fell apart."

"Things that fall apart can still be fixed." Molly lets go of my hand to wave toward the bathroom around us. "Like this inn. We brought it back. You could do the same for your career. You can still get what you want."

"Maybe." I wipe the tears from Molly's cheeks and kiss a patch of freckled skin. Could what she said about fixing things that fall apart be true for our marriage? Do I want it to be? Eureka Springs and Molly seem like my past, not my future. But in this moment, with her in my arms, vulnerable and honest and hopeful, I have to wonder. "For right now, all I want is to enjoy my time here with you, for as long as I can," I say, the only thing I know to be true.

Molly looks from my eyes to my lips, then leans in and kisses me. It starts slow and soft, but a rhythm and heat rises behind it, and soon her robe drops to the floor, our bodies pressed together, hers clean and mine still covered in murky gray droplets. She pulls her lips away for a breath. "Then let's live in the moment, yeah?"

I don't know how we went from fighting to a teary heart-to-heart to being so hungry for each other, but this could be one of our last chances. I pull Molly into the shower with me, my hands searching out her most sensitive places. I want to kiss her until every past pain has disappeared, make her heart race enough to drown out the fear of what's ahead, touch her in the right spots to make us both believe there's nothing left in the world but us.

I'M JOLTED AWAKE BY A buzzing near the bathroom door, where I left my pants.

I gently pull myself from Molly's softly snoring body and find my phone in the pocket. Seeing my manager's name on the screen, I quietly shut myself into the bathroom. "Hey, Edgar," I say. "How's it going?"

"Are you sick?"

"No?" I say in a confused voice.

"You sound weird," Edgar says. "Your voice is all hoarse and low."

"I, uh, just stepped away from something." I clear my throat. "But I can talk for a minute. What's up?"

"Amazing news," Edgar says, more chipper than I've heard him in a while. "Are you sitting down?"

I perch on the closed lid of the toilet. "I am now." Edgar's been dying to get me to L.A. for some guest spots, but once Molly and I made the agreement with Clint, I told him I was

out of commission until we sell the inn. He's still been email-
ing me at least once a week with fresh ideas for what I can
do next. I get it. Asking someone who's so good at his job to
sit on his hands is pretty cruel.

"Anders Prescott is leaving his role on *Blue Plate Special*," Edgar tells me.

"Wow, really? He's the face of that show. How is it going
to survive without him?" I say before I begin to realize why
Edgar's calling.

"With you," Edgar says.

"With . . . what?"

"They want you to be the new host-slash-judge of *Blue
Plate Special!*" Edgar says gleefully. He lists a few key details,
including a jaw-dropping financial offer that makes my previ-
ous TV wages sound like peanuts. "This is huge," he continues. "It's an established brand with a big viewership, so it's
unlikely it'll be canceled anytime soon. The producers love
that you've won before as a contestant, and your appearance
as a guest judge back in 2019, and they were big fans of *You
Can Take It with You*. They want to get you to L.A. as soon as
possible to shoot promos. What do you say? How soon can I
get you on set?"

"I . . . I have to think about it," I say, feeling a disconnect
between my brain, my heart, and my mouth.

"What?" Edgar says, flabbergasted. "This is a career-
defining opportunity of a lifetime. What on earth do you
have to think about?"

"Like you just said, it's a career-defining decision," I say,
just as shocked as Edgar that I'm not jumping at this chance
like I would've five months ago. But I'm not the same Robin
I was then. "It's an incredible offer, really. I know that. Thank

you for the negotiating I'm sure you've already put into it. But it also deserves thorough consideration."

I hear Edgar's heavy exhale and can picture him at his desk in his L.A. office, face-palming. "Okay, I hear you," he says with all the patience he can muster. "Take a few days. A week, even. Maybe the suspense will make them want to pay you even more. But get back to me ASAP, okay?"

"I will," I promise. After my conversation with Molly, I'm unclear if looking back or looking forward is what will put me on the right path. I don't know which I'd be doing by taking the *Blue Plate Special* role. And I'm not sure which I'm doing here at the inn. It feels like both. Or maybe looking within instead of outward. The only thing I'm clear on is that I've got more thinking to do.

"All right. I'll send over the details for you to review," Edgar says, the clicking of his keyboard audible through the phone. "Talk soon. I'm sure you'll make the right decision."

He's already hung up by the time I say, "I hope I do."

43

MOLLY

I LEAN AGAINST THE DOORFRAME OF KEYANA'S STUDIO, WATCH-ing silently as she dabs colorful details onto the wings of a moth on her canvas. It's been a busy week of tying up loose ends at the Hummingbird, now that Robin and I have moved past our fight. My fear and anxiety about what happens next is fading into a calm acceptance of the unknown, and every-thing's falling into place, including the glasswork I came here to do. A few minutes go by without Key noticing me, but even-tually she steps back to consider her work from a different angle, and I take the opportunity to make my presence known.

"It looks fantastic from here."

Key jumps. "Jesus Christ, Molly. How long have you been standing there?"

I shrug. "In the grand scheme of the universe, not long."

Key rolls her eyes and wipes her hands on a towel hung from the pocket of her smock. "What's up?"

"I have a surprise for you," I say, smiling coyly. "Remember what I taught you about installing a window?"

Key squeals and runs into the gallery space at the front of her store, looking around for what I brought. She spots the large, flat object covered with an old blanket near the front door. "Show me!" she demands, making grabby hands in the direction of the package.

I whip off the blanket with a "ta-da!" Key gasps, then drops to her knees to examine the detail work. I watch as she traces the copper outlines of the glass shapes.

When I sat down to sketch out ideas, I thought of the beehive painting I saw her working on the first time we met. That became the basis of the window: a tessellation of hexagons in golds and yellows. Every other hexagon holds an image from Key's art. Some are flowers she's painted on murals at the inn and on canvas, brilliant red amaryllis and pink peony and the soft purple Ozark wild crocus we saw that day on our hike. Other hexagons highlight insects she's depicted in her works: bumblebees, of course, and praying mantises, ladybugs, and fireflies. It took almost as long as the windows for the board-game store and the donut shop combined, but it was worth it to see this look on her face.

"Can we hold it up to the light?" Key asks.

I nod. We each take a side of the frame, hoist it level with the giant windows of her storefront, and watch as the afternoon light sparkles through the panes, creating dancing dots of color throughout the gallery.

"So . . . you like it?" I ask Key, who has been uncharac-teristically quiet.

She turns to me with tears trailing down her round cheeks. "It's perfect," Key says. "It's . . . it's me. It's my art. It's my brain made of glass and copper."

"It's not quite as intricate as your paintings that I used for inspiration," I say, preparing to apologize for the inexact color matching and lost details, but I stop myself. Even if it's not perfect, it's the most impressive piece I've ever made.

"There's not a single thing I don't love about it," Key says, colorful patterns from the window dancing across her face. "Dammit, set it down so I can hug you."

Laughing, we carefully place the window back on the dolly and embrace. Key kisses me on each cheek, leaving a little moisture behind from the happy crying.

"So are we installing this thing or what?" I ask.

A brilliant smile stretches across Key's lips. "Hell yeah."

A COUPLE HOURS LATER, ROBIN meets me and Key for tacos at our favorite food truck. It's the day before Halloween, a be-loved holiday in haunted Eureka, and everyone has deco-rated accordingly. The weather has turned lightly chilly, which feels amazing after sweating our way through the in-stallation.

We chat for a while as we eat. One of Key's eyebrows arches judgmentally when I hold up my al pastor taco for Robin to take a bite.

"So," Key says, wiping a stray bit of salsa from her lips, "y'all seem pretty cozy to be getting divorced next week."

I ball up the foil from my tacos before replying. "It's been good. Getting closure."

"Mm-hmm, closure." Key takes a judgmental sip from her margarita. "Sounds very healthy."

I squint at her, telepathically yelling, *You recommended the lesbian way.*

Robin shifts on the wooden bench. "We actually wanted to ask you for a favor," she says. "Our court date is next Friday afternoon, right after we're supposed to finish signing over the inn to Clint, and we need a witness to testify that we've lived in Arkansas for the past sixty days and that we make each other's lives, um, what was the word?"

"'Intolerable,'" I finish for her. "Consistent indignities that make your life *intolerable.*"

Key looks from Robin to me, skepticism all over her face. "Aren't you tolerating each other pretty well?"

"Well, she leaves her tools all over the place," Robin says, looking at me with a teasing grin. "I stubbed my little toe on her power sander yesterday, and it still hurts."

"And *she* always tries to talk to me about random crap while I'm reading," I add.

"See?" Robin says, turning back to Key. "We fight. It's intolerable." I wonder if, like me, she's thinking about our fight after Clint's tour. About how fighting can sometimes end with understanding ourselves and each other better.

Key sighs. "What exactly does testifying entail?"

"It will be easy," I say, pulling a folder from my bag to hand to her. "I already typed up a letter with some evidence. I can send you the digital file in case you want to make any edits before you sign it."

Key skims the text. "But this makes you out to be the bad guy. Hostile behavior? Refusal to help cover Robin's living expenses? Playing cruel pranks on her?"

"It's a fault-based divorce," I explain. "It was my idea. One of us has to be the villain. And since Robin's more of a public figure, if we made it her, it might get noticed. We don't want an Ali Krieger and Ashlyn Harris–style publicity storm on our hands."

"I don't like it either," Robin says, grabbing my knee under the table. "But after talking it all through with Danica, this is our fastest and easiest route."

"Even though it involves asking your Black friend to lie in court, potentially putting herself at risk?" Key asks, examining us over the top of the folder.

I inhale, my hands going clammy at the idea of anything bad happening to Key because of us. "Oh my god, Key, I'm so sorry, I didn't even think about it like that," I say, feeling like the worst best friend on the planet. "We can find someone else—"

"No, I'll do it," Key says, her mind made up. "Because nothing in this letter is technically a lie, and I know more than anyone else how much you *did* make each other's lives hell back in 2018. And because I think a state telling you what decisions you can and can't make about your adult relationship is bullshit. But you should've thought about that before asking."

"We absolutely should've," Robin says, contrite. "I'm sorry, Key."

Key sets the papers down on the picnic table and laces her fingers together. "Are you sure you want to go through with this? I obviously had my doubts at the start, but you two seem happy together. Why throw that away now? Why not see where it goes?"

It's a fair question, one I've been asking myself a lot in the past week. Why *do* we insist on following the plan when things have felt so good?

I give Key the same talking points I've used on myself lately. "We care about each other, deeply. And we want what's best for each other," I say, looking only briefly at Robin's encouraging smile. "Which means letting Robin find her inspiration as a chef and open a new restaurant as soon as she figures out what and where it should be. And it means letting me get back on the road to keep honing my craft and making windows and seeing new places. We got what we wanted out of this arrangement. We've made up. We've learned a lot about who we are now. And we're mature enough to know we should let go before it turns sour again."

Key looks at Robin. "And you agree? This is what you both want?"

Robin clears her throat. "Yes. It's going to be hard to say goodbye, but we made this decision for a reason. We're on the same page."

"So you came back to Eureka, rediscovered parts of yourselves you'd thought you'd lost, reconnected with old friends and with each other, you're happier than you've been in years, and you take that all as a sign that you should break up and leave the town that healed you?" Key asks, straight-faced.

Robin and I are both silent for a moment, looking anywhere but at each other. "We'll come back to visit?" I say awkwardly.

"God, y'all are exhausting." Key closes the folder I handed

her. "But fine. I'll testify. And I'm holding you to that promise to visit. You'll always have a home in Eureka Springs."

Before June, I thought coming back here would rip me in two. Now it's the idea of leaving the inn behind that unsettles me. Walking away from everything we rebuilt, all the memories, old and new. Waking up in some strange hotel bed without Robin beside me. The thought feels like a black cloud drifting overhead. I wave it aside and say, "Deal. How about another round of margaritas?"

44
Robin

I SNAP A LID ON THE LAST PLASTIC CONTAINER AND STOW IT IN the walk-in fridge. "All right, that will do it," I announce.

"That went fast," Jesse says, piling dishes into the industrial dishwasher. "So I can bring all of it to the inn tomorrow at four? Any special equipment you need?"

I point to a stack of crates near the back door. "I put everything in those, and I put green labels on the stuff we need from the fridge and freezer." I glance around the kitchen to make sure I haven't forgotten anything. "You might want to put a sign on the door tomorrow afternoon telling folks who didn't read the email to go to the inn."

"Smart." Jesse turns off the faucet and dries his hands on a towel. "Should we grab a drink at One More Round?"

I shrug. "I'd love to, but I've still got packing to do."

"No worries. We'll toast tomorrow." Jesse maneuvers around a giant stand mixer to pat me on the shoulder. "I can't believe you won't be in the kitchen here anymore. What are we going to do without you?"

"You'll be fine. You were before I got here." I unbutton my white chef's coat and toss it in the laundry bin. "Luisa has been killing it on the line. With a little mentoring, she'd make a great sous-chef."

"Luisa is fantastic," Jesse agrees. "Doesn't mean I won't miss you."

"I already promised Key I'll make it back to visit soon," I say.

"Figured out what's next yet?" Jesse asks, gathering his jacket and bag from his locker along the back wall.

I grab my bag as I say, "Getting closer. I've found so much inspiration being here with you. I think I'll do some traveling, visit other cool new restaurants, see what speaks to me."

"That sounds like it could be a TV show in itself."

"It probably could." I can't help but smile saying it, knowing the decision I've made is the right one. I haven't told anyone about the *Blue Plate Special* offer. I didn't want anyone else telling me what they thought I should do. Instead, I'm listening to my gut. I've taken twice the time Edgar suggested to reflect, and after a full day thinking about it while prepping for tomorrow's dinner, I'm ready to call him with my answer.

"Well, keep me updated once you figure out what's next," Jesse says after realizing I'm not going to give him any hints. "I never got a chance to visit your restaurants before. I don't want to miss out on the next one." He points to the crates loaded up for tomorrow. "Can't wait to get a taste of Kindling."

"It'll be even better all plant-based, which I can only do because of what I learned from you," I say honestly. "When I got here, I was so creatively drained I could hardly fry an egg. Who'd have thought cooking without meat and dairy and eggs is what I needed to get my groove back? The way you let natural ingredients guide you and push you out of your comfort zone is seriously inspiring, Jess. You're a wizard in the kitchen, and it makes me want to try out my own magic. I can't thank you enough."

"Well, the respect is mutual." Jesse opens the back door onto a stone staircase. "Shall we?"

"One minute," I say, turning back for a last look at this kitchen that I entered while at rock bottom, where I rebuilt myself tablespoon by tablespoon. I take a deep breath in, let it out, then flip the light switch.

I take the long route home after parting ways with Jesse, walking slow, admiring Eureka's quirky architecture, listening to the cricket songs. Halfway, I duck into one of my favorite natural springs, down a few steps into a circular grotto. It's less green than it was in the summer, but there are still a few late-blooming flowers. I kneel down by the small pool collecting at the bottom of the spring. Directly against the advice on the sign telling me this water is unsafe and I shouldn't touch it or put it anywhere near my face, I put my hand under the trickle and bring drops to my forehead and both of my cheekbones. I feel a sense of calm wash over me, an inner voice assuring me that I'm doing the right thing. With that assurance still in my head, I pull out my phone and call Edgar.

WHEN I GET TO THE inn, my feet autopilot me to the back garden. I sit on the bottom step of the gazebo, leaning back on my elbows. Marmalade saunters over and sprawls in the grass next to me, belly up. The early-November air is crisp and cool against my skin. I've pruned the gardens back for the coming winter, but I still smell the rich, earthy fragrance of things growing.

I'm not sure how long I've been out here when the kitchen door creaks open. Molly pads across the grass in house slippers, a thick knitted throw blanket wrapped over her flannel pajamas. She stops in front of me to pet Marmee, then asks, "Whatcha doing?"

I exhale heavily. "Soaking it all in."

Molly settles next to me on the gazebo steps, wrapping one end of the blanket around my shoulders. I didn't realize I was cold until I feel Molly's warmth next to me. We stare up at the sky for a couple minutes, listening to the wind shift the leaves on the trees and the chirp of crickets who have no clue the first frost will soon send them underground.

"Do you think the stars are different here?" I ask eventually.

Molly looks at me like she's worried I've officially lost it. "I'm pretty sure we've got the same stars here as everyone else on the planet."

"Right, I know," I say quickly. "But don't they, like, *feel* different? Closer? Maybe it's the altitude. Less light pollution. Or maybe it's just me."

"No, I know what you mean," Molly says, staring thoughtfully upward. "Everywhere else, stargazing feels like observing a big unknown galaxy *out there*. But here it feels like we're part of that galaxy, in the middle of the big swirl of lights instead of just watching from afar."

"Exactly!" I look at Molly, surprised that she so accurately put my feelings into words when I couldn't. But then I remember she's known me for going on fourteen years, listened to thousands of my random thoughts, finished thousands of my sentences. What a gift it is to be witnessed like that. After this week, there's no guarantee I'll ever be seen as clearly by someone again. But if these five months have taught me anything, it's that life is long and full of surprises. I turn back to the sky. "I got a big career opportunity the other day," I say, feeling light and free, like I'm floating a few inches off the gazebo. "Anders Prescott is retiring, and they want me to take his place on *Blue Plate Special*."

Molly gasps and pulls back, the blanket moving with her, exposing me to the cold breeze. "Rob! Are you serious?" she says, clearly elated for me, not an ounce of bitterness in her voice. "It's everything you've been working toward. Congratulations! You must be—"

"I told them no."

I didn't think Molly's expression could get more shocked, but I think her eyeballs might pop right out. "You what?" she squeaks.

"Being here in Eureka, getting my hands dirty fixing up the inn, cooking with Jesse at Counterculture . . . it may not have given me all the answers for my future. But it's helped me realize what I don't want," I say, tucking the blanket back around my shoulder and looking up. "I don't want to be the one tasting other people's food and nitpicking their art. I don't want to spend more time in a chair getting my makeup and hair done than in the kitchen. I don't want to focus more on how food looks for the screen than how it smells and tastes to real people in real time. I don't know how people will react to my dinner tomorrow night, but I'm so hyped preparing for it and imagining it that I know this is what I have to do. I have to be in a kitchen, pushing myself creatively, and watching people enjoy it. That's what I love about being a chef. Not the fame or the sponsorships or the followers. The food. And the moments it creates."

I turn to Molly and find her looking at me like I've hung the moon. "That's the most you thing I've ever heard," she says. "I'm so proud of you. It must have been really tough to turn down an offer like that."

"My manager, Edgar, took it pretty hard," I admit, remembering how crushed he sounded on the phone. "But me? I feel like I'm in control of my own destiny. And it's fucking awesome."

Molly kisses me on the cheek and scoots in closer to my side as we both look at the stars above us.

"I'll miss this view," I say.

Molly leans her head on my shoulder. "I will too. But it's almost one A.M., and we've got a big day tomorrow. Maybe we should get some sleep."

I rest my head against Molly's and ask, "Five more minutes?"

Molly nods gently, and my head moves up and down with hers. "Five more minutes."

45
MOLLY

ON THURSDAY MORNING, I TRY TO PRETEND IT'S NOT THE SEC-
ond to last time I'll ever wake up in the Hummingbird's penthouse apartment. I could get buried in all the lasts piling up
around me. But I think I may have finally learned what Gram
tried to teach me all those years ago about living in the moment, not grieving everything I'm about to lose.

Of course, it's harder to ignore what's coming when I
open my eyes to a stack of boxes and suitcases. With most of
our furniture deconstructed or moved, none of this room
looks how I want to remember it. Robin, sleeping peacefully,
is the only mental image I'd like to keep. I don't want to dis-
turb her, but I can't resist running my fingers through her
dirty-blond mop of hair. I lightly drag my nails across her
head, smoothing her bangs away from her forehead.

A slow, sleepy smile forms on Robin's face as my fingers reach the back of her head. Her lashes part and she looks at me with those big golden-brown eyes that never stopped appearing in my dreams, even after all the years apart.

"G'morning," Robin says, her voice hoarse.

"Hi," I say with a sappy smile. "Sorry. I didn't mean to wake you."

"'S'my favorite way to wake up," Robin says as I massage her scalp. "And we've got a lot to do."

"Not so much that we can't spend a few more minutes in bed."

Robin pulls me closer so that we're on our sides facing each other, nose to nose. We relish the warm nest of the bed, wordlessly absorbing every detail of this feeling in case it's our last chance.

Our gaze builds in intensity, and our hands start roaming beneath the blankets. It starts gently, sweetly. There's nothing like the fuzzy edges of morning sex, the haze sharpening into a vibrant rush of pleasure with aftereffects I can ride out all day.

But now this connection feels different than ever before. Beneath our physical desire for each other, there's a tangle of emotions: gratitude, nostalgia, yearning, anguish, elation, certainty, fear, hope, and so many other feelings I don't think words can describe. Our pace changes frequently, but we follow the shifts in tempo, rocking together with a swiftness before slowing to an agonizing waltz before racing to a crescendo but halting right on the edge and holding tight until neither of us can wait another second and start the dance all over again.

And then we get a call that the rental company is here with the chairs, tables, and firepits for tonight's dinner, and we can no longer ignore the world outside our bed, beyond the sloped ceilings of our penthouse apartment. It's time to get moving.

WHEN ROBIN TOLD ME HER plan to re-create the Kindling experience in the Hummingbird's gardens for her dinner-series night, I was immediately on board. I knew the logistics would be tough. But I figured we'd build a campfire, set up some folding tables, and everything would work out.

It turned out to be a little more complicated than that. Jesse's special dinners have been limited to thirty people each month. We've got more space than the restaurant, and our old friends and neighbors are treating the event as an unofficial goodbye party. But when the RSVP list crossed sixty diners, I think all of us were a little shocked.

The rental company we used to work with for weddings set up all the tables and chairs, plus tablecloths and place settings. Jesse, Robin, and the Counterculture crew have taken over the kitchen and dining-room area to prep vegan skewers, sides, and desserts to be cooked over the fires by guests. My job is greeting everyone as they arrive and stoking the fires in the pits dotted around the gardens. Robin taught me how to stack the logs and fan the flames for a nice, even heat source.

There are so many familiar faces here. Clint, who we're meeting tomorrow to sign the closing documents, is here with a whole crowd of gay lawyers and assistants and boyfriends past and present. Dorothy, the ghost-tour guide, and our old employee Eleanor are seated next to the owners of the hardware store, who offered us a friends-and-family discount on supplies for our renovation. Key is here, of course, along with Thembi and Louis, and a handful of other folks from the Eureka Springs Black Business Bureau. Local artisans, poets, shop owners, city council members, retired hippies. Even the people I don't know look thrilled to be here at our beautiful old inn for a once-in-a-lifetime dining experience.

I make the rounds, making sure everyone has a drink in hand and checking on the campfires, until Robin comes out for her opening remarks. We direct everyone who isn't already seated near the gazebo to gather around, then pause the music so Robin can begin.

Robin looks, honestly, more stunning than ever. She never needed the professionally styled hair, the TV-ready makeup, the hyper-trendy clothes. Just put her in a white chef's coat and a backward baseball hat and I'm a goner.

"Welcome, all!" Robin says into a microphone, her voice projecting through speakers around the yard. "I'm Robin Lasko, sous-chef at Counterculture and co-owner of the Hummingbird Inn. Well, for one more day."

She has to pause for a thunderous round of applause, looking grateful for the support. Robin smiles toward Clint's table, then waves down the noise and continues.

"Thank you all for coming out for tonight's dinner series. When Jesse— Jesse Montoya, owner and head chef of Counterculture, over there. Wave, Jesse! When Jesse put me in charge of our November dinner, he probably knew I'd do something unexpected. But I'm not sure he pictured uprooting his whole kitchen and bringing it here to the inn so y'all could cook your own dinners over open flames." The crowd laughs. "But of course, being the incredible culinary artist he is, Jesse jumped on board. Let's hear it for Jesse."

The audience reacts immediately, clapping and cheering. I smile at Jesse, who grins back from across the porch where we're both standing.

"Tonight's meal is inspired by my old restaurant Kindling," Robin continues. "And Kindling was inspired by my childhood, when I fell in love with cooking. A lot of kids learn their first recipes from their parents or grandparents. That wasn't my story. *I* first discovered the magic of food at Girl Scout camp."

The audience, enraptured, titters with surprise.

"I know, you're probably thinking hot dogs and s'mores. Which are awesome, don't get me wrong," Robin says. "But I was more fascinated by the unexpected things you could cook over a fire. I tried just about everything you could put on a stick: pineapple, peanut butter and jelly sandwiches, granola bars. I experimented with flavor combinations and textures, fascinated by how soft marshmallows expanded and grew even squishier with heat, how soft bread turned dark and crusty. How you can take one thing, put it on the flames, and watch it emerge as something completely different."

Robin's got the whole audience on the edge of their seats. Even I, knowing this part of her story, am hanging on her every word.

"That's the kind of creativity and joy I hope this experience sparks for y'all in tonight's hands-on experience," Robin says, shifting into instruction mode. "Servers will come

SUSIE DUMOND

around with vegan skewers and sides in cast-iron pans. Each of your tables has a variety of sauces for brushing over your food as it cooks and for drizzling on top afterward. Your server can help if you need any guidance. I encourage you to get out of your comfort zone, try something new, and play. Oh, and remember to save room for dessert. Thank you."

The audience applauds as Robin descends the steps of the gazebo, headed toward me. By the time she reaches the porch, servers are circling with large trays of food ready for the flames.

"How'd I do?" Robin asks, eyebrows tilted up.

"You were perfect," I say, squeezing her hand. "I think everyone's dying to dig in. Feels weird that you're not running back to the kitchen, though."

"That's the fun part," Robin says, watching people pick out their first courses. "My work happens up front. Now it's up to them."

We observe as the guests select skewers loaded with varying combinations of artichokes, squash, peppers, shallots, locally foraged mushrooms, seitan, tempeh, and more. The first brave people take turns at the firepits, then their moans of delight once they start eating tempt everyone else to get cooking. The servers make another loop with family-style sides in cast-iron dishes to be heated over the firepits. Robin and I chat with friends and neighbors as they drop by, complimenting the food and telling us how much they'll miss us. My cynical side would normally roll her eyes and assume none of them really cared about us that much. But the way they welcomed Robin and me back to town with open arms, even after so many years away, made me realize their kindness wasn't just for show. So instead I hug folks and tell them, truthfully, how much we'll miss them too.

Once the guests have had their shot at the campfires, Robin runs to the kitchen and comes back with a couple skewers and a cast-iron pan for us. We huddle around a firepit on the side of the inn, enjoying the warmth on this chilly November evening. Robin instructs me to slowly rotate the skewer over the flames until the oyster mushrooms get dark and crispy at the edges and the scallions and shishito peppers are lightly charred. Meanwhile, she sets a pan of baba ghanoush and a few slices of bread on the metal grate positioned over the heat.

When our food is ready, Robin drizzles a spicy pomegranate sauce over our skewers, and we dig in. It's a spectacular combination of flavors, textures, and heat levels. The baba ghanoush has a smoky flavor to it, which Robin explains comes from pre-grilling the eggplant over a wood fire. I could spend forever asking questions about how she chose the ingredients and sauces, but she keeps getting pulled away by different guests and servers, so I grab a couple bottles of wine and circle the tables, refilling glasses.

With the drinks flowing and the music playing, time flies. Soon the servers start bringing out the dessert course. I help them set up three stations with vegan marshmallows, crackers, cookies, and chocolate bars for our guests to make their own mix-and-match s'mores. If I thought people were thrilled by the hands-on experience before, that was nothing compared to their childlike joy with the playful sweets.

I can't wait for Robin to try the s'mores myself, so Caro and I go together. I opt for snickerdoodles, dark chocolate, and a sea-salt-caramel marshmallow. They grab matcha crackers, white chocolate, and a strawberry marshmallow. As we hold our roasting sticks over one of the fires, Caro says, "You must be so proud of Robin for pulling this off."

"I am," I say. "But she'd be the first to say she couldn't have done any of it without Jesse. He's brilliant. Eureka may be pretty liberal, but it's still in rural Arkansas. Only he could build a thriving vegan restaurant here."

"I've always known he could do it. He just needed someone like Robin to believe in him." Caro shifts their eyes from the flames to me. "I wish y'all weren't leaving. It's been so good for Jesse having Robin around. He can't stop talking about all the wild dishes they've come up with together, and Counterculture is booked up for the next three weeks. I've loved seeing you both too. And you've seemed so happy together lately. I've been secretly hoping things would work out and you'd stay here to reopen the inn."

I don't admit that I've been picturing the same thing. Renovating the inn brought back so many memories from the first time, it's bizarre not to be gearing up to reopen like we did back then. "Our time here was always meant to be temporary," I say to Caro. "I've got to get on the road for some commissions. Robin has to move on to her next restaurant. And the inn will be in good hands with Clint."

"Good Hands *is* what all my exes call me," Clint says, appearing beside me with his own s'mores supplies. "Whatcha talking about? How I'm probably going to turn the Hummingbird into a gay bathhouse?"

"It can be whatever you want it to be," I say, wrapping an arm around Clint's shoulders. "As long as you don't burn it down. Or turn it into a parking lot. That was Miss Addy's greatest fear."

"This town *could* use more parking," Clint says with a fake musing expression. "How much do you think renting one of those wrecking-ball trucks costs?"

I shove him playfully.

"Kidding, of course," Clint says. "I love the inn just like it is. The only thing that could make it better is if you and Robin were running it instead of me."

"That's what *I* said," Caro adds.

Noticing my marshmallow has reached the perfect shade of golden brown, I pull it from the fire. "The inn has taught me everything I needed to learn from it. It's someone else's turn now. I have to let go at some point, don't I?" I say, sandwiching the molten sugar goo between my snickerdoodles and chocolate.

"Says who? Hold on tight like the rest of us lifers," Caro says as they construct their own s'more. We each take a bite, then look at each other with wide eyes. "Holy shit," Caro says through a sticky mouthful. "This is ridiculously good. Like, it should be illegal."

I laugh. "I'm glad it's not, because I really want another one."

Caro, Clint, and I chat for a few more minutes before getting pulled away by other guests. At some point, Robin pauses the music to thank everyone again for coming, and the applause is so loud that I worry we might get a noise complaint from the neighbors—until I remember most of the neighbors are here. Robin looks so moved by the outpouring of love that I think she might cry.

I feel a rush of guilt for all the times I've been jealous of how Robin talks to fans. She shouldn't act demure or embarrassed by the attention when she's this absurdly talented. And I shouldn't feel threatened by her accepting the praise and opportunities she deserves. Robin is an incredible chef. I've always known that. Other people ought to see it too.

Even with dinner completed, no one seems ready to leave. Most of the guests stick around well past ten P.M., chatting, dancing to the music, and drinking the ever-flowing wine. I can't help but remember our wedding day all those years ago, when I felt like an outsider looking in on the event. Maybe this is how I was supposed to feel back then: like I'm at the center of the action, busy but also content, wrapped in love by everyone here.

I'm standing near the emptied shed, observing the party, feeling a rush of gratitude for all this inn has brought me, when a strong burst of wind rushes through the trees. I watch in what feels like slow motion as an ember from the nearest campfire swirls into the air, floats across the yard, lands in a pile of fallen leaves near the porch, and immediately crackles into a shockingly large flame.

46

Robin

"ROBIN!"

I'm in the middle of a conversation with a group of Counterculture regulars near the gazebo when I hear Molly's panicked voice call my name. I know her tone means trouble because Molly doesn't freak out easily. Without making any apologies, I run.

I find her within seconds, only about fifty feet away, at the back corner of the porch near her shed. She's pulled off her knee-length camel coat and is using it to bat at a pile of flames dangerously close to the porch railing.

"Extinguisher!" Molly yells toward me, but I'm already on it. We prepared for this, knowing fire was a risky thing to have so close to a historic building. The firepits were strategically placed as far from the house and other structures as possible, and we stocked up on extinguishers just in case. I grab two from their spot by a dessert table and run back to Molly. I roll one toward her, then pull the pin on the other and start spraying toward the base of the flames.

The whole thing is over in a couple minutes. Once we're sure the fire is out, Molly and I look at each other, chests heaving, then drop our fire extinguishers and grab each other in a tight embrace. I feel like I'm holding on for dear life as I wait for her breathing to slow. "We're okay," I say into her ear, feeling her shake in my arms. "The inn's okay. The shed's maybe a little singed, but everything is fine."

"It happened so fast," Molly says, voice quaking. "There was a pile of leaves from the wind, and then an ember, and a leaf floated up onto the porch, and, oh god, Robin, it could have gone so wrong."

"It didn't," I say, rubbing circles on her back. "You didn't panic and you acted fast and you saved it."

"*We* saved it," Molly murmurs into my shoulder.

I notice some of our guests clustering around us with concerned looks. It was over so quick, the ones on the other side of the house probably don't even know anything happened. I gently pull away from Molly, still holding her by the arms, as I announce to the group, "We're all good! Everything's under control!"

Clint pushes through the crowd, asking in a loud, worried voice, "Wait, was that a fire?"

"Just a scare, really," Molly says, voice tight, stepping toward Clint. "But we'll get the inspector back out tomorrow before we sign the paperwork, just to be sure."

"Looks like there wasn't much damage," Clint says, leaning over us to check. "Don't worry about the inspector. We can still close tomorrow, and I'll have my contractors take a look afterward. Seems like that honeysuckle bush might not make it, though. Or Molly's fashionable coat." Clint uses the end of a discarded extinguisher to poke at the mess. "But it's more important that you two are okay."

"Um, I wouldn't write off an extra inspection so fast," Clint's lawyer says, appearing behind him.

"Not now, Jonathan," Clint says, pulling him away. "Let's go make sure the shed is all clear. Ladies, we'll talk tomorrow. Thanks for looking out for the inn one last time."

As Clint and his lawyer walk around the side of the shed, Jesse takes their place. "What can I do?" he says.

"Can you get everyone back to their tables?" I ask. "Nothing they can do now besides give us space. And let's stop adding logs to the firepits and let them burn out."

Jesse moves the onlookers back to the party and directs servers to bring out the last of the wine. Molly and I take a deep breath together, then grab a hose and a broom to clear away the fire-dampening foam and examine the porch. It really isn't as bad as the blaze made it look; there are some scorch marks on the handrails and Clint was right about the bush, but there's no structural damage. A little paint touch-up will make it look like nothing ever happened.

Molly and I put our party faces back on and make the rounds to assure folks that everything is truly fine. While the near catastrophe didn't really put a damper on the mood, it did cause people to realize how late it's gotten. We spend an hour saying goodbyes, trading hugs and phone numbers and promises to stay in touch. I watch as Keyana and Molly share a long embrace, whispering into each other's ears and laughing through tears in the way best friends do. Then we spend

another hour packing up with the restaurant team and loading supplies borrowed from Counterculture into Jesse's van.
The line chefs leave the kitchen spotless. Jesse and Caro
stick around to help us stack the tables, chairs, and firepits
near the driveway, where the rental company will pick them
up in the morning.

It's a bleary two A.M. by the time we part with Jesse and
Caro, swearing we'll find a way to get together again someday. And then it's just Molly and me, both still shaken from
the adrenaline of the fire. And Marmee, meowing grumpily
at us for keeping her up past bedtime. The cat follows us
from room to room as we gather our things in the entryway,
making sure the inn is ready for its new owners. We work
through the early hours of the morning, cleaning up the
main-floor bathrooms, sweeping away shoe prints, checking
the yard for trash. Through it all, we discuss how lucky we
were that the spark didn't land on the roof and take the whole
building down. We trade memories of the Hummingbird's
glory days, or at least the ones we were here to see. After all,
the inn was here long before us, and with any luck, it will
outlast us.

The sky is turning soft shades of pink and orange when I
join Molly on the back porch to clean, sand, and paint the
fire-damaged section of the porch. She watches in silence as
I finish the final coat, erasing the reminder of what tragedy
could have occurred.

When I'm done, Molly steps back to examine our work,
hands on her hips. "What do you think?" she asks.

"Can't even tell anything happened," I say. It surprises
me how quickly evidence of us being here, of our successes
and our mistakes, can be painted right over.

Molly puts the lid on the paint can. Something wet hits my cheek, and at first I think it's a splatter of paint, but then I realize it's tears. *My* tears. I try to brush them away, but it's no use. There are too many. It's a waterfall, one I realize I've been holding back for weeks.

As soon as Molly sees, she drops her supplies and rushes over to hold me. I immediately feel better from her touch. But the tears come harder and faster as I fully absorb the fact that we're about to walk away from this inn and from each other. I'm a blubbering mess in her arms. We sink down together, resting on the porch steps, my head on Molly's shoulder as she rocks me back and forth. I slowly catch my breath, and when I shift away from Molly, she's teary too.

"What's wrong?" Molly asks, an arm tucked around my waist.

"I was thinking about the fire," I admit. "And how quickly this whole place could have burned down. What would have happened if we weren't here?"

Molly tilts her head at me. "Well, technically, the fire probably wouldn't have started if we weren't here, because there wouldn't have been a bunch of tiny fires to set it off."

"Sure," I say. "But anything else could've happened. A fire next door. A flood. A tornado."

"Tornadoes don't really come through the mountains as much."

"You know what I mean," I say, bumping my knee against hers. "In that moment, when I saw you and the flames on the porch, everything we've built together flashed before my eyes, and . . . and it scared the hell out of me. I *need* the inn to be okay. I *need* it to always be here. I could only walk away last time because I thought you'd still be here to take care of it."

Molly sniffles, and I turn to see tears running down her face too. "And I could only leave because I thought the management company and Caro and Jesse would be here," she says. "But now we're leaving it with Clint. He loves this place. He won't let anything happen to it."

"I don't know how to leave it again," I say, shaking my head. "It's a part of me now, and I'm part of it. You know? I thought I'd done all my growing up before I moved to Portland, but coming back here showed me I've still got a lot of shit to learn."

"I know what you mean," Molly says, wiping her face with the back of her hand. "It's like as long as the Hummingbird keeps going on, I can keep going on. But we don't have to be here for that to happen."

"The fire also made me think about losing you," I say. "Seeing you there, trying to put it out with the coat off your back, I was terrified. What if you'd gotten hurt?"

Molly's green eyes soften, wrinkles deepening at the corners. "It was a tiny fire," she says gently. "I'm okay."

"I know you are." I pick up Molly's right hand and kiss the peak of each knuckle, exhilarated and afraid to reveal what's been weighing on me for at least the last few days, but realistically since the moment Molly and I made our agreement. "To be honest, I think I've been lying to myself for a long time, that I can walk away from all of this, from you." I tuck Molly's brown and teal locks behind her ears and cup her cheeks and open my heart wide for her, hoping with every cell in my body she'll feel the same way. "I don't want to lose you again, even if it's not from some freak accident, even if it's a reasonable decision we've made together. Going to Portland, opening my own restaurant, having my own TV series, I did it all because I thought it would make my life feel more meaningful. But the whole time we were apart, even if my career was bigger, I felt smaller. Less whole. I didn't realize how much of me was missing until I was back here with you, working on the inn, cooking with Jesse. I don't want to leave half of my heart in Eureka again."

Molly's lips are parted in surprise, her eyebrows raised. "What are you saying?"

"I want to stay," I say, confidence in my decision building. "Here. With you."

"We're . . . we're supposed to meet with Clint and the lawyers in two hours," Molly says, her voice unsteady.

"Fuck the lawyers," I blurt out, smiling through the tears still clinging to my cheeks. "I mean, Danica seems great. And I obviously love Clint. The closing paperwork is ready, but we haven't signed on the dotted line yet. Let's blow them off. Reopen the inn ourselves. With a team, of course. We're older now. We can't do it alone. Maybe we can convince Caro to come back. Or maybe Clint can still invest and help us hire someone. Then you can keep taking commissions, with Eureka as your home base. We can work out the details."

"But what about your career?" Molly says, inching away from my touch. "Don't you want to move to a big culinary city and open a new restaurant? How can you give up everything you've ever wanted?"

"*You're* everything I've ever wanted," I say, simple and sure. "I didn't realize it before. I needed to see for myself what I could do, what was out there. But it's always been you, Molly. It's always been us, here, together." With a heavy breath, I shift to the terrifying part, where this dream could completely fall apart. I grab Molly's hands in mine and look directly into her uncertain but hopeful face as I say, "This is a huge, life-changing choice that involves both of us. Your career, your art, your life away from Eureka Springs, I can't ask you to give it up. I know without a doubt this is what I want, but if it's not what you want, I understa—"

Molly puts her thumb to my lips, stopping me in my tracks. "I see things differently now too, Robin. As afraid as I was of change, that time apart showed me what I'm capable of. I didn't go with you to Portland because I was scared of wanting more, of leaving my safe haven. But your leaving forced me to be brave. To see new places. To create new art. Art that's in museums now." She shakes her head as if she still can't believe it. "I made art in Louisiana, Georgia, Alabama, Oklahoma. But it was usually chasing someone else's vision. I can make art anywhere. Here, I can keep making it on my own terms."

I take a jagged breath in. "You mean, you want—"

"—to stay here with you." A brilliant smile bursts across Molly's face like sunlight breaking through clouds, and I'm reminded of the first time she smiled at me like this, that day at Home Depot all those years ago. "It's always been you, Robin. You and me," she says.

I grab Molly in a passionate kiss, our bodies immediately tangled together. We get lost kissing each other, like it's the first time and the millionth time all in one. When we stop, sunbeams are streaming through the gaps in the mountains. We lace our fingers together and watch the light shift, listen to the birds sing.

"You know," Molly says, her voice its own music in my ears, "everything we wanted from our agreement came true.

We both have huge career opportunities offered to us. We've got a trustworthy friend willing to buy the inn for more money than either of us ever expected to have. We hashed out what happened and understand why we fell apart. We have every reason to follow the plan to the end and say good-bye."

I freeze, worried Molly is changing her mind. If she does, I think I might crumble to dust right here and spend the rest of my non-life hanging with the Hummingbird Inn ghosts.

Molly gently caresses my cheek, turning my face toward hers. "But we have one reason to blow off the plan and stay here together. The most important reason: because we want to."

I smile so hard that my cheeks ache. "Fuck the plan."

WE WRITE NOTES TO CLINT, Keyana, and Danica, brief but sincere apologies for bailing on them at the last minute. We explain that sometimes love makes you do foolish things. I tuck them into a basket filled with leftover cookies, chocolate, and marshmallows and drop it off at the front desk of the law office where we were supposed to sign over the deed to the inn and meet Key before our court appearance for the divorce.

Then Molly drives us down a familiar highway. We turn up the music, belting along to the songs that played on the radio back in 2012, when we first fell for each other. By the time we arrive at our destination on a narrow gravel road, the sun is fully risen, lighting up the brilliant oranges and yellows and reds of the autumn leaves in the Ozarks.

Molly and I hike to the top of a stone ledge, our hands

clasped the whole time, even when it makes moving over uneven ground harder. We're wearing our wedding outfits, and I still can't believe we both held on to them for a decade. Then again, I guess it makes sense when you consider we're just a couple of sappy dykes who couldn't find the nerve to file for divorce all these years.

We find our footing on a dry patch of rock at the top of the rushing waterfall at Lover's Leap. I try to brush the chilly mist from my face, but it's a losing battle.

Molly laughs as we both shiver. "This is what we get for being two fools who didn't figure out we should stay together in August, when the water was warm," she says.

I shrug. "As long as we're two fools together, I can handle anything."

I pull a stray leaf from Molly's lacy white dress, and she straightens the collar of my tux, my jacket unbuttoned because of my rounder midsection. We say some words, unplanned but from the heart, about how this time it's for us. This time we'll face our problems side by side, grow together, bloom right here where we've decided to put down roots.

And then we leap.

ACKNOWLEDGMENTS

This book—its characters, setting, and themes—is very near and dear to my heart. That also made it immensely difficult to write. Much like the Hummingbird Inn, my manuscript had good bones, but needed a lot of love and hard work to become something other people could enjoy. I'm eternally grateful to my editor, Katy Nishimoto, for her sincerity, clear eyes, and determination to get this story right.

None of my books would be possible without my agent, Jamie Carr, who champions my work with passion and perseverance. Thank you, Jamie, for seeing me through this process, as well as Elisabeth Weed, DJ Kim, and the good folks at the Book Group for their support while Jamie welcomed a new tiny book lover to the world. (Hello, Isaac!)

I'm honored to be a part of the Dial Press and Random House family. Thank you to everyone at my publishing house who helped craft this book and got it into the hands of readers: Whitney Frick, Andy Ward, Avideh Bashirrad, JP Woodham, Debbie Aroff, Maria Braeckel, Madison Dettlinger,

Hope Hathcock, Donna Cheng, Susan Turner, Meghan O'Leary, and Cara DuBois. And all my gratitude to cover designer Sarah Horgan for her dreamy illustrations of Molly, Robin, and the Hummingbird Inn.

With each book published, my book community grows, and my life (if not my bank account) is richer for it. Thank you to all the authors and writers sharing this wild journey with me: Andie Burke, Timothy Janovsky, TJ Alexander, Ginny Myers Sain, Jess Pryde, Amelia Possanza, Thien-Kim Lam, Malik Thompson, Courtney Kae, Tirzah Price, and so many more who have inspired me and commiserated with me along the way. I'm also grateful to the *Book Riot* community and for all that their staff and contributors do to celebrate books.

I wouldn't be the reader and writer I am today without the magic of independent bookstores. Thank you first and foremost to my beloved Loyalty Bookstore in D.C., especially Hannah, Christine, Shady, Chardai, Brandi, Sandie, Rebecca, and Noah, who gave me a very well-timed editing pep talk. Some other bookstores and booksellers who have embraced me and make a huge impact on their communities: East City Bookshop in D.C. (Laynie-Rose, Destinee, Maggie, and so many others), Little District Books in D.C., Magic City Books in Tulsa (Pat), WordsWorth Books in Little Rock (Lynne and Hannah), the Ripped Bodice in L.A. and Brooklyn, and Meet Cute Bookshop in San Diego. If you've made it this far, this is your sign to run to your local indie bookstore and buy a few new books.

A huge shout-out to the many other wonderful bookish people who have championed my work and make the world a more readerly place: librarians (especially Carissa and

Ellen at the Tulsa City-County Library), educators, book reviewers, Bookstagrammers, and BookTokers.

I'm extremely grateful for the beta readers, Annika Barranti Klein and Catherine Roberts, who gave me their gentle and honest thoughts at a crossroads in this book. You are brilliant and wonderful, and your input made this story stronger. Thanks also to the many friends and loved ones who put up with me through the stress of writing *Bed and Breakup*: Trey, André, Jordan, Addy, Danielle, Meredith, Noura, Amy, Elaine, Alyssa, Andy, Gaby, Paige, Moto, Diane, Anne, Donald, Frances, Molly (whose name I borrowed and with whom I share many fond Eureka Springs memories), and others who hopefully know who they are.

None of this would be possible without my parents, April and Ralph Dumond, who indulged my book obsession from a young age and never denied me a trip to the library. Mom and Dad, thank you for introducing me to Eureka Springs so many years ago and reminding me that I can always come home.

Finally, thank you to my spouse, Mickey. Most romance novels end just as the seeds of love are planted. Our fifteen years together have shown me that the real magic happens once you put down roots. It's been the gift of a lifetime to grow alongside you, whatever the weather, and watch you blossom into a truer version of yourself each day. When taking a big leap, there's no hand I'd rather hold than yours.

Bed and Breakup

Susie Dumond

Dial Delights

*Love Stories
for the
Open-Hearted*

A NOTE FROM THE AUTHOR
ON EUREKA SPRINGS

EUREKA SPRINGS TAUGHT ME TO BELIEVE IN MAGIC.

Yes, my dear reader, Eureka Springs is a real place, even if it sounds like something I dreamed up. My earliest memories of Eureka do have a dreamlike quality to them, though. Natural springs trickling down decorated limestone formations, cotton-candy-colored Victorian houses towering over me, street performers plucking at dulcimers, pillowy pink taffy spinning in shop windows, peculiar grown-ups in flowy caftans peddling magic crystals and tarot readings. It's a place that never failed to spark my imagination.

I was only six months old the first time my parents brought me to Eureka Springs. It was a fairly easy and affordable destination for them, only a three-hour drive along winding mountain roads, but vastly different from our home in Little Rock. My dad, a pharmacist, and mom, an oncology nurse, saw the quiet, lost-in-time town as a perfect escape from the high-stress environment of the hospital where they both worked. Eureka Springs became a familiar haunt for our family, somewhere we returned at least once a year, my dad drawn to the various food and wine festivals, my mother and I happy for any excuse to wander around, visiting the natural springs and browsing the gift shops.

We'd often bring along my paternal grandmother, whom I called Guy. A skillful quilter, Guy lived for her sojourns to Eureka Springs' fabric and quilt shops, where she would buy enough supplies to last her until our next trip. Guy was a somewhat reserved and serious woman, born during the Great Depression in rural Arkansas farming country. Eureka brought out a rare sense of whimsy in her. She'd even agree to pose in silly costumes at the old-timey portrait studios, donning frilly dresses very different from her usual jeans and sensible button-down shirts. (As you might have guessed, Guy was a big inspiration for me in writing Molly's gram.)

Our adventures in Eureka Springs became less frequent as I grew older, my schedule packed with theater rehearsals, dance classes, and school clubs. By the time I finished college in Oklahoma, Eureka Springs had become a fond memory. The winter after graduation, my partner and I were browsing low-cost destinations for a weekend trip to celebrate our two-year anniversary when we came upon a deal at a historic hotel in the heart of Eureka Springs, one where my parents and I had stayed many years before. It seemed like the perfect opportunity to show my new beloved the town that had always so delighted me.

I was pleased to find Eureka was spellbinding in all the ways I remembered. But I also noticed some things about the town that I hadn't had the context to understand before. Eureka Springs, in short, is queer as hell. Rainbow flags hung from every other doorway. There were not one but *two* LGBTQ+ bars. I now recognized the owners of my favorite boutiques and galleries to be queer elders. Same-sex couples walked down the street hand in hand, something my partner and I hadn't often risked in Oklahoma, but now were delighted to do in the safety of this strange little town.

I began to wonder if some part of me had always recognized Eureka as a queer oasis, even when I was a kid. If that was why I felt more myself there than anywhere else in my home state. I still have some of the rainbow jewelry I begged my mom to buy me on our trips in the nineties. But at the age of twenty-two, I'd come to terms with my own sexuality, been embraced by a queer community, and fallen deeply in love with my partner. Eureka became not just a place I'd enjoyed as a child, but a portal to a strange world where I could be myself and love whom I loved out in the crisp mountain air, a freedom I'd yet to find anywhere else in Arkansas.

My first two books feature cities I love that have shaped me in some way: Tulsa in *Queerly Beloved* and New Orleans in *Looking for a Sign*. So when I started thinking about the story I'd like to tell next, it was only natural that I consider Arkansas. But I must confess to a complicated relationship with my home state. Although Little Rock is a city I treasure in many ways, it's also a place where I struggled to feel comfortable or picture a future for myself. Even in fiction, I couldn't imagine a happily-ever-after for a queer couple in Arkansas.

But then I thought of Eureka Springs. From infancy to adulthood, I'd always felt myself come alive there. It was a place that felt full of possibilities, where the old mingled happily with the new, where eschewing traditional expectations was celebrated. Once I decided on Eureka Springs as the setting of my next novel, everything fell into place as if by magic.

With *Bed and Breakup,* I wanted to tell a story about what it means to love someone over years, how it feels to grow into adulthood alongside a partner and grapple with the choices you make together and apart. I wanted to dig into the messiness of building a life with someone and the beauty that blooms from those challenges. Historic bed-and-breakfasts— one of Eureka's biggest attractions—were a perfect thematic fit for this second-chance romance. And while exploring these themes of loving someone, something, someplace, for both its virtues and its faults, I saw Arkansas in a new light.

While working on this book, I had the wonderful opportunity to spend a week in Eureka Springs at the Writers' Colony at Dairy Hollow, a place that offers authors the "write time, write place" to focus on their craft. I'm extremely grateful to the good folks at WCDH, as well as the many Eureka Springs residents who enthusiastically shared their experiences living in the town and showed me some of its hidden gems. I hope that I did them justice; any misrepresentations of Eureka Springs are solely mine.

If this book inspired you to make a trip to the Ozarks to

see Eureka Springs for yourself, here are a few recommenda-
tions:

- *Cliff Cottage Inn:* I stayed here while working on this
  book for historic B&B inspiration. It's a delight, and an
  easy walk from downtown.
- *Basin Park Hotel:* I stayed at this historic hotel as a kid
  and later with my partner. It's got a metric ton of Eureka
  charm.
- *Crescent Hotel:* Historic hotel known for its ghost legends
  and hauntings.
- *Beaver Lake/Hogscald Hollow/Lover's Leap:* A real place,
  and even more beautiful than I described it! A hidden
  gem worth a short trip outside town.
- *Eureka Live:* This queer-centric club offers epic drag
  shows and a light-up rainbow dance floor.
- *Missy's White Rabbit Lounge:* This location was previously
  a gay bar that I deeply loved, and it inspired One More
  Round. While it's no longer a queer-specific bar, it's still a
  great place to hang out and very queer-friendly.
- *Gravel Bar at Wanderoo Lodge:* Not to spoil the locals'
  best-kept secret, but this queer-owned bar is where the
  true Eureka lifers hang out, and it's got excellent live
  music.
- *BREWS:* I love this spot for the coffee, beer, music, and
  vibes. (It's also a great place to edit a book for a few
  hours.)
- *Mud Street Cafe:* I truly can't visit Eureka Springs without getting a fancy latte and a slice of quiche from Mud
  Street. My favorite breakfast in town.

- *Local Flavor Café*: An eclectic and artsy café that serves up bold, fresh dishes.
- *MoJo's Records/B-Side Cafe*: An excellent queer-owned record shop with lots of niche finds, plus delicious food and a patio with a gorgeous mountain view.
- *Crystal Waters*: Mystical crystal shop located on an iconic rainbow-painted stone staircase between downtown Eureka's two busiest streets.
- *Oracle & Sage*: A great place to get a tarot, astrology, or aura reading.
- *GameMakers*: My favorite board-game shop in the world, which inspired Wild Card in *Bed and Breakup*. Buy literally anything the owner recommends to you.
- *East by West*: Quirky gift shop with a friendly "working bunny" who will help you check out. Yes, a real bunny!

Robin's Anniversary Cake

EARL GREY, LEMON, AND HONEY–FLAVORED CAKE

INGREDIENTS

For the Earl Grey Syrup

½ cup granulated sugar
½ cup water
2 sachets or 2 tablespoons loose-leaf Earl Grey tea

For the Earl Grey Milk

1½ cups milk (whole milk preferred)
2 sachets or 2 tablespoons loose-leaf Earl Grey tea

For the Cake

2½ cups all-purpose flour
2 teaspoons baking powder
1 teaspoon salt
¾ cup (1½ sticks) unsalted butter, at room temperature
1½ cups granulated sugar
3 large eggs
1 teaspoon vanilla extract

Zest of 1 lemon

1 tablespoon honey, plus more for serving

1 cup Earl Grey milk

¼ cup Earl Grey syrup

Fresh blackberries, for serving

For the Buttercream Frosting

¾ cup (1½ sticks) unsalted butter, at room temperature

24 ounces powdered sugar, divided

Juice of 1 lemon

½ teaspoon vanilla extract

¼ teaspoon salt

2 tablespoons Earl Grey milk, plus more as needed

1 teaspoon Earl Grey syrup

2 teaspoons honey

INSTRUCTIONS

For the Earl Grey Syrup

In a small saucepan, bring the sugar and water to a gentle boil, then immediately pour into a glass jar over the Earl Grey tea. Steep for 10 minutes, then remove the tea bags or remove loose-leaf tea by straining through a fine-mesh sieve. Set aside.

For the Earl Grey Milk

Place the milk and tea in the same small saucepan and bring to a simmer, stirring frequently to avoid scalding. Once the milk is steamy and beginning to bubble, remove from heat and steep for 10 minutes. Remove the tea bags or remove loose-leaf tea by straining through a fine-mesh sieve. Allow the milk to cool to room temperature.

For the Cake

Preheat the oven to 350°F. Mix together the flour, baking powder, and salt in a small bowl and set aside. Prep three 6-inch cake pans (or two 9-inch cake pans) using your preferred method. (I rub them with cold butter and dust with flour. Parchment paper or nonstick spray is also fine.)

Using a stand mixer with a paddle attachment, cream the butter on medium until light and fluffy. Add the sugar and mix until combined, about 2 minutes. Add the eggs one at a time, blending between each addition. Add the vanilla, lemon zest, and honey, and blend on medium until fully incorporated.

Add half of the flour mixture to the butter mixture and mix on low until almost incorporated. Add the Earl Grey milk and stir until almost incorporated. Add the remaining flour mixture and blend until just combined, being careful not to overmix.

Divide the batter equally into the cake pans and bake for 30 to 40 minutes, until the cakes are golden brown and bounce back when lightly pressed. Let cool for 5 minutes on a wire rack.

Loosen the edges with a knife and remove the cakes from the pans. Brush the smooth bottoms of the cakes with Earl Grey syrup (about 1 tablespoon each). Let cool to room temperature.

For the Buttercream Frosting

Using a stand mixer with a paddle attachment, cream the butter until light and fluffy. Gradually incorporate roughly half of the powdered sugar until thick and thoroughly combined, about 3 minutes. Add the lemon juice, vanilla, salt, Earl Grey milk, Earl Grey syrup, and honey, and blend until combined. Add more powdered sugar in small batches until desired texture is reached. (You might not need the full amount. If the consistency gets too thick, add extra Earl Grey milk.)

To Assemble

Slice off the domed tops of the cakes to make them even and flat. Place a small dab of frosting on the center of a cake plate and place your first cake on it. (This prevents sliding while you frost.) Spread roughly ½ cup frosting on the first cake, then add a second cake and repeat, ending with the final cake layer on top. Stabilize the cake by inserting a thin wooden skewer or plastic straw through the center and trimming off any excess at the top (optional). Frost with the remaining buttercream. Top with fresh blackberries and a drizzle of honey.

PHOTO: ELLIE MERRITT

SUSIE DUMOND is a queer writer originally from Little Rock, Arkansas. She is the author of *Queerly Beloved, Looking for a Sign,* and *Bed and Breakup,* and she also talks about books as a senior contributor at *Book Riot* and a bookseller at her local indie bookstore. Susie lives in Washington, D.C., with her spouse, Mickey, and her cat, Maple. When she's not writing or reading, you can find her baking cupcakes or belting karaoke at the nearest gay bar.

susiedumond.com
Instagram: @susiedoom

ABOUT THE TYPE

This book was set in Fairfield, the first typeface from the hand of the distinguished American artist and engraver Rudolph Ruzicka (1883–1978). Ruzicka was born in Bohemia (in the present-day Czech Republic) and came to America in 1894. He set up his own shop, devoted to wood engraving and printing, in New York in 1913 after a varied career working as a wood engraver, in photoengraving and banknote printing plants, and as an art director and freelance artist. He designed and illustrated many books, and was the creator of a considerable list of individual prints—wood engravings, line engravings on copper, and aquatints.

ABOUT THE TYPE

This book was set in Fairfield, the first typeface from the hand of the distinguished American artist and engraver Rudolph Ruzicka (1883–1978). Ruzicka was born in Bohemia (in the present-day Czech Republic) and came to America in 1894. He set up his own shop, devoted to wood engraving and printing, in New York in 1913 after a varied career working as a wood engraver, in photoengraving and banknote printing plants, and as an art director and freelance artist. He designed and illustrated many books, and was the creator of a considerable list of individual prints—wood engravings, line engravings on copper, and aquatints.

DIAL DELIGHTS

*Love Stories for the
Open-Hearted*

Discover more joyful romances that
celebrate all kinds of happily-ever-afters:

dialdelights.com